Immersed in Paradise

Tom Conway, Sr.

iUniverse, Inc.
New York   Bloomington

Immersed in Paradise

iUniverse books may be ordered through booksellers or by contacting:

iUniverse
1663 Liberty Drive
Bloomington, IN 47403
www.iuniverse.com
1-800-Authors (1-800-288-4677)

Because of the dynamic nature of the Internet, any Web addresses or links
contained in this book may have changed since publication and may no
longer be valid. The views expressed in this work are solely those of the
author and do not necessarily reflect the views of the publisher, and the
publisher hereby disclaims any responsibility for them.

ISBN: 978-1-4401-8764-3 (sc)
ISBN: 978-1-4401-8765-0 (dj)

Printed in the United States of America

iUniverse rev. date:12/04/09

Contents

Chapter 1

A Migraine in
a Baseball Cap

Brandy Barton's naturally curly honey blonde hair flowed gently down her back to just below her shoulders. Her cobalt eyes were accented by long sleek lashes, and gave the appearance of two huge saucers of water from the bluest oceans in the world, with a large black pearl in the center of each. Her slim, athletic frame was the product of many years of intense competition in a myriad of sports while she was growing up in the Shenandoah Valley.

On February 29, 2004, minutes before its scheduled departure time of 5:30 pm, Eastern Time, she settled into her window seat aboard United Airlines Flight 951 at Dulles International Airport. After the plane thundered into the sky, she started to read a magazine she had purchased for the trip, but soon put it down, and began thinking of how much her life was changing, and why she was flying to Costa Rica.

Brandy was the oldest of the three children of Stonewall Jackson and Mary Beth Barton. "Stony," as her father was called, was a police officer until she graduated from middle school, when he resigned to go into the real estate business. She remembered that when he announced his decision to the family, she had said, "Daddy, you love being a policeman! You've always told me that protecting people, and keeping the bad guys from hurting them was the most important thing someone could do. That's why I want to be a cop!"

He had answered, "I know, honey, but I have to look out for my family, and this way I can be more of a part of your lives, and I'll be able to give you more. We'll be able to buy a nicer house, and we'll have a better life."

During the next three years, Brandy played volleyball and basketball at Echo Mountain High School. She also broke several records as a sprinter on the track team, and was lauded by the local press as a phenomenon. During the summer before her senior year, Stony bought a house on the edge of the country club, and she transferred to John Singleton Mosby High School in Newmarket.

On her first day at Mosby, as she was arranging her things in her wall locker, she heard a male voice say, "So you're our new girl jock! You're too pretty to be very good at sports!"

When she turned around, she was face to face with a husky six foot tall boy who was wearing a baseball cap atop his dark brown, closely cropped hair. His hazel eyes and infectious smile caught her immediate attention.

She pretended to ignore him, and silently continued to sort through her books. Then she locked her locker, and started down the hallway.

"Hey, lighten up! I'm only kidding! My name is Chuck Harper, and I'm the Captain of the baseball team. I'm a pitcher, and I'm going to be a big leaguer someday."

"Gee, I'd be impressed, but I have a terrible headache!"

"You have a headache?"

"Yes, and it's six feet tall, and wearing a silly baseball cap! Now, if you'll excuse me, I have to find my English class."

"Hey, that's where I'm going! We can walk together!"

"Okay, but no more crap a about girl jocks! If you were a little brighter, you'd know that girls don't wear jocks! Besides, if being pretty means you can't be good at sports, then you can't be much, because you're cute!"

"Hey, that's funny! You're okay! I like you. Would you like to go out sometime?"

"Maybe, but I'll have to think about it, and there's one thing you need to know! I love to compete, and no matter what I'm doing, I want to be the best! That includes school, and when I graduate from college, I'm going into law enforcement! When that happens, I'm going to try my best to make the world better."

That afternoon, when Brandy shouldered her back pack, and walked to her mountain bike, Chuck followed her.

"Can I give you a ride? My van is over in the lot." She hesitated, then said, "I rode my bike, but if we're going to go out sometime, you ought to meet my dad."

She laughed quietly to herself, and thought, *Wait until daddy sees this guy! He'll run right for his shotgun!* I can hardly wait!

Chuck said, "I remember your dad; he was a policeman. He was always nice to us kids."

"Did he ever arrest you? If he did, he'll remember, and you'd better not get close to him when he sees us together."

"Heck, no! When I played little league, the Police sponsored a couple of teams, and he showed up at our games a few times. Wait here and I'll go get my van."

"No, I'll ride my bike to the parking lot. You lead the way."

When the reached a 1989 Chevrolet van, Chuck opened the back door to load Brandy' s bike, and she noticed an inflated air mattress behind the driver's seat. She exclaimed, "My, my, that's convenient! I bet the cheerleaders love you!"

"Hey, don't get the wrong idea! I go camping a lot!"

"So do I, but I usually back pack, and sleep alone in a sleeping bag."

When Chuck started the van, he said, "I could go for some ice cream. Would you like to stop at Dairy Queen? I'll buy!"

"Sure, but don't expect me to jump onto your mattress!"

"What if I buy you a coke, too?"

They laughed and teased each other for the next thirty minutes. When they reached Brandy's house, Stony was getting into his car, and Brandy said, "Oh, there's my Dad! Don't let him see that damn mattress or you'll never see me again, except at school!"

When he saw the van, the large man left his car, and headed in their direction. He called out, "Hey, honey, where's your bike? I thought you rode it to school."

"I did, but Chuck offered me a ride. We met at school today. He's really nice, and I might go to the movies or a dance with him."

Chuck got out of the van, and said, "Hello Sir, I'm Chuck Harper."

"Well, I'm Brandy's father, and I might say I'm pleased to meet you, but I'm not sure yet!"

When Chuck opened the back door of the van, and reached for the bike, Stony was looking over his shoulder.

"Son, if you plan to see my daughter much, you'd better lose the mattress, and if you don't treat her right, you might find yourself looking down the barrel of my shotgun!"

Having so spoken, he returned to his car, and drove slowly away, laughing to himself, and thinking, *I hope I scared that kid into thinking I'm a real bad-ass! I remember him*

from little league. He's one hell of a pitcher, and he can hit, too!
He seems like a nice kid!

When the car had disappeared down the road, Brandy said, "Don't worry, I know where he keeps his guns, and he's only trying to scare you."

"Yeah? Well, it worked! He looks like Lee Marvin, and he sounds like Dirty Harry!"

"Oh, don't be a wuss! You're a big strong jock, and I'm beginning to like you. Let me put my bike away, and I'll show you around."

After she had taken her bike into the garage, she walked into the backyard, where her father had set up a basketball court. She picked up a ball from under the basket, and threw it to Chuck.

"Want to play some one on one? You can take it out first. We'll play to twenty two."

Chuck dribbled the ball to half court, and then started to drive straight for the basket. Brandy raised her hands high in the air, blocking his path, as she moved swiftly backward. When her adversary started to lay the ball up to the net, she leapt like a cat, and plucked the ball out of the air just as it approached the rim. She swiftly took the ball back to mid court, and then dribbled it to the right, behind her back, faked a move to the left, and neatly slam-dunked the ball into the net. After several encores involving similar moves, she was ahead by twelve points. Chuck, gasping for his breath, moaned, "Where did you learn to move like that?"

"I've been playing basketball since I was four, and I started running track in elementary school."

"I know that, because I've read the papers, but you can jump, too!"

"Well. I'm a sprinter, but I'm also a high jumper."

"So you set me up? You're getting even because I teased you!"

"Something like that! Want to finish the game? "

"No, thanks! I'll see you in school tomorrow."

The next day, he asked Brandy to go steady, and from that day until they graduated, they saw as much of each other as they could, despite her father's early curfews and close surveillance. In her senior year, she lettered in track, volleyball and basketball, played first violin in the school orchestra, was queen of the senior prom, president of the student council, and valedictorian of her class. Chuck led the baseball team to the conference championship, playing right field when he was not pitching, and managed to get good enough grades to join Brandy in the National Honor Society.

The summer after graduation, despite Stony's objections, Brandy and Chuck spent a week camping in the mountains, hiking, biking, and making love under the stars. In September, although she had been offered grants in aid by two college in West Virginia to plat basketball, Brandy decided to take advantage of an academic scholarship to Mary Hays Mc Cauley College near Fredericksburg. Chuck decided to play baseball at Spingwater College, a short drive from his home. He had tried to persuade Brandy to enroll at Springwater, so they could remain together.

"If you stay here, we can see each other all the time. Besides, you could run track, and I'm sure you could make the basketball team. In fact you're good enough to start on the guys' squad!"

"Hey, I'm going to miss you, but if I stay here, I'll have to live at home, and I couldn't handle four more years of my dad monitoring every move I make. Besides, I want to concentrate on my studies. I'll miss sports, but they aren't my life. I'm going to go into law enforcement when I graduate, hopefully with the U.S. Marshall's Office, the Border Patrol, or the FBI! I want my life to count for something!"

Brandy got straight A's her first semester, and in the spring, she went out for track. The four by one hundred relay team went to the NCAA Division III finals in her Junior and Senior years. She and Chuck got together whenever they could; sometimes he would drive to Fredericksburg, and they would spend the weekend camping at Lake Anna, or she would drive home.

In May, 2001, Brandy graduated from McCauley Magna Cum Laude with a Bachelor's degree in Psychology. Chuck received his degree from Springwater, and, though he was not drafted, he was signed by the Atlanta Braves to pitch in the low minors. Midway through the season, he tore the ulnar lateral ligament of his right arm, and was released outright, bringing his baseball dreams to an abrupt end.

On September 11, 2001, terrorists flew hijacked airliners into the World Trade Center and the Pentagon, ending the lives of hundreds of innocent people, and changing the lives of every citizen of the world forever. In November, Brandy became a special investigator with the Department of Homeland Security. After training, she was assigned as the only female member of an eight person anti-terrorism task force. She moved into an townhouse with three college friend in suburban Virginia, and started working ten to twelve hours a day, six days a week. Despite her arduous schedule, she volunteered to work with children four hours a week at a local hospital.

In December, Chuck began working for the Department of Defense in the Pentagon, and began studying Criminal Justice at Marymount University. He and Brandy considered moving into an apartment together, but she knew her parents would not be pleased if they did so. Chuck decided to share a rented house in Arlington with Gus Delaney, a baseball teammate from Springwater, who was a Secret Service Agent, and three Capitol Police officers. With Brandy in mind, he selected a room with a full bath in the basement.

Chapter 2

Love Endures

From the day she started, Brandy relished her job, despite pulling twelve hour shifts. She often worked undercover, or on stakeouts, sometimes wearing a wire, and occasionally finding herself in dangerous situations. Although the agents carried weapons, she was given mace, and cautioned to use it only if she were faced with imminent death. Chuck, who generally worked eight hour days, five days a week, was very patient and understanding, and spent much of his free time studying, or hanging out with his roommates. On New Year's Eve, 2002, Brandy was on duty, tracking four suspected terrorists through Southeast Washington, and Chuck went to Georgetown with Gus. When she entered Chuck's house, shortly after noon on New Year's Day, he was sitting on the couch watching a football game on television.

"Hello, honey, did you and Gus get lucky in Georgetown?"

"We had a few beers, and then I came back here. I was worried about you, out on the street with those seven horny guys. How did it go?"

"We got the bad guys, and those horny people are all really nice. Besides, they're all married except for Brick, and he thinks I'm a dyke, because I put him down when he came onto me the day we met!"

Chuck took her in his arms, kissed her, and said, "You know that I love you and I'll marry you any time you say the word. Heck, you won't even let me buy you an engagement ring! After all, you're my girl! "

"I love you, too, but I'm going to be an Federal Agent, and 'till death do us part,' is a commitment that I'm not ready to make right now!"

In February, despite the demands place on Brandy by her job, Chuck continued to be very understanding, and his love for her grew with each moment they were together. Nonetheless, they continued to engage in a friendly competition as to who would be the first to land a job as a full fledged law enforcement agent with the Federal Government.

Chuck was very proud of Brandy, and was genuinely interested, albeit somewhat envious when she described her involvement in cases like that of the infamous "Beltway Snipers," who, in the fall of 2002, ruthlessly shot down innocent people at gas stations and shopping malls in Virginia and Maryland.

"You must feel great just to be a small part in helping get trash like that off the street! I really envy you! My job involves too much ass sitting, and no ass kicking!"

"Well, you've got time to go to school, and I don't usually have time to take a pee, but I really do like what I do."

On New Year's Eve, 2003, Brandy found herself working again, sitting in a battered pick-up truck, watching a farm-house through binoculars. During the months that followed, she and Chuck managed to remain together, despite the demands of her job, her volunteer work at the hospital, an almost manic obsession with running, which they often did together, and working out at the gym, whenever she could find the time. In the early summer, she was assigned to aerial surveillance, which meant long hours in light aircraft or helicopters.

One day, one of the pilots, Mark Maynard, approached her at the airfield and said, "How would you like to ride in a Blackhawk?"

"I'd like that very much, but why are you asking?"

"Because I'm about to return one to Andrews, and the boss said to pick someone to go along, so I picked you, if you're interested."

Within the hour, the helicopter was several thousand feet over the Maryland countryside. "Would you like to fly her?"

"You're kidding, right?"

"Just do what I say!"

He chuckled, and said, "Now that the ship is flying herself, would you like to join the mile high club?"

"Well I like to do new things, and I'll try almost anything once! You're cute, but my boyfriend would not like it. I bet your wife would not be too happy about it, either! No, thanks, I'll pass!"

"Relax, I'm just kidding; besides, I'm not allowed to hover her that high! We're right over the base. I'm about to take her down. My car is on the lot, and I'll take you back to the office."

When Brandy was parking her car in front of Chuck's house, he came running out the door waving an envelope in the air. She said, "You look like you've just won the lottery! What's going on?"

"My Criminal Justice degree was in the mail when I got home. Now maybe I can get a real job like yours. I'm going to apply to the Joint Services Criminal Investigation Department first, and see what happens. They have a guy at the Pentagon who thinks I have a shot!"

" What great news! Why don't I take you out to dinner to celebrate?"

"Sure! How was your day?"

"I got to ride in a Blackhawk. Mark had to take it back to Andrews, and asked me to go along for the ride. He even let me hover, and then he asked if I wanted to join the mile high club, but I turned him down after he told me he wasn't allowed to fly that high!"

"Well, he has good taste, but you're my girl!"

"Oh. It wasn't that! My back is killing me, so I passed!"

"Yeah, right! You know I'm the best, and didn't want to be disappointed by some old guy!"

"Actually, I also had to pee so badly, I needed to get down to the ground fast!"

In mid-summer, Brandy and the task force were sent to California to gather information about a terrorist cell operating out of a surfing school in Southern California. She and the rest of her team spent most of their waking hours in bathing suits, and she learned to surf. When she returned and told Chuck of her adventures, he said, "What a job! You just got a month's pay for running around on the beach in a bikini with a bunch of horny, muscle-bound surfers, while I was buried a half-mile down in my office in the Pentagon! Life just ain't fair!"

Chapter 3

Chuck Rocks the Boat

In late October, Chuck greeted Brandy with an announcement that he had been accepted for training as an agent by the Joint Services Criminal Investigation Department."

"Gee, Babe, that's great news, and I'm really happy for you! I'm also very jealous. Do you know where you'll be working? I hope it's in DC."

"That's the bad part. I'll be reporting to Fort Story after I am trained. I'll be down in Georgia for three months before that."

"But I'll still be here! I work in Washington, and anywhere else the team is sent! I love you, and don't want to lose you. You're my guy!"

"We could get married, you know!"

"I'm not ready for that, but not seeing you all the time we were going to different schools was a real bummer, and I don't want to go through that again."

The following Monday, Brandy went to see her supervisor, Jerry Evans. When she walked into his office, he smiled, and exclaimed, "Well, hello Tiger! What can I do for you?"

"My boyfriend has been accepted for training as an agent by the JSCID, and then he'll be working out of Fort Story. I'm thinking about trying to transfer to Norfolk . You know that I've got my application in to be an agent, and I haven't given up on that, but I want to be with Chuck, too!"

Evans said, "Well, you're a bright kid, and very important to the team. I'd like you to stay with us, but I'll see what I can find out. We don't want to lose employees who have potential, and try to do what we can to keep them happy. Go back to work, and come see me when you have all the details."

That night, Brandy met Chuck at the Burger King, and while they were eating, he said, "You have a look on your pretty face which is making me worry a little bit! It usually means that you've come up with one of your wild ideas. What's up?"

"I talked to Jerry about a transfer to Norfolk, and he's going to check it out for me. Also, while you're in training, I thought I might go away somewhere to think; maybe even try to improve my Spanish. I might go to Costa Rica while you're away. There are some schools there that I've heard about, and I'm going to see what I can find on Google."

" I knew it! My problem is that it sort of makes sense, which makes me worry a little bit!"

That evening, Brandy logged onto the internet, searching for language schools in Latin America, and found a website for "CASA" (Central American Spanish Academy) in Costa Rica." She read, "The only way to really learn Spanish is to live it. If you're serious about learning Spanish and want to learn, quickly, efficiently and professionally, and you want to be totally immersed in the language and the culture of one of the most enchanting and safest countries in the world, then you've come to the right place!"

She called to Chuck, saying, "I found a school which will 'totally immerse me in the language and culture' of Costa

Rica! That's for me! Now all I need to know is exactly when you'll start training, so I can apply for a leave of absence."

On the first day of December, Chuck received his orders to report to the Federal Law Enforcement Center in Glynco, Georgia on March 1, 2004 to begin training. He was also advised that after successful completion of training, he would report for duty at Fort Story. The next day, when Brandy went to see Jerry Evans, he said, "Hello Brandy, If you're still interested in a job in Norfolk, there's an opening down there for as a computer analyst. You'll be stuck behind a desk, and you seem to like the action, but you'll be with your guy. When will he finish training?"

"He got his orders yesterday. He'll be reporting to Glynco on March the first, and when he finishes, he'll go to Fort Story in June. When will I have to report to Norfolk?"

I'd like to take some time off while he's in Georgia. I think I'd like to get away for awhile, and travel somewhere. Of course, I wouldn't expect to be paid."

"Actually, the position won't be available for a few months. Maybe you should take some time to think everything out. I'll find out if you can take administrative leave without pay. Where do you think you'd be going? If you leave the country, you'll have to report all contacts with foreign nationals, and you'd be up to your butt in paperwork. But in our line of work, that's a given!"

"I've found a Spanish school in Costa Rica. I minored in it in college, but would like to be fluent, if that's possible. I'd be living with a host family, and speaking only Spanish most of the time.

"Well, being able to speak fluent Spanish wouldn't hurt your career, and Costa Rica is a country that's considered reasonably safe for gringos. Their constitution forbids an organized military. I'll check it out, and get back to you."

"Thanks, Boss! I really appreciate it."

"No problem! Now get back to work! The team is waiting for you."

On Friday night, February 27, 2004, Brandy and her friends threw a going away party for Chuck, and they spent the night together. In the morning, she kissed him goodbye, and he climbed into his car to drive to Georgia, in order to report for training by 4:00 pm on March1, the day prior to commencement of training.

Chapter 4

Brandy Arrives in Paradise

The pilot's voice came on the intercom, and Brandy was suddenly brought back to reality. "Ladies and gentlemen, we are preparing to land at San Jose International Airport. It is now exactly Nine-twenty-five in the beautiful city of San Jose. The sky is clear, and as you can see, the moon is full. Please keep your seatbelts fastened until we are safely parked outside the terminal. Thank you for flying United and I hope you enjoy your time in Costa Rica."

After Brandy claimed her baggage and cleared customs, she found the exit, and walked outside, where she saw a small Hispanic male holding a white cardboard sign on which was neatly printed with the acronym "CASA" in bold black letters, standing beside a large black van. She walked up to him and said,

"Are you looking for me? My name is Brandy Barton."

"Si, senorita, I am Pepe, and I am here to take you to your host family!"

At that moment, a voice directly behind Brandy announced, "Then you are also looking for me! I'm Paul Travers, and I'm a new CASA student, too!"

Brandy turned to face a tall, handsome man with curly brown hair and a neatly trimmed mustache.

"Then we're going to be classmates! You said your name is Paul? It's nice to meet you. My mane is Brandy. Were you on my flight? I didn't see you on the plane?"

"No, I arrived about twenty minutes ago from Houston.

After the driver had loaded the luggage, Brandy slid into the seat behind him, and the young man sat down beside her. No sooner than they had fastened their seat belts, the monstrous vehicle lurched forward, and began frantically threading its way through the heavy traffic, narrowly missing pedestrians and a variety of other conveyances, including an ox cart full of melons. Despite the turmoil around them, Brandy and her fellow traveler managed to engage in a conversation.

"So you're from Texas! Are you a cowboy?"

"No, I'm originally from Saint Louis. I've been a basketball coach for the past five years at a small school near Houston, but last summer a buddy of mine talked me into becoming his partner in the restaurant business. We both decided that I needed to improve my Spanish, so I'm down here to try to get better at it, and have some fun. Where are you from?"

"I live in Virginia, but I work in Washington."

"Are you a politician?"

"No, but I'm a government worker--actually, I've taken a three month leave of absence to come here, so I guess you could say I'm unemployed! Of course, for the next three months, I'll be a student!".

Before Paul could speak again, the van came to a stop in front of a long row of single story houses surrounded by high ornate iron fences, with separate gates leading into the driveway of each unit. The buildings were painted white, and there were decorative bars on the windows of each dwelling. Pepe turned his head and spoke. "Senorita, this will be your home while you are here. Your host family will be Guido and Rosita Macano. They came here from Italy many ears ago."

At that moment, the coach lamp by the front door came on, and a white haired, slightly plump woman came out and opened the gate to allow the van to come into the driveway. She spoke in Spanish before anyone else could say anything.

"Buenos noches, Senorita Barton! I have been expecting you. Your room is ready. Please come inside. Pepe will take care of your bags."

The driver unloaded Brandy's luggage, and followed the two women into the house. As they walked away, Paul, who was still seated in the van, called, "Goodnight! I'll see you in school!"

She turned and waved, then stepped through the door. When she did, she was greeted by a muscular light brown dog with a pug nose, which sat up and extended his right paw, to shake hands. "Hi, there handsome!" She took the paw in her hand, and then turned to Rosita. "What a cute puppy! Is he a Mastiff?"

"He is a Cane Corso, an Italian Mastif. We bought him as a guard dog, but Guido has spoiled him. He even trained him not to bark at strangers. Now he's only a house pet, but we love him. His name is Tuffito, but we call him Tuffy."

She told the dog to leave, and he obediently sidled to the rear of the house. The driver placed the bags on the floor of the foyer, excused himself, and left the house. The lady smiled, and said, "My name is Rosita Macano, and my husband, Guido, and I will be your host family while you are here. Guido has gone to bed, but you will meet him tomorrow. It is late now, and we'll be rising early in the morning. Classes begin at eight o'clock. I will fix your breakfast, and then we'll walk to the school. You will have breakfast and dinner here, and will eating lunch somewhere near the school. I'll show you to your room in a moment, but come and sit in the parlor with me. Do you have any questions?"

Brandy was surprised that, although she had not spoken Spanish much since she was in college, she understood most of what Rosita was saying. She answered, "Not at the moment, but I'm sure I will be asking about many things before very long." "

The woman laughed, and said, "Oh yes, I'm sure you will, and I will be very happy to answer any questions you might ask. One thing you should know is that my husband and I are Italian. That is a problem sometimes, because we occasionally slip, and use Italian with our guests, and it drives them crazy."

"That is wonderful! Maybe I will learn some Italian, too!"

"That is true, but I'm sure you're tired! I will show you your room now."

She picked up the two heaviest bags, and started down the hall. Brandy gathered the rest of her belongings, and followed. As she walked, she noticed the walls were adorned with paintings, mostly pastoral scenes or houses, or churches, except for one canvas which bore the face of a gorgeous young girl with intense dark eyes exactly like Rosita's. Brandy paused and said, " I love your artwork! Are you the girl in this picture?"

"Yes, my husband is an artist, and I was his model. I will tell you all about it before you go back to your country"

She took a step forward, and opened a door. Then she walked into the room, set Brandy's suitcases on the floor, and stepped aside, saying, "This will be your room, and I hope you will find it to your satisfaction."

"I love it! This is really nice!"

"I am very happy that you like it. I will leave you now, and I hope you sleep well, and I will see you in the morning. Good night."

"Good night and thank you!"

Brandy picked up one of her bags, set it on the large brass bed by the wall just inside the door, and opened it. She removed a pair of pajamas and a small bag of toiletries from it, and placed them on the desk which stood in front of a huge window. When she opened the blinds, she saw the mountains in the distance, with a full moon lurking above, in a cloudless sky. In the garden, her eyes fell upon the shadow of a mango tree, in which several birds were sleeping. As she surveyed the scene, she thought,

Gosh, what a sight! It reminds me of home. I have a feeling that I am going to like it here! I wonder what Chuck's doing now. He would love this!

She walked into the bathroom, where she quickly showered. She donned her pajamas and lay down on the bed next to her suitcase. When she awoke, she heard a tapping on the window, and when she sat up, a gigantic Macaw was peering at her through the glass, and making strange sounds, as if to say, "Wake up, Gringo lady, you can't sleep all day!"

She climbed out of bed, and walked to the window, through which a warm breeze carried the scent of the flowers which grew under the window sill. She walked over to the dresser, glanced in the mirror, put on her robe and when stepped into her slippers, there was a knock on the door. When she opened it, she was greeted by Rosita, who was wearing an immaculate white apron. "Good morning, Senorita, I just want to tell you that breakfast is ready. You can dress later, and then I will walk to school with you."

She followed Rosita to the dining room, where a huge walnut table was set. In the center was a large platter, filled with assorted fruits, including fresh mangoes, papayas, melon wedges, and pineapple slices. A short, white haired man, who appeared to be in his mid seventies, was seated at the head of the table. He appeared to be very fit, and there was a twinkle in his enormous brown eyes. He arose as soon as she entered the room, and winked at her with a mischievous smile on his face. He was wearing a tropical white linen shirt, ecru trousers, and sandals.

"Buenas dias! You must be Senorita Barton, and I am so pleased to see how beautiful you are!"

"Well, you must be Guido, and you can call me Brandy! If I had known you would be here, I would not be in my pajamas. Rosita, you should have told me how cute your husband is!"

Rosita was standing in the doorway with a plateful of toasted homemade bread in one hand and a pitcher of freshly squeezed orange juice in the other. She laughed heartily, and said, "I didn't tell you what an old fool he is, either, and if he pinches you on the backside while you're here, he'll spend the rest of his life sleeping in the streets! By the way, you can call me Rosa, if you wish."

"Oh, Rosa, I'm sure he wouldn't pinch me! He looks like a perfect gentleman!"

"Child, you are very young and naïve, and obviously have not been to Italy. You don't know much about Italian men!"

Brandy thought, *What sweet people! I feel like I've found a second family. I only wish that Chuck could be here. I wonder how he's doing now. If there are women in his classes, I hope they look like Shaquille O'Neal!*

Chapter 5

The First Day of School

After breakfast, Brandy got dressed, then she and Rosita started out for the school. As they walked along the pothole filled street, past shops and row houses with beautiful flowers sharing space with piles of garbage in front of them, she thought, *So this is paradise! I wonder if Adam and Eve threw their trash on the ground! There is beauty everywhere, but thoughtless humans have found a way to give it zits!*

"Rosa, how far is the school from your house?"

"It is only seven blocks, but the traffic is treacherous, and you must be very careful crossing the street."

"I've worked in Washington, and I know about traffic! By the way, I really like Guido. You told me last night that he was an artist, and you were his model. Is that true?"

"Yes, I grew up in a small village near Torino; you North Americans call it Turin! I met Guido there when I was sixteen, when my mother and I were visiting friends. He was almost thirty years old, and very handsome. He asked me to pose for him, and at first I said no, but he was very persistent. After that, I was an angel, a princess, and the Virgin Mary. The painting in our house is the first he did of me, I was very young. I married him six months after we met."

"How did you happen to come here?"

"The Catholic Church commissioned him to restore some murals at the Basilica in Cartago, and I came with him. Later, he was hired to do frescos in other churches, and we liked it here so much, we never went back to Italy. Most of my family has moved here since. You will meet them before you go home."

Soon the two women were standing in front of a large two story white concrete building. The entrance was at street level, with a sculptured archway, under which were two patio tables, several matching chairs, and a glider.

"My, I've talked so much, and we're here already! I will introduce you to the director, and then I well go. Your dinner will be ready when you get home."

When she saw the furniture, Brady asked, "Is this a café?"

"No, it is what the school calls 'the break area.' There are drink and snack machines inside."

She led Brandy across the gleaming ceramic surface, through the double glass doors, and into the building until they were in front of the director's office, where a tiny well dressed, smiling woman, who appeared to be in her mid-forties was standing. She addressed Rosita in Spanish.

"Good morning, Rosa, it is nice to see you! I assume this beautiful young lady is Miss Barton."

Before Rosita could answer, Brandy said, "Yes! That is me, but please call me Brandy."

"Very well, Brandy, it's very nice to meet you! I'm Glenna Castillo. You may call me Glenna--or Maestra! You're right on time. There are some other new students in the lounge, and we'll join them in a moment."

Brandy said goodbye to Rosita, and followed Glenna into the next room, in which there was a coffee table, three overstuffed chairs, and a sofa. Paul was sitting in one of the chairs. A young blonde woman wearing a red halter top and tight white shorts was seated in the chair next to him. A muscular man in his thirties was sitting next to a slightly plump, mostly bald, man about fifteen years his senior. Glenna directed Brandy to the only unoccupied chair, and began to speak.

"Welcome to CASA! I have already introduced myself to each of you, and now it is your turn to meet each other, if you are not already acquainted. Brandy, you were the last to arrive, so you may go first. I know some of you know some Spanish; this meeting will be in English. However, no English will be spoken in the classroom, and when you are on your own, you will learn faster if you speak Spanish while you are in thus country, particularly when you are traveling, and I would suggest that you use your weekends for that purpose."

Brandy said, "I'm Brandy Barton, and I'm on a leave of absence from my job with the United States Government in Washington, DC. I live Virginia, and I met Paul at the airport."

Paul introduced himself, and the next to speak was the other young woman.

"Hi, I'm Kerry Stevens, I just graduated from college, and I'm going to start teaching kindergarten in Jackson, Mississippi next fall."

The muscular man said, "I'm Ted Corrigan, and I'm a police officer in Chapel Hill, North Carolina. This guy next to me is Mike Farelli, and he's my Sergeant."

Glenna spent the next half hour explaining how to exchange currency, buy stamps, and where the students could send e-mails home. Then she described the teaching methods, and conducted a short tour of the building. She stopped at a small room in which there were two computers. "Here are our computers, and you are free to use them whenever they are available. However, there are many computer cafes all over the city, from which you can send messages at a minimal rate. Now you can take a break, and return in fifteen minutes, at which time you'll be briefed on your class schedules. You'll also be given your textbooks and study materials. In addition, you have been advised that 'total immersion' includes travel. Savanah Sanchez is the person in our office who arranges tour packages, if you choose to travel that way. However, you will find that she is very eager to advise you on any travel you choose to do on your own."

Paul, who was shadowing Brandy during the tour, nudged her with his shoulder and said, "Let's go sit outside in the break area. I'll buy you a coke, and we can watch people getting killed trying to cross the street."

"Thank you, Paul. That sounds like fun, but one of the computers is open, and I want to send a quick e-mail"

After she sent the message, she walked outside to join Paul and the others. After the break, each of the new students went to his or her placement interview. Brandy found herself in a small classroom, talking to Amanda Ruiz, a middle aged woman with silver highlights in her shimmering coal black, hair.

"Senorita Barton, you seem to have considerable knowledge of the Spanish language already."

"I studied Spanish in high school, and college, but I want to become fluent, and please, call me Brandy."

"If you wish, and you may call me Amanda, or Maestra!" After she learned that Brandy had taken Spanish in high school and college, the teacher advised her that she would be at an advanced level of instruction, then said,

"Classes will start in the morning, and if the weather is nice, they will be held outside in our beautiful garden behind our building. Dress casually, because we want you to be comfortable. I'll be your teacher, and I'll tell you tomorrow who will be your instructor for private lessons, which are held in the afternoon. Also, I'll speak to you only in Spanish, after your lessons start!"

She gave Brandy her work assignments, a textbook with a workbook, and a white tee shirt with "CASA" printed on the front, in large black letters. The phrase, "Total immersion is the best way to learn!" appeared on the back in smaller letters.

After Brandy put her materials into her backpack, she thanked Amanda for her time, and walked out in the hallway, where Paul and the two policemen were waiting. Each of them had already put his tee shirt on, and Paul said, "Well, we made the team! How about you? Where's your jersey? Didn't you make the cut?",

Brandy replied, "It's in my back pack!, and I'm saving it to wear to church on Sunday! You guys look like a bunch of overgrown kids on a field trip! I'm hungry! How about lunch? There's not much more for me to do today, except to pay the balance of my tuition. I hear there's a decent place to eat across the street, if you guys don't mind risking your lives dodging taxis and ox-carts!"

Ted grinned, then said ,"I used to be a traffic cop, and these people scare the hell out of me, but we have to eat someplace."

By that time, Kerry had joined the group, and, in a slow, syrupy southern drawl, said, "I heard about the same place, and I'm starving! Why don't we all go there together, and get to know each other?"

Brandy, after noticing that Kerry's sparkling green eyes were fixed on Paul's muscular frame, smiled sweetly, and said, "Yes, why not? Of course we have to cross the street first!"

They managed to weave their way through a plethora of assorted vehicles, and reached the café safely. Soon they were inside the eatery, in which there were several tables and a lunch counter. Half a dozen booths were lined up in front of the widow. They crowded unto a booth, where Kerry maneuvered her way beside Paul, and Brandy found herself seated between Ted and Mike.

Brandy glanced at the menu, and said, "I'm going to have the plate lunch special--grilled chicken with beans, rice, salad, and the juice of the day, for two dollars in our money!"

Ted grinned, and said, "That sounds good to me!"

Kerry spoke next. "I'll have that, too! It sounds yummy!"

Mike laughed boisterously, and quipped, "Hell, I'm a sergeant; I can pick up every body's tab, and neither of you ladies will have to do me any favors, unless you want to! I'll go for the special, too, and I hope beer is the juice of the day!"

Ted responded immediately. "I'll pay for my own lunch, because I have to work for you. Besides, these girls are obviously interested in the coach!"

Paul looked directly at Brady and said, "Maybe, but some women aren't impressed by us jocks!"

Brandy remained silent, but Kerry said, "I can't speak for Brandy, but I love athletes. I was a cheerleader at Mississippi State."

Brandy didn't react verbally, but thought, *I'm sure that's true, and I'll just bet the football team really liked her!* While they were eating, Brandy learned that Ted and Mike were on a drug task forge in North Carolina, that Kerry had been the runner-up in the Miss Jackson beauty pageant, and that Paul had taught English in addition to being head basketball coach. Mindful of the security requirements of her job, she told the group that she was on a leave of absence from the Department of Immigration.

After lunch, Paul said, "Since we don't have much to do for the rest of the day, I'm going to check out at the school, then look for a cantina!"

Mike said, "Coach, I think you've got the right idea! Teddy, what's your vote?"

"I'm in, let's do it!"

Kerry squealed, "Goody, maybe we'll find a bar with a dance floor! Let's party!"

Brandy said, "Count me out, guys, the food was good, and all of you are fun, but I have to pay the balance of my tuition, then I'm going to go back to my new home and unpack. After that, I'm going to go for a run, try to find a gym, and get ready for tomorrow's class before dinner. See you in school!"

Brandy left the café, and after she paid the remainder of her tuition at the cashier's office, she was walking towards the door when Glenna called to her.

"Brandy, if you have a moment, there's someone here I'd like you to meet!"

She saw that Glenna was stranding next to a petite, smartly dressed woman with long, shiny black hair, who was carrying an armload of books. She strode over to the women and said, "Hello Glenna, I've paid my tuition, and I'm on my way home. Is this the teacher for my private lessons? I'm eager to get started1"

"Yes, this is Vicki Soza, your private instructor."

The two women exchanged pleasantries, and then Vicki said, "We'll start tomorrow afternoon. I'm going to a meeting at the University of Costa Rica, and I'm going to take you with me. I'll give you the details after your morning classes."

Chapter 6

Brandy Takes
Cooking Lessons

Brandy quickly donned her running shoes, a pair of shorts, a tank top, and a baseball cap, then went into the kitchen, where her hostess was peeling potatoes. "

"Rosa, I'll be back in about an hour. I'm going running, and I want to check out a gym near the school. I have a daily routine, and want to try to stick to it as much as I can! When I get back, I'll help you fix dinner, if you wish. Maybe you can teach me to cook!"

"I'd like that very much. Be very careful when you're running in the street. I'm sure you noticed how treacherous the traffic is!"

"Don't worry! I won't take any chances, and I'll see you soon."

As she trotted along, Brandy found it necessary to keep looking down to avoid the gaping potholes in the pavement, while trying to keep an eye on the cars and other conveyances which hurtled through the streets around her. When she returned to Rosita's house, about one hour later,

Guido was struggling to stay awake while watching a soccer match on television. When she stepped into the parlor, his eyes opened wide, and he exclaimed,

"Ah, my beautiful angel has returned! Come sit with me. We will watch the football match together. I saw the American women win the World Cup in 1999. Do you play football? I watched you run when you left the house, and you move like the wind!"

"No, I've played many sports, but not soccer--I mean football! I ran track in high school and college."

"I am not surprised, you have a superb figure, and I would have loved to have you pose for me. Please, come join me."

"I wish I could, but I must take a shower, finish unpacking, and do my homework. After that, Rosita is going to teach me how to cook."

"Then it is my loss, but if you watch and listen carefully to Rosita, you might become a famous cook like her."

Later, Brandy joined Rosita in the kitchen, and as soon as she walked through the door, her hostess handed her a spotless white apron.

"If you're going to cook, you must be properly dressed. I wouldn't want you to ruin your nice clothes."

Brandy smiled as she tied the apron around her waist, and said, "Thanks, but I don't think a little grease would do much harm to my tee shirt and cutoff jeans!"

"I heard you talking to my husband earlier, and I hope you don't take him seriously. He's harmless, but when he was young, he was so handsome and charming that many women fell in love with him, and like many Italian men, he took full advantage of the situation. I did not like that, but I knew that he loved only me, so I learned to live with it. He is a wonderful man, and I will love him until I die. I just hope he doesn't upset you with his silliness."

"Rosa, I've worked closely with seven men for the past two years, and they all act like fools sometimes! There is an old man at the hospital where I used to do volunteer work. He called me the only woman in his life!" He is over seventy years old, and has been married to the same woman over half his life. He was fun! I even took him out to dinner to celebrate his seventieth birthday, then, when I took him home, he introduced me to his wife. I think men act silly, because they don't want to feel old. Most of them are that way. I think Guido is cute, and as full of it as any other man!"

"Young lady, you are very wise. Now it is time to cook."

While Rosita was showing her how to cook pasta to the right consistency, and adding pinches of many seasonings to the poultry dish she was preparing, or mixing dressing for the salads, Brandy was thinking, *How lucky I am to be here! I love these people, and I've only been here for two days! I may not want to go home when my visa expires!*

After dinner, she helped wash and put away the dishes, then she and Rosita went into the parlor, where Guido was sound asleep in front of the television set while Clint Eastwood was dealing with the bad guys in "Fistful of Dollars" in Italian, with Spanish subtitles. Rosita soon chased him off to bed, and she and Brandy chatted and watched television until it was almost midnight.

When Brandy started to walk to school the next morning, she met Mike, Ted, Kerry and Paul, who stepped in beside her and said, "Well, I see that you made your way back home yesterday!"

"And it's apparent that you and the party group did the same. Did you get to dance with Kerry?"

"Hey, she's cute, but she's a twit! By the way, I was talking to a girl from Iran yesterday after school. Her name is Nora. She lives with her dad, and not in a host house. She's trying to put a group together this weekend to go to the Arenal volcano. I told her I wouldn't mind tagging along."

"That's a coincidence! I was looking at travel literature that Savannah gave me yesterday after lunch, and met the same person. I told her I was interested, too! I want to see everything while I'm here, and traveling alone isn't recommended, especially for a woman. It would be good to have a big strong man around to protect me. We can talk to the Iranian lady together, and make some plans."

"You look like you can protect yourself! I'll talk to Nora, and tell her she has at least two fellow travelers for the weekend."

"Okay, so when you see her at school, tell her I'm in. We can go to lunch together tomorrow and make our plans."

"Tomorrow? Why not today?"

"Can't make it today, because I'm lunching with my private instructor, then she's going to take me to the University to look around."

"Okay, we'll do it tomorrow."

Together they dodged cars, pedestrians and large holes in the pavement. The morning passed quickly, though no English was spoken. If Brandy or one of the other students did not understand something, Glenna would explain it differently in Spanish. At noontime, after four hours of instruction interrupted only by a ten minute break, Brandy thought, *I heard a slang expression yesterday--"Estoy como las vacas" and it means "you have the brains of a cow!" That's me! My brain hurts!*

Chapter 7

Senor Sloth and
a Friendly Stranger

After class, Brandy met Vicki, who was just leaving her office. "Hello Brandy, as I told you yesterday, I have to go to the University this afternoon. We'll have lunch, and then take the bus to the campus. I'll show you around, but then I have to attend a meeting of language teachers later in the afternoon. There are many things to see, and we can talk about anything you wish. It will give you an insight into our culture, and our system of education."

"Wonderful! I want to learn everything I can about your country."

After the two women ate together at a tiny coffee house, they boarded a bus bound for the University. When they arrived on the campus, the first thing that caught Brandy's eye was a giant sloth, sleeping in a mango tree. Her eyes widened, and her mouth dropped open.

"Oh, my gosh! Isn't he cute?"

Vicki began to laugh, and said, "That's Senor Sloth, but most of the students cal him El Maestro, and sometimes, they call him El Presidente! I think they're implying that he's smart enough to hold either of those jobs!"

"Is he a pet? Was he brought here as a tourist attraction?"

"No, he just showed up on campus a few years ago, and decided to live here. Maybe he likes to be around creatures who aren't as smart as he is!"

While Brandy continued to gawk at the hairy denizen of the mango tree, passing students began to look at her as if she was deranged. When she realized that she was attracting more attention than the lounging primate, she said," These people must think I'm muy loco! I guess to them that guy is not unusual, but I've never seen a sloth before!"

"No, they just don't understand why anyone would be so entranced by a sight they see every day."

"I can relate to that! I once brought a school friend from New York home for the weekend, and she reacted about the sane way I just did, when she saw a cow!"

"Well, you're going to see many unusual things during your stay in Costa Rica, so you might as well get used to it. Are you planning to travel much while you are here?"

"Yes, I want to see everything. In fact, I'm going with two classmates to see the Volcano Arenal this weekend."

"Well, that's a magnificent sight, but the bus ride will be an adventure in itself! Speaking of seeing sights, we're in front of Museum of Insects. Would you like to learn about the bugs which are native to our country?"

"Yes, that sounds interesting, and if I get bitten by anything while I'm here, I'll know what to call it!"

Inside the building, Brady was astounded by the beauty of the numerous varieties of butterflies, and the enormity of some of the creatures on display, which to her chagrin, she learned were not extinct. She was particularly interested in the strain of bees which originated in Africa. Of these, she thought, *If one of those things ever attacks me, I'll at least know what it was!*

When they left the museum, Vicki said, "I have to leave you now. Can you find the way back?"

"Yes, and I think I'll walk. It is such a gorgeous day."

"That isn't a bad idea; I've walked back to the institute many times myself. It usually takes about thirty minutes."

Soon after Brandy began walking briskly along the sidewalk, she noticed that a neatly dressed man who appeared to be in his mid-thirties was almost walking in step with her. Like most of the Costa Rican males, he was short in stature. He didn't seem aware of Brandy's presence, and since she was a head taller than he, she decided to try her Spanish out on him.

"Buenos Tardes, Senor!"

"Good afternoon! You are from Estado Unidos, no?"

"Si, I mean yes, I am, and I'm here to learn your language. We seem to be heading the same way, would you mind if I walked along with you? I'm going to meet a friend at the mall."

"No, I would like the company; and maybe I can learn some English."

"Sure, I can help you with English; you can help me with Spanish!" Then she thought, *Great! He wants to speak English! Maybe I can teach him some curse words! No, I can't do that! Wouldn't want anyone to do that to me! He seems nice, and I can probably kick his butt, so I'll be nice too! He thinks I'm going to the mall, and when we get close, I'll ditch him, in case he should try to follow me.*

As she walked with the man, she pointed to people, and vehicles, saying, "bus," or "child," or "shop," and he would counter with the Spanish word. He didn't ask her name, and she didn't mention it, nor did she ask his. When they were within a few blocks of Rosita's house, she excused herself, waited as the man walked away, then she fell back on her training, and did a surveillance detection route, using a restaurant as her cover stop. When she was sure she was clear to go, she continued on her way. W hen she reached the house shortly after 3:00 pm, Rosita was waiting at the door.

"You received a phone call a short time ago from the director of the San Pedro daycare center; and she said you had called her on Tuesday to inquire about volunteering to work with some of the children. She left her number, and wants you to call her."

"Oh, yes, I volunteered at the children's ward at a hospital back home, and am very anxious to work with children while I'm here. I'll call her right away."

She entered the house, and called the number Rosita had given to her. When she learned that she would be able to start right away, she went to the parlor where Rosita and Guido were watching an opera on television, and said, "Rosa, I'm going to the daycare center now, but will be back in time for dinner. The three of us can spend the evening together, because you're my family now, and I want to get to know you both."

Chapter 8

Mugged by Moppets

When Brandy entered the daycare center, she was met at the door by the Director, Penelope Pena. "Senorita Barton, it is so nice of you to come here for the children, and I think you'll like the ones I've chosen for you to meet. They are all eager to meet you. The oldest is eight, and the youngest, who is one, is just starting to walk. I told them you would teach them English, and they're very anxious to meet you."

"Gee, I don't know how good I'll be at teaching them much, but I'll try my best."

"That's all you can do. We might as well get started. Please come with me."

When they reached the end of the corridor, a group of screaming little children burst through the door. After Penelope introduced them to Brandy, a four year old, who said his name was Luis, took her by the hand, and led her into a room in which there were several small tables and chairs. She spent the next three hours listening to the children taking turns telling stories about dogs, cats, school buses, monkeys, and ice cream. Marisa laughed at the way Brandy spoke Spanish, and Luis spent most of his time on her lap. Lulu, the one year old clung to Her leg, when she was not on the floor pulling at her shoe laces. When she walked back outside, she thought, I'll keep trying. *Ouch, my brain hurts! Those children are so sweet, but they talked so fast! The kids back in Virginia talked slowly to me, and they spoke English! Anyway, we all laughed together, and it was really fun! Maybe next time it will be easier.*

The moon was beginning to show itself above the mountains behind Rosita's house when Brandy entered the parlor. Guido, who was very bright and alert, greeted her.

"We were beginning to worry that the children may have decided to keep you, and I would not blame them, for you are so beautiful. I would love to paint you, but my old hands cannot hold a brush."

Rosita walked through the kitchen door, laughing gently. "Pay no attention to him, Brandy! Remember what I told you about Italian men. We are having pasta with a special sauce tonight. It is Guido's favorite. He claims he married me because of my cooking, but he never gave me much time to cook when we were young!"

"That's true, she was quite beautiful, even then, but she never protested to me for keeping her from her pots and pans!"

Brandy laughed, and thought, *These two people really love each other. I hope someday I'll know that kind of love and maybe it will be with Chuck. I really miss him, and I'm sure he feels that way. The problem is that I have so much I want to do, I'm not ready to be a stay-at-home wife. I want to live my life in a way that when I die, I will not feel I missed out on anything!*

She followed the couple into the dining room, and sat at the table. Guido opened a bottle of Italian wine, filled the three wine glasses, and sat down at the head of the table, to Brandy's left. When Rosita joined them, he said the blessing. Brandy marveled at how delicious the food was, and exclaimed, "Rosita this food is the beast I have ever eaten, and what did you do to the broccoli? It's scrumptious!"

"It's steamed, and seasoned with lemon juice. It's nothing, really, but I am glad you are enjoying it."

When they had finished the meal, Guido returned to his television. Brandy helped Rosita clear the table, and wash the dishes. Not long after that, Guido excused himself and retired for the night. Brandy told Rosita that she was going out for the evening,

"I'm going to El Pueblo with several of my classmates, and will probably be back very late, so don't worry, or wait up for me. Two of my classmates are police officers, so I'll be safe!"

"El Pueblo! There are many clubs there! That is nice. You should spend time with young people, but be very careful!"

"Oh, don't worry. I can take care of myself! Besides, there'll be many of us, and there's safety in numbers.

Chapter 9

Checking Out the Night Life

Brandy walked to the corner, where a taxi was waiting, from which Ted emerged. "Hi Brandy! Mike, Kerry, Paul, me and you, are going to share this cab. We'll meet the rest of the gang there. The driver says El Casa Caliente is a real good spot, so we'll start there. Hop in, we're burnin' daylight!"

Burnin' daylight? Where did you get that?"

"From my hero, John Wayne, in the movie, 'The Cowboys!' It's one of my favorites!"

Brandy joined Paul and Kerry in the back seat, and then said, "We're going to El Casa Caliente? That sounds like a hooker hangout!"

"Naw! It's supposed to have hot music and dancing. Mike is a wild man on the dance floor."

About ten minutes later, after four or five brushes with death, the cab arrived at a strip of bars and restaurants, where Karen Bristol, a social worker from Newark, Tracy Riggs, a dance instructor from Kansas, Trevor Beasley, a geologist from Colorado, and Fred Sims, a Chicago lawyer, exited.

They gathered together, and surveyed their surroundings. Ted said, "This looks like a little town I saw in Spain, when I was on Embassy duty in with the Marines!"

Brandy asked, "You were a Marine?

"Semper Fi, doll face!"

"Doll face? Boy, are you full of shit!"

"Once a Marine, always a Marine!" Anyway let's check this place out. There's the joint the cabbie recommended, El Casa Caliente. Want to start there?"

Brandy said, "Well, I don't know. Cabbies steer tourists to any place that pays them to do it. I'm betting it's full of hookers and I don't care how they earn a living, I just have no use for their services"

"Semper Fi! Where's your sense of adventure? We'll have a drink, maybe a dance or two, and then move on.

There are a lot of bars here, and so little time."

When the group entered, they were ushered to three tables which the hostess had hastily pushed together, across then dance floor from a Salsa band. About two dozen unescorted females in very sexy outfits were either sitting in pairs at tables, or on stools around a massive bar. There were several couples gyrating wildly to the music, some of whom seemed to know what they were doing, and others did not appear to care. A waitress in a very short white skirt, and a scarlet tube top, came to the table to take their orders. Brandy and Kerry ordered margaritas, and the others order beer, except for Karen, who meekly asked for a diet cola. As soon as the waitress left the table, Ted asked Brandy to dance. When the number ended, she led her partner back to the table, and was very happy to see that the drinks had arrived. She lifter her glass, and took a sip. When she noticed that it was quite potent, she decided to nurse it, and was delighted to see that Kerry was almost gulping the contents of her glass. She said, "Kerry, you have to dance with this Marine, he's really hot!"

Ted, who had begun chugging his beer as soon as he sat down, jumped to his feet, and dragged the long legged blonde out to the dance floor.

Paul, who had been sitting next to Brandy, said, "This is a clip joint!"

Brandy agreed, "I think you're right, and I don't want to hang around here too long. I strongly suspect that all those ladies in butt shorts with their boobs hanging out of their tops are not tourists! I 'm ready to move on, and so are some of the others."

She and Paul finished their drinks, and when Ted and Kerry finished dancing, she said, "We're going to find another bar. Of course, you may want to stay; maybe you'll meet the right girl, and bring her home to your mom!"

Ted lifted his beer, drained the glass, and dragged Kerry, who was "working it" for all it was worth, back out to the dance floor. Then Paul picked up the check.

"This round is on me!"

Fred, the Chicago lawyer, fished into his wallet, and extracted a bill, which he stuffed into Paul's shirt pocket.

"Thanks, but I'm going to stick around here. I think I see someone I know at the bar. This should cover my end, and I'll catch up with you later."

Paul called the waitress to the table and paid her. The group headed for the door, leaving Ted and Kerry bouncing about to the deafening sounds of the band. As she was leaving, Brandy noticed that Fred was talking to a short, very well built brunette with pink highlights in her hair. She was perched on a bar stool with her legs crossed, and she was wearing a gold lame halter and matching skin tight shorts.

"Hey, guys, catch a look at the counselor's friend! Does any one want to bet on whether we'll see anymore of him tonight?"

During the next two hours, the group went from one club to the other, and even though she sipped them slowly,

slowly, Brandy began to feel the effects of her Tequila laden cocktails. Kerry and Ted had rejoined them in the first bar they had found after they left Casa Caliente. Kerry, who was still not sipping her drinks, was ignoring Ted, and openly pursuing Paul, who continued to direct his attention to Brandy. As midnight approached, Ted lifted Brandy from her chair, and carried her out to the dance floor. She began to dance, playfully exaggerating her moves. Ted pulled her close, and said, "I really think you're hot, and we're just a short walk from the Holiday Inn! What do you say?"

"Boy, are you a smooth talker! Why not ask Kerry?

She's feeling no pain, and might even give you a piggy back ride! I think you're really a nice guy, and it's just the beer talking, or I'd kick you where it hurts! I'm going home, now. See you at school!"

She walked back to the table, finished her drink, and then shared a cab with Paul back to the corner where they had assembled earlier.

While they were in the taxi, Paul said, "You really seemed pissed back there, what did that jarhead say to you?"

"He graciously invited me to shack up with him at the Holiday Inn, and I said no thanks! He's drunk, but I know he's a nice guy, and all he really did was ask. Maybe I overreacted."

"Well, you're beautiful, and what he did was pretty crude, but guys do get out of line every once in a while."

"I know that, but he knows I have a boyfriend back home, and even if I was that horny, I wouldn't mind a little finesse!"

"I'll bear that in mind. Remember that we're traveling together in the morning."

"And you remember what I said about finesse! Of course, Nora will be there to chaperone! "

When the taxi reached Rosita's house, Paul paid the driver, and got out to walk with Brandy to the gate. She kissed him on the cheek, and said, "Thank you for helping me get out of that mess. I'll see you tomorrow. Can you find your way home?"

"I sure hope so, it's five houses down the block, and I don't have the best sense of direction, but I'll try!"

Bandy laughed, and said, "Oh, that's swell, considering that we'll be traveling together in just a few hours. Goodnight!"

She went inside, and went directly to bed. A few hours later, she arose with the sun, took a quick shower, and packed her duffel bag for her trip to Arenal, being careful to include her backpack. a poncho, and the biohazard bag complete with snake bite and bee sting kits which Chuck had given her the day he left.

Chapter 10

The Traveling Trio

After breakfast, Brandy joined her fellow students for the walk to school. Ted approached her timidly, and muttered, "Hey, Brandy, I know I made an ass of myself last night, but like you said, it was the beer, and you can't blame a Marine for trying!"

"I don't. Just don't get any wrong ideas. I think you're a pretty nice guy, and I like you, but I have a boyfriend. He has been my steady since high school, and someday when I'm sure I can handle a permanent commitment, I'll probably marry him, and have children. I'm here to learn Spanish-- I'm not looking for action!"

Ted joined Mike and two detectives from New Jersey who had arrived on Wednesday. Brandy walked with Paul, and when they reached the school, Nora was waiting in the break area. Brandy greeted her. "Hello Nora, are you all set for our journey? I'm going to run back for my bag on the lunch break, and we'll grab a taxi to the bus station."

When her classes ended, Brandy sprinted back to pick up her bag and say goodbye to Rosita and Guido. She hugged them both, and they each kissed her, and told her to be safe. As she ran out the door, Guido was mumbling in Italian about crazy kids and volcanoes. On her way back to school, she thought, *Those people are so cute! I feel like I have a grandma and grandpa right here!*

Back at the school, she joined Paul and Nora. They hailed a taxi to go to the Coca-Cola bus station. After they climbed aboard, the cab lurched away from the curb and began speeding through the crowded streets, narrowly missing pedestrians, potholes, and avoiding t-boning scores of other cars. It sped past clothing stores, souvenir shops, and outdoor meat, fruit and vegetable stands, none of which had the benefit of refrigeration. The hair-raising journey ended moments after the driver narrowly avoided a young man who had unwisely stepped in front of the car, the car came to an abrupt stop. Paul, after looking around, asked, " Is the station? I don't see any signs."

"No, it's three blocks straight ahead. I don't like to drive in that neighborhood. I only charge you to here, not all the way."

Paul laughed, and then paid the fare. When the three of them and their belongings were safely out of the car, he said, "I only tip what the trip is worth!"

He walked to the sidewalk and they started out in the direction of the station.

Brandy said, "What a delightful neighborhood! If it's not safe to drive through, it will be a real treat to walk around in! My, what a lovely aroma, everything smells like urine!"

They entered the bus station and went to the ticket counter, where they purchased tickets to San Carlos from a smiling, baldheaded, little man, who reminded Brandy of a Hispanic Homer Simpson. He gave them directions, speaking so rapidly in Spanish that Paul and Nora walked away in bewilderment. Brandy remained at the counter to try to conceal her money from potential wrong doers. While so engaged, she heard the clerk laughing, and talking his friend, who was seated next to him. "Those crazy American kids didn't understand a word I just said to them. They'll end up in San Pedro!"

After the two men had enjoyed their moment of laughter, they smiled coyly at Brandy. She returned the smile, stretched her statuesque figure to her maximum height, and said, "I understood every word you just said, and if the crazy American kids go to San Pedro, it is because of your wonderful directions!"

She winked at the two men, and as she wiggled tantalizingly away, she heard them laughing hysterically. She went to the waiting area to join her friends, and a few minutes later, they were aboard the bus in comfortable seats, without air conditioning, but with large windows, through which a warm, fragrant breeze flowed. It was not long before they were out of the city, and winding their way through the beautiful countryside. Flowers and trees bloomed everywhere--along the road, and on the sides of very steep hills. More than once, the bus passed an eighteen wheeler load with wood or other commodities on a single lane, blind curve or its rear wheels came close to plunging it into the one hundred foot gorge below. Nonetheless, when Brandy looked out the window at the mesmerizing scenery, felt the warm breeze on her face, and realized that two honks of the horn meant the bus was head-on with another around a curve in the road, she began to relax, with no fear of that over which she had no control. Just seeing the cows on the distant hills, the sun slowly descending behind the mountains, the plethora of purple, pink, orange, or red flowers, the coffee, bananas, melon, and orange crops made her forget that she was hurtling down a mountain road in a tin can on wheels.

Though Paul and Nora had slept through much of the three hour bus trip, the time passed quickly for Brandy. Each time the bus climbed to the top of a ridge, she marveled at the lush, fertile land below, as the sun set, and a full moon rose above the majestic mountains to stand the night watch in the sky. Soon, when the rolling behemoth was nearing San Carlos, it passed through several tiny barrios, where impoverished children ran alongside the bus, so close to the rapidly rotating wheels that Brady prayed they would not be killed. The sight of plywood shacks, and rusted out metal huts with trash piled in front of them, surrounded by the delicate petals of beautiful flowers made tears well up in her eyes, and caused her to think,

What a contrast! It is a combination of rich and poor; ugliness and beauty! Coming here should make Americans grateful to God that they have what they have!

Soon, her eyes found a sign which said: "Welcome to San Carlos", and she noticed that Paul and Nora were both awake. When the bus stopped, and after they had secured their luggage, they entered the station, where Brandy paid a hundred colones for a fistful of toilet tissue, and used the bathroom. When she returned, she was less than happy to learn that the bus to La Fortuna would not leave for two hours. While they stood discussing what to do while waiting, a man driving a 1990 Nissan Sentra pulled to the curb, and emerged partway from the battered vehicle.

"Hola! I see you wait for bus to La Fortuna. I am going there now. Would you like a ride? I will give you a cheap price!"

"No thank you, we'll wait for the bus."

Paul, who was very impatient, said, "Don't leave yet, we'll talk it over."

Then, speaking in a low voice, he said, "I'm for going with this guy. Ticos--Costa Rican men, give rides all the time to help support their families."

This guy could really be taking us for a ride, I vote for the bus!"

Paul said, "Okay, but I'm going with this guy. Two hours is a long time. See you in La Fortuna! "

He walked to the car and opened the back door, then turned to Brandy, and said, "If you're coming, hop in. I'll protect you ladies!"

Brandy crawled onto the seat, and Nora silently followed. Paul climbed into the front seat, and closed the door. When Brandy looked at the dashboard, she noticed a statue of the Virgin Mary, below which was taped a picture of the driver, his wife and four children. She thought, *Now, that is comforting! He has a figurine of the Virgin Mary, and a photo of his family. Of course, I never rode with Charles Manson, and he might have had things like that in his car!*

She surreptitiously removed her Swiss army knife from her pocket, along with her compass, so, if threatened, she might use the compass cord as a garrote, or defend her self with the knife. Not long after that, she began to enjoy the friendly conversation with the driver, tranquilized again by the warm breeze wafting though the window and the reflection of the moon on the small rivers and streams which wound their way through the fields. Cows grazed along the roadway, and the moon drew an outline of the distant mountains. When they reached their lodgings, a long row of little box like cabins which reminded Brandy of those she had seen in old movies from the 1930s, extending along a ridge overlooking the volcano. Just before they entered the office, which also housed a small restaurant, a pungent odor filled the air, which Brandy was soon to learn was the smell of volcanic ash. When they reached their quarters, she looked at the volcano and saw that the top was obscured by the clouds.

Once inside, they discovered there was a bathroom and two small bedrooms with picture windows facing the volcano. Brandy and Nora selected one bedroom in which there was a double bed. Paul carried his bag into the other, stretched, yawned, and said, "I don't know about you ladies, but I'm going to sack out. I'll see you in the morning. Good night!"

He entered his room and closed the door. Brandy told Nora she could shower first, and sat in a chair with a bottle of water, in hopes of seeing the volcano erupt. When her roommate finished in the bathroom, she showered quickly, pulled on a clean shirt and a pair of shorts, and returned to her vigil. In a short time, she was sound asleep, but woke up at 1:00 am to discover that the volcano was still not visible. After that, she slept until 6:00 am, and, one hour later, she and the others were ready to start the day.

Chapter 11

Journey to Arenal

Brandy looked out the window, and the sun was shining. A thermometer outside the window showed the temperature was 85 degrees Fahrenheit. When she started out the door, she realized that she had neglected to apply protection from the sun. She retreated to the bathroom, put sun screen on every exposed area, and started out the cabin door. At that precise moment, torrents of rain began to descend. She called to the others, "Guys, it's pouring rain out there, what should we do?"

Then she looked at Paul, who had a wistful smile on his face, and said, "Besides sit around in here and drink beer?"

He grinned good naturedly, and said, "Hey, I'm still recovering from yesterday's hangover! I vote we get a cab, and go check out the resort at Catara La Fortuna."

Nora said, "Well, I sure don't want to stay in here all day. I say we go with Paul's idea."

Paul called a taxi, and a few minutes later, a Nissan Sentra, which could have been a twin of the one they had traveled in from San Carlos, appeared outside. Once they were underway, however, they became painfully aware of a significant difference. It had no shock absorbers, and could not have passed a safety inspection anywhere in the United States. After it had literally bounced its way up dirt roads until it reached the park, Brandy commented, "I feel like I've ridden a horse for forty kilometers over rocks!"

Inside the park, the three young adventurers, with a guide in the lead, began the descent into the ravine on a very steep, flooded and precarious trail, while the rain continued to pour, and, though the canopy of the rainforest provided some shelter, the downpour made the descent even more dangerous. At one point the hikers stopped to look around. Brandy gazed at the canopy above, and excitedly exclaimed, "This is gorgeous! Look at that lush, green foliage! The vines hanging from the trees, the small plants and little flowers dancing from the weight of the raindrops make me feel like I'm on a movie set!"

As they continued down the trail, Paul said, "Yeah, there is beauty everywhere, and the nice thing about the rain is that the snakes won't be out to bite us. I do not care for snakes!"

Nora, who usually had little to say, smiled and remarked, "That is good, because I'm terrified of snakes!"

Brandy said, "Well that is one thing we all seem to have in common! I don't even like to think about snakes!"

After speaking, she thought, *So we all would shit if we even saw a snake. Well, I don't have the heart to tell this big, cute, jock that the pythons who live here like to hang from trees, which means I'll be the only person who gets nervous each time a vine slithers down my back, and slides under my poncho! Anyway, it's more likely that I will fall to my death into the ravine, than to get my butt bitten by a Fir de Lance or one of his relatives!*

Soon they were halfway down the trail, and a beautiful, powerful thread of sparkling water, dropping over one hundred feet from the top of the forest, came into view. Paul shouted, "La Catarata! Will you look at that! Only God can do that!"

They continued to the bottom of the trail, and then stood in silence as they watched the water thundering from the pinnacle of the forest to fall into a shimmering turquoise pool. The mist that sprayed into their faces felt refreshing, in contrast to the 85 degree temperatures. The trees around them dripped with rain, and scores of smaller waterfalls were visible all around them. The water was tempting, but the force of the falls made swimming impossible. As the water hit the cool azure pool below, its impact created a large splash, which changed directions with the wind.

While Paul, Nora, and the guide wandered around the area, Brandy sat down on a large flat rock, and listened to the raindrops pounding rhythmically on the trees above, the crashing of the waterfall, the babbling turquoise stream, and the cry of a bird somewhere in the treetops. As she marveled at the beauty, she began to think, *I wish Chuck could be with me now to share this! He would love it. When I decide to marry, I hope he'll still be in my life.*

When the others came back, they sat on the rocks for an hour, admiring the sights around them, and then the guide said, "Let's head back up the trail."

He started the arduous climb up the pathway, which was so steep, that it was necessary at times to grab the rocks above to pull themselves up. As she struggled upward Brandy thought, *It would be just my luck to reach for a vine, and discover that I had a very unhappy viper in my hand!* When they reached the top, they returned to La Fortuna, where they ate lunch, and arranged for a guide to pick them up, to take them to Arenal National Park. A short time later, an old truck with a club cab arrived. Brandy and Nora climbed into the back seat, and Paul sat next to the driver.

At the park, they hiked Los Tucanes trail, which the guide said would take them to the area of devastation from the 1968 eruption of the volcano. When they reached it, they found that it was overgrown by a tall plant which resembled sugar cane. They passed through the field, and entered a dark secondary growth forest. Under the watchful eye of their guide, the trio climbed the hill in darkness, and were greeted by a spectacular view when they reached the top. Immense black lava rocks covered the entire surface, as far as the eye could see. Jorge, the guide, said, "This is where the 1992 eruption occurred. If we clime the rocks to the top of this peak, the view is magnificent. Follow me, and be very careful."

Paul stepped in behind him, and the two women followed. Soon Brandy could see the volcano stretching into the clouds. The mountains with steam rising from them were on one side, and the sparkling blue waters of Lake Arenal were on the other. Volcanic ash covered the ground, and the angry volcano emitted a loud rumble, as if to say, "You are close enough, stay where you are!"

The party stood in silence, with an area of total devastation on the right, and one of spectacular beauty on the left. Suddenly a hard wind began to blow, and an eerie sound resonated through the area.

Brandy said, "What is that sound? It gives me goose bumps!"

Jorge laughed, and said, "That is just the howler monkeys serenading us."

"I'm glad to hear that! I thought it was the Chupacabra!"

Paul laughed, and said, "Do you like Rock Music?"

"I like almost any kind of music, but I wasn't talking about the Rockers, I was talking about that thing that eats chickens!"

"Oh, that Chupcabra! I thought about the band because I played lead guitar when I was in college. We had our own guitar attack!"

Jorge interrupted their discourse, saying, "Don't stand too close. Arenal is very dangerous. There are steam vents and abysses, everywhere, and lava flows continuously from the crater." A few minutes later, he said, "We must go now, it's about to rain again."

By the time they had climbed back up the rocks, the rain began pouring down on them, and continued until they reached the truck. Once inside, Jorge said, "Now we'll go to the resort at Tabacon."

While they bounced along on the rock infested road, Jorge spoke about the resort and its facilities. "Thermal waters, warmed by the volcano, run down through the resort, and when you sit in the water, all the aches and pains flow out of your body. You will see!"

Brandy thought, *If I sit down in the warm water before I find the bathroom, aches and pains will not be the only thing flowing from this body!*

The three tourists entered the resort, changed into their bathing suits, and walked to dimly lit area with numerous rocky pools of thermal water and waterfalls, surrounded by a variety of trees. Brandy exclaimed, "This is amazing, and breathtaking! I might stay here all night."

Paul chuckled, and said, "Well, you'd better get your butt wet quick, because the guide said we have one hour!"

He sat down beside her, and said, "Nora went looking for bottled water, and I want to say something to you before she gets back. I hope you don't take it the wrong way. I came here to learn Spanish, but I also came to think. Four months ago, I broke up with a girl I met in college. She was a cheerleader, and a lot like Kerry. We were together for five years, but neither of us spoke of marriage. Then one day, out of the blue, she told me she wanted to get married, but never intended to have children. I want to be a father some day, and since I'm almost thirty, I can't wait forever. When I first saw you, I felt that you might be the girl I'm looking for. I feel that I could spend the rest of my life with you, and I've only known you for a week. I'm talking long term, here. I'm not out for a quickie, like Ted, and I'm sober!"

Brandy started to speak, but Nora was walking towards them with three bottles of water.

"Paul, you're sweet, and I'm flattered, but you've got the wrong girl, and I'll tell you why when I get the chance."

Nora handed each of them a bottle of water, then sat down in the pool next to them. When Jorge called them, they changed their clothes, and returned to the truck. Back at the cabin, they called for pizza, and after they had eaten, Nora excused herself and went to bed. Paul sat down next to Brandy to join her in her hope s of seeing a volcanic eruption. When she was sure that Nora could not hear, she spoke softly, and said, "Paul, you're a real nice guy, and a lot of girls would have loved to hear what you had to say back at Tabacon. Unfortunately, I'm not what you're looking for. I've been with the same guy since high school, and I love him very much. The problem is that I'm not sure that I'll ever get married, but I love kids, and that part usually works better for married people! I set a goal when I was a freshman in high school. I want to have a career in law enforcement, if I can get into that line of work, and I don' plan to marry any time soon!"

"Hey, that's cool, but I'm no quitter, I'm used to pissing in the wind. If you don't mind, I'm going to hit the sack. Goodnight."

"Goodnight. Remember, we're going kayaking in the morning before we start back!"

Paul slowly walked to his room, and closed the door. Brandy decided to sleep on the couch, in hopes that she could see Arenal erupt, and lash out at the sky above, with smoke and flames, like a dragon in the days of old. She began to doze, but woke up several times, hoping in vain to see the volcano do its thing, but her hopes did not materialize, and by the time the rising sun was scheduled to appear, it was raining. She was grateful that the torrents outside meant that the kayak trip would be cancelled, because she had been awake most of the night.

She stumbled into the bedroom, quickly showered, then put on fresh clothing and put her back pack into her duffel bag with the rest of her gear for the journey back to San Jose. The scenery on the alternate route they had chosen was similar to that which they had encountered when they were heading out, except that they crossed the Catarata River. Brandy could see the bridge through the front window of the bus, and a sign which said that it was three hundred feet above the stream. No sooner than the bus had started thundering across the wooden plank surface, Brandy remembered an old cliché about 'termites holding hands', and thought of how perfectly it described the decrepit span. Just as the vehicle's wheels cleared the last plank, Brandy looked back and saw a huge crocodile who seemed very disappointed that he had been deprived of a tasty snack!

Chapter 12

The Fish of the Devil

When Brandy got to her class on Monday morning, she discovered that another colleague of Ted and Mike's had arrived. She also learned that Ted, and Mike would be leaving on Friday. After Ted had introduced her to Jimmy Roach, he said, "The good news is that Jim is a very nice married man with four kids, who won't get drunk, and try to get in your pants. The bad news is that I'll be leaving with Mike, and I won't get a chance to try one more time, but with a bit more finesse!"

Jimmy, whose face reddened slightly, said, "Corrigan, you're reprehensible! This lady is way out of your league."

Brandy said, "Don't waste your time; Ted knows that I know how full of crap he is! What he doesn't know is that bad boys turn me on, depending on how crude they are."

"Well, old Ted didn't invent crude, but he's taken it to a new level!"

At that point, Amanda called the class to attention. When it ended at noon, Brandy and her three classmates went to the café for lunch. When Ted and his cohorts ordered the special, Brandy said, "You guys know by now that I like to live on the edge, and eat something different There is something here 'Pescado del Dias, the catch of the day, which I can't pronounce or translate. I'm going to ask the waiter about it." When she did, the slightly bald little man said that it was a very special fish dish, and she said, "Ah! It's fish! I'll have that!" When her food came, she noticed that it had an odd taste about it, but she drenched it with picante sauce, and washed it down with pineapple juice. The rest of the afternoon was uneventful, and she had no problem until dinner time, when she began to feel weak, and nauseated. She told Rosita that she felt as if she was going to die, and that she might not be able to keep any food in her stomach if she had dinner.

"What did you have for lunch?"

"I had the 'Pescado del Dias. It tasted funny, but I ate it anyway, and now I'm dying."

"Oh, my goodness! You should never eat fish in this country! The menu should have said, 'Pescado del Diablo' -- the fish of the devil!' I'll make you some toast, and manzanilla tea."

After she finished her tea and had taken a few bites from the toast, Brandy went to her room where she rummaged through her biohazard bag, removed a large bottle of Pepto Bismol, gulped down the recommended dosage, and went to bed. Despite frequent trips to the bathroom, she managed to make it through the night, and was content in the morning with the fact that she was able to keep down crackers and ginger ale. She went to her morning classes, but her condition worsened, so she skipped her afternoon lesson, and went back home, where she slept for five hours, until her hostess awakened her. "Brandy, I brought you a bowl of chicken soup. It is best to have something in your stomach."

When Brandy sat up in bed, Rosita placed the tray in front of her, and sat down beside her. When the bowl was empty, she went to her desk, and worked on a class assignment for an hour, then retired for the night. On Wednesday, she felt better, and walked to class with Paul, Terence Sullivan, an Australian, who taught school in Japan, and his Japanese wife, Mikasa.

As they walked, Mikasa said, "You seemed very ill yesterday at school, and I did not see you in the afternoon. What is your illness?"

"I ate some bad fish, and I've been worn out and nauseous. I also have diarrhea."

"Bad fish is sometimes a big problem in my country. I have some herbal medicine I always carry in my purse."

She reached into her handbag, removed a small flask, and handed it to Brandy. As soon as Brandy arrived at school, she poured it into a cup, and drank it. Within the hour she felt that she was fully recovered. She ate soup and salad for lunch, attended her private lesson, and set out for the daycare center.

When Brandy entered the room where the children were assembled, the jubilant tykes began yelling, "MaestraBrandy, Maestra Brandy!" They began running about, and jumping with excitement. When Brandy heard them, she thought, *Maestra! I know that's the Spanish word for teacher, but they probably think it means the same as big, dumb cow!*

During the next hour Brandy and the children colored and painted. Then, after she taught her charges English words, they all went outside to play "Simon dice" (Simon says). Luis gave the first command which was "Simon says, sit! The next was, "Simon says, play dead!"

Brandy thought, *This is a piece of cake! I've been half dead for two days anyway, going the rest of the way will be easy!*

No sooner than she had reclined and closed her eyes, Luis shouted, "Simon says, make a hamburguesa!"

When she heard the command, Brandy who was peacefully enjoying her pretended demise, opened her eyes to see a herd of screaming urchins careening toward her defenseless abdomen. Fabio, in the role of a slice of cheese, was the first to land, followed by the lettuce, portrayed by Danielo, a tomato named Fredrico, a pickle named Consuela, Rudy as a dab of ketchup, and finally the top half of a bun called Magdalena. Then the cheese accidentally kicked Brandy in the ribs when the pickle jumped on top of the tomato and squashed the head of the lettuce. In the turmoil, the ketchup was dumped on the pavement, but managed to climb back onto the top of the bun. Then, though no command was given, scores of little hands began tickling Brandy's sides.

Mercifully, the torture ended, and Brandy was able to get a game of tag started. When the play session ended, she said goodbye to her playmates, and was leaving the center. As she started out the door, one of the nurses, Melinda Salazar was walking down the hallway. "Buenos tardas, Brandy, I hope the children did not wear you out. They love you very much."

"I love them, too. No, I'm fine; in fact, I'm on my way to the gym, to work out. I've been eating so much, I have to do something, or I'll have to buy new clothes."

"I think you look very trim, but it is important to stay fit. What gym do you go to?"

"Believe it or not, it's called the Musculoso Fitness Center. It's close to the school, but I think it was built by the first Spaniards who came here, and I think Columbus brought the exercise bikes over on one of his ships!"

"I know that place. Yes, it's old, but the people are nice."

"Yes, they are, and I have fun with the trainers. We kid each other a lot. 'I'll be back, soon. Buenas tardes."

"Buenas tardes, Brandy! We'll be looking forward to your next visit. The children love you!"

When she finished her workout and was leaving the gym, Brandy noticed that a step class was about to begin, and asked if she could sign up. The instructor told her that she could join in with the other women, and make her arrangements after class. Shortly after she had started, she began to think, *This is really hard! The commands given to the beat of the techno music aren't getting through to me. I'm two steps behind, and turning backwards, when the little girls in front of me are turning forward. When they leave, they'll probably be laughing about the big fat gringo girl in the back row! They actually seem very nice, and if nothing else, I've made a few new friends!*

As Brandy was walking back to Rosita's house, she passed a computer café, and thought, *I'm sure that I'm cured, but I think I'll drop a short e-mail to Chuck, and then see what I can find on the internet about fish poisoning.*

In the café, she sent a short message to Chuck, then went to a search engine and typed in, "food poisoning-- fish." In a very short time she learned that she probably had gotten a disease called Ciguatera which could be caused by eating any fish caught in tropical waters, and manifested by symptoms which, included dizziness, nausea, vomiting, diarrhea, and numbness, which were identical to those she had experienced. Reading on, she learned that there was no medicine that would cure the illness, but that it was treated by medicines which would alleviate the symptoms, which could last as long as two weeks, depending on the amount of poison which had been ingested.

She signed off the computer, and then went home, where she finished her homework. She went to bed, confident that she had been cured. To her dismay, when she awoke the next morning, she was more miserable than she had been a day earlier, and that the remedies she had used had simply resulted in temporary relief. She drank a can of ginger ale, and went to her morning class.

In the afternoon, she and Vicki went to the Mercado Central, and while they were passing a fishmonger's booth, she held her breath, and tried to avoid looking at the fish. Her efforts were to no avail, and she was certain that one fish, which she had presumed to be dead, had winked at her. She thought, *I'm being taunted by El Pescado del Diablo, and he has forced me over the edge! I need to find some fresh air, and then I can die in peace!*

She looked ahead, and was pleased to find that they had reached the exit. Soon after she parted company with her teacher, she went directly home. She decided to go to bed right after supper, in the hopes of recovering by the weekend, in time for a planned trip with Paul and Nora to Manuel Antonio Playa. To her surprise, she slept though the night, and woke up refreshed as the sun began to rise, and a Toucan in the garden peered at her through the window for a few minutes before he flew away to start his day.

Chapter 13

Sun, Sand, and Surf

On Friday, Brandy, Paul and Nora decided to skip their morning classes to get an early start. As soon as she finished breakfast, she shouldered her backpack, lifted her duffel bag from the floor, and headed outside. When she reached the gate, a 1999 Land Rover pulled up, driven by a young Costa Rican woman. Paul was seated in the front passenger seat, and Nora was in the back seat, surrounded by luggage. Brandy paced her duffel bag on the floor, took off her back pack, and climbed into the vehicle. Paul said, "This is Juanita Perez, my host's daughter, and she has offered to drive us to the bus station."

"I'm pleased to meet you Juanita, and thank you for saving us from a killer cab driver!"

It soon became apparent that Juanita was not very familiar with stick shifts, and the group finally arrived at the bus station after stalling twenty times in less than fifteen minutes. Brandy and the others were gratified to have arrived safely at the station, and hopped aboard the bus bound for Manuel Antonio Playa National Forest. The bus rolled up and down the mountains for over two hours, passing palm trees, and a wide variety of tropical vegetation, before it screeched to a stop in front of a long weather-beaten building with an ancient rusty corrugated metal roof, where several busses and trucks were lined up in the parking lot. After the driver announced a fifteen minute rest stop, he and his passengers went inside, where he joined three drivers from other busses. While the driver and his colleagues ordered rice and beans and flirted with the waitress, Brandy walked around looking at assorted souvenirs, magazines, and cheaply made tropical clothing. As she wandered about, she thought, *Great, the driver is pigging out on beans and rice! Boy, am I glad we're sitting near the back. That's a very dangerous diet for a long bus ride!*

When the break was over, everyone trooped back to the bus, and the monotony of crawling up, and rolling down the seemingly endless rows of mountains, made more interesting by an occasional close encounter with oncoming traffic, continued for two more hours. Suddenly, the bus's transmission failed, just as the pavement seemed to end at what appeared to be a dried up riverbed rather than a road. After everyone had gotten off, Paul said, "The driver says our hotel is just up the road. Why don't we hike the rest of the way?"

Brandy and Nora agreed, and they retrieved their belongings and walked to the hotel, only to discover that their suite would not available for several hours. They left their bags at the desk, then changed into bathing suits, and went out to the pool to have lunch and swim. They found a table in the shade, and Paul ordered a beer. I'll buy the first round. Anyone interested?"

Nora told him she would like to have bottle of water. Brandy said, "It's a bit early. If I start drinking now, I'll get sleepy. Order me a bottle of water. I'm going to get wet!"

When she stood up, she noticed that two small boys on the terrace above the pool, where a bald man in his mid-thirties was paddling about, enjoying the sunshine, were prodding a huge Iguana with a stick. She sat back down just as the homely creature plummeted into the water below, missing the man's head by inches. The terrified man decided at that point to set an Olympic record which could never be broken, and began swimming as though his life was in peril. If his nationality had ever been in doubt, it became obvious that he was German, because, with every stroke, he screamed, "Ach du lieber, mein gott, mein gott!" His screams became louder when he and the Iguana emerged from the water at the same time, and in the same spot.

A waiter, who was laughing uncontrollably while witnessing the spectacle, calmly grabbed the hapless animal by the tail scooped it up, and offered the man an Iguana steak on the house. By that time the man had regained his composure, but meekly declined the offer. Brandy walked to the edge of the pool, and jumped in. Paul and joined her a few minutes later.

After they had frolicked in the water for close to an hour, Brandy said,

"It doesn't look like we'll be able to check in anytime soon. I'm going to scope out the beach. Anyone want to come along?"

Nora and Paul nodded their approval, and put on their shoes and socks. Soon they were heading about eight hundred meters uphill on a path which crossed several pastures where cows were peacefully grazing. When they reached the top, they were treated to an incredible view of the ocean 400 feet below. Huge palm trees lined the beach in front of the sparkling blue water, in which there were numerous rock islands about two hundred meters offshore. Brandy gasped with excitement, "Wow! Paul, do you remember the scene in Jurassic Park, where the helo was flying onto the island? This is it! It's breathtaking!"

"Yeah, I saw the movie, and you're right. This is awesome!"

Brandy turned to her left, and saw lush green rolling hills, with the rainforest further off in the distance. A moment later, the group reached a private road, then turned back to the main road. As they walked, they were awestruck by the sight of the sun sinking slowly into the water. They soon reached a cluster of shops and restaurants, and after a man they met recommended Diego's Barbeque Grill, they decided to try it. Brandy asked the waiter what he would recommend, and he answered, "We have the best tuna steak you will find anywhere in the world."

Nora rolled her eyes, but did not speak. Paul chuckled, looked at Brandy, and said, "I'm betting you won't ever eat fish again after last week."

The waiter said, "Did the senorita get some bad fish?"

"Yes, I was sick all last week in San Jose."

"San Jose does not get fresh food! We have the best produce, meat and fish in all of Costa Rica."

"Okay, then I'll have tuna."

Paul cast an apprehensive eye at his companion, but made no comment, and ordered barbequed chicken. Nora ordered a vegetable platter. While they were eating, Paul said, "If you're not heaving your guts out, what do you plan to do tomorrow? A fishing trip might be fun."

Nora said, "I think I'll go to Quepos and walk around. There are many curio shops, and I want to find as Catholic Church."

Brandy spoke. "I really want to go surfing, if I can; I learned to ride the waves in California." Turning to Nora, she said, "I didn't know you were a Catholic. That explains why you don't wear a veil! I thought All Iranians were Muslims."

"No, I'm not Muslim! In fact, my family left Iran because many people there did not treat us well. Many Muslims are very nice, but the fanatics are in control. Regarding tomorrow, I'm terrified of jelly fish, and I get seasick, so I won't be going fishing, and if I swim, it'll be in the pool! You two can do your thing, and I'll do mine."

Paul said, "Well, Brandy, I'd like to hang out with you if you're not dying from food poisoning! Surfing sounds cool! I've never done it, but I was a terror on a skate board when I was a kid."

"That will help, and surfing is really fun. I'm not going fishing tomorrow, that's for sure. You can go and we'll eat dinner together when you get back. Speaking of fish, this is the best tuna I've ever eaten!"

"Well, if you're sick tomorrow, I'm not going to stick around to hold the bucket for you!"

"Gee, I wish you would! That sounds very romantic! Anyway, I'm sure this fish isn't the Pescado del Diablo! By the way, we'd better head back to the hotel, and I think we should take a taxi."

When they reached the hotel, the desk clerk checked them in, and had their luggage taken to the suite. When they reached the suite, they were surprised to learn that their was one double bed, and on the far side, behind an ornamental lattice work near the sliding glass door which opened onto a small balcony, there was a pull-out sofa bed, a table and a desk. Paul walked to the sofa and set his bags down. "Don't worry girls, I know my place!"

Chapter 14

Brandy Wipes Out and Paul Passes Out

When Brandy woke up, Paul and Nora were still sound asleep. She decided not to disturb them, and, after dressing for the beach, she put her beach towel, sunblock, and two bottles of water in her backpack, she left a note for Paul that she would meet him on the beach. She decided to have breakfast while she waited for the bus, and after eating toast and mangoes, she began her journey to Manuel Antonio Playa. She found it difficult to contain her excitement, and as soon as she got off the bus, she began her search for a prime location to go surfing.

She was taken in by the beauty which confronted her as her eyes surveyed the lush rain forest, as it blended with the white sand of the beach. Along the coast there were many coves, and a small river ran from the rain forest to the far corner of the beach. Near the juncture of the stream and the ocean, she saw a sign which read, "Caution Crocodiles." When she read it, she decided to move farther down the beach. She walked across the beach front until she spotted a truck full of surfboards. She approached the compact, muscular, olive skinned man who was sitting cross-legged on the tailgate, and asked, "Will you rent me one of your boards?"

The man looked at the blue-eyed beauty like a hungry man sitting down to a steak dinner, and said,

"You want to go surfing; I'll go out with you. I have a longboard you can use. Have you been surfing before?"

"Yes, I learned last year when I was in California. I love it, but you should know that I'm interested in surfing, and nothing else!"

'Hey, don't get me wrong, my offer was to lend you a board, and go surfing with you. My name is Gerardo Lopez, and I've been a pro-surfer. I was free -style champion of Costa Rica. Now I'm retired."

He pulled a surfboard off the truck, and gave it to Brandy, then secured another for himself. After he called a teenage boy over to watch the truck, he said,

"Okay, let's hit the water, and you can show me what you got! If you've surfed the waves in California, you probably know your stuff!"

Though Brandy had no idea as to whether or not her new friend had lied about being a professional, he impressed her enough with his surfing that she trusted his advice. The darkly handsome young man was very skilled, and obviously putting on a show for her benefit. They cavorted on the waves for two hours, until Brandy decided to take a water break, and headed back to where she had left her beach blanket and back pack. Geraldo returned to his truck where other surfers were gathered. She sat down and secured a bottle of water from her pack. Before she had removed the cap, she heard Paul's voice. "I've been watching you out there, you were really awesome! Where did you get the board?"

"From that Tico I was out there with. He lent it to me, but you'll probably have to pay for yours!"

"That's okay by me! I wouldn't want to sleep with him anyway!"

Don't be a smartass, he's just being nice. He told me he was a professional surfer, and whether he is or not, he sure knows what he's doing!"

Twenty minutes later, Brandy decided to return to the water, and Paul said, "Go for it, but I think I'll just watch you."

Brandy started to walk towards the water, but paused at edge of the beach to look at the waves, and thought, *All I know is big and small, rip currents or no rip currents. These waves look pretty small, and I'd like one long ride before I quit.*

Gerardo must have read her mind, because he came running to where they stood, and said, "Since you're going back out, you should know that the waves are smaller, the currents are stronger, and the waves are slightly inconsistent. If you want me to go back out with you, I'll go get my board."

"That's very nice, but I'm a big girl and I'm sure I can handle it."

He laughed, and said, "Okay, do your thing!"

She waded out into the surf and Gerardo returned to his friends. After she had caught several waves and rode them in, she was so impressed with her success that she broke one of nature's Cardinal Rules, which is, "Never turn your back on the ocean!" She was posing proudly, while admiring the beauty around her when she heard male voices screaming,

"Bueno, Bueno!"

She saw a gigantic wave coming towards her, and began paddling frantically, like a possessed woman. Her efforts were successful, and she managed to catch the incoming wave, but when she rose to a standing position, she realized how enormous the wave was, and that the entire nose of her board was completely submerged. She tried to lean back as far as possible, hoping for redemption, but was thrown high into the air. When she hit the water, she went completely under the waves, striking the left side of her rib cage on a rock, cutting her right leg open, and scratching her left leg from the thigh to the knee. When she finally surfaced, and limped out of the water, Gerardo came running to assist her, with Paul on his heels.

"Bravo! Bravo! That was a magnificent attempt, and an awesome wipeout!"

When he noticed that she was bleeding, he told her that he had a first aid kit in his truck. She said, "The only thing that hurts is my pride. I really wanted to ride that wave!"

"Well, we can go back out in the afternoon, and you can try again. You are a very brave woman!"

"Maybe I will, but I'm going to walk along the beach and think about it."

She went back with Paul, gathered her belongings, and they found a food stand. After eating a taco, which she washed down with a cold beer, she looked out at the ocean, where monstrous waves were wildly crashing towards the beach. She decided not to take Gerardo up on his offer to go back out in the afternoon, and spent the rest of the day walking along the beach with Paul. Finally they sat in the sand admiring the orange sun as it descended into the ocean from the blue, pink, and purple tapestry of the sky. When the fiery sphere was barely visible above the water, they walked to the bus stop, and rode back to the hotel.

When they reached the pool Nora was swimming laps. Brandy called to her, as she finished her lap, and started to emerge from the water.

"How was your shopping trip?"

"I didn't buy anything, but I found a church, and want to go to mass before we leave. I've been back here for over an hour. How was your day?"

"I went surfing, and it was great, except I had a humongous wipeout! I'm too embarrassed to talk about it, but I'm sure that Paul will be glad to tell you all the gory details! Have you eaten yet?"

"No, I haven't, but I think I'll grab a bite here, then go back to the room and read for awhile. I want to go to early mass in the morning. What are your plans?"

"Well, I sort of racked up my poor body in that wipeout, but Paul wants to go to a nice restaurant. Why don't you come along?"

"No. thank you, I think I'll stick with my plans. You two go out and enjoy yourselves."

Paul seemed pleased that Nora had her own plans for dinner, and was clearly disappointed when Brandy said,

"You know, I'm really hurting. Maybe we ought to eat here with Nora, then go for a swim and call it a day."

"Oh, come on, don't be a party pooper! We'll go some place nice. We don't have to check out until 2:00 pm! You can sleep in if you want to!

'Oh, what the heck, I'll take a shower and get dressed, then we can look for a place."

"If it's okay with you, I've heard that the Fuente de la Juventud is one of the most popular places around. I'll call and reserve a table for two."

"The place is called the Fountain of Youth? Sounds interesting, but don't get the idea that this is a dinner date! It can be my treat, or we can split the bill. "

She took a shower, and then rubbed Neosporin on her legs, wiped them dry with gauze, and put on a pair of designer jeans and a blue tank top. When she joined Paul, he was wearing Dockers and a Hawaiian shirt. Once outside, they found a cab, and headed for the Ponce de Leon Hotel. As they rode up in the elevator, Paul said, "I just found out today that Ponce de Leon had an important place in Costa Rican history."

"Well, I knew about Columbus, because my hosts are Italian, but I didn't know much about Ponce de Leon either."

When the elevator doors opened, she said, "Wow, this is beautiful. There's an Aviary in the middle of the room! I wonder if the fountain the birds are crapping in will really make old people young again."

"I doubt it, but this place is something else!"

The headwaiter led them to a table by the panoramic window, with a view of the beach and rainforest. Paul ordered a beer; and Brandy ordered a margarita. When the waiter told them that the special was pork medallions with a red wine and cranberry sauce, they decided to order it, with small salads on the side. When they were halfway through the meal, a Salsa band began to play. Brandy decided to drink her margarita slowly. She began wishing that the man opposite her at the table was Chuck, as she thought; *I wonder what he's doing right now! This place was made for lovers, and margaritas make most people horny! I'd better switch to water.*

She continued sipping her drink slowly, but Paul was on his fifth beer by the time they finished eating. She said,

"Paul, I'm ready to go back to our hotel. I ache all over from my wipeout, and the margarita has made me sleepy. I want to pay my share of the tab. I'll even pay for your dinner. I don't want you to get the idea we're on a date. You are really nice, but I'm not here for romance!"

"Yeah, you've told me about what's his name back in the states. Well, don't worry; I'm looking for a long term relationship, not a one night stand. Hey, that music is hot! Let's dance!"

"Okay, but it'll be our last dance of the night, then I'm leaving, and you can share the cab if you want too, or you can stay here and try your luck at the bar!"

She led Paul out to the dance floor, just as the band stopped playing, and she said, "This has been fun, and I'm glad that I let you talk me into this, but it's time to leave, now! Let's pay our bill and call it a night."

During the taxi, ride back to the hotel, Paul fell asleep, and rested his head on her shoulder. She put her arm around him to male him comfortable, and did not awaken him until they reached the hotel. When they got on the elevator, she said. "Thank you for this evening; you're a very sweet guy!"

He didn't respond, and remained silent until he had entered the suite. Then he walked to the couch where he reclined, without opening it, and said, "Goodnight! I had as great time. Thank you for dinner, and I'll see you in the morning!"

She walked to the other side of the room, where Nora was sound asleep. Then she put on her pajamas and went to bed, but soon discovered that she couldn't sleep on her left side, or her stomach, because of pain around her rib cage, which, combined with Paul's snoring kept her awake for close to an hour. When she finally she managed to fall asleep, she slept until the sun came up, when a mixed chorus of bird calls, and the shrill ranting of howler monkeys reached her ears. She heard the shower running, and then noticed that Nora had left a note that she had gone to early mass, would be taking the bus from Quepos back to San Jose, and would see them at school. The left side of her body was aching, and she began to suspect that she had bruised a rib when she collided with the only rock in the ocean. She had just gotten out of bed, when bathroom door opened.

Paul came out with a towel wrapped around his lower body. When he saw Brandy, he said, "Oops! Excuse me; I didn't know you were awake. I decided to go fishing since we don't have to check out until this afternoon. Want to come along? I promise that I won't propose to you any more on this trip. Nora has checked out, but if you saw her note, you know that! We don't need to check out until mid afternoon, so we've got plenty of time, although a late bus won't get us back to San Jose until about midnight, but we can sleep on the bus and in class tomorrow!"

"Thanks for inviting me on your fishing trip, but I'm really in pain, and decided to eat breakfast; then I'll spend the day soaking in the hot tub and the pool. Also, I'm going to fly back. I want to see the mountains, especially volcanoes, from the air. Why not come with me?"

"I don't know about flying. You do your therapy; I'll go fishing, and we'll talk about it when I girt back!"

Brandy went into the bathroom to put on her swim suit, and when she came out, Paul had left. When she got to the pool area, she walked to the hot tub, and sat down. As she felt her muscles respond to the warm, swirling water she began thinking about Chuck, and whether or not they would be together after she returned to Virginia. It was-not long, however, before her silent meditation was interrupted, when a waiter approached her. "Would the pretty senorita like to have breakfast? I'll have a table ready for you, if you want order something."

"Why, yes, I'd like that very much. I'm going to swim to cool off after I get out of this stew-pot, then I'd like a tall glass of orange juice and some black coffee. Then I'll check out your menu."

Brandy stayed at the pool, following the shade, until almost 1:30 pm, and then returned to the suite to begin packing.

Chapter 15

Flying Through
the Valley of Death

A few minutes after Brandy starter packing, Paul arrived, sat down in a chair, and said, "I've decided to fly back to San Jose with you. I'm not sure that I want to fly over a volcano in a plane flown by a Tico pilot who probably learned to fly in a hang -glider powered by a surplus lawn mower engine, but I'll go with you. Frankly, I don't like flying in small planes, and I can't help wondering what kind of aircraft we'll be flirting with death in down here."

"Don't worry, I've been told they're all twin engine turbo props. It'll be fun."

When they checked out of the hotel, they called a cab to go to the airport. As they approached the field, Paul stammered,

"This is an airport? It's just a Tiki hut with a long runway! God help us, please?"

"Silly, see those planes coning in? They're Caravans, and they look like they're brand new. This is exciting!"

"Yeah, right! I just hope I don't get so excited that I crap in my last pair of clean shorts. I probably should have taken the bus."

"Don't worry; I have some clean panties in my bag. I'll lend you a pair if you have an accident."

"Great! When they find my body, I'll be wearing women's skivvies! My mom will love reading that in the papers!"

They purchased their tickets, and then carried their bags out to the tarmac. When they reach the plane, a beautiful blonde woman climbed out of the cockpit.

"Hello. I'm Kathy Porter, and I'll be your pilot today. Where are you from in the states? I'm from Indiana, myself."

"I'm Brandy, and this is Paul. I'm from Virginia, and he's from Texas."

Paul laughed, and said, "We were expecting a Tico pilot, but you'll do!"

"I get that a lot. These planes are a bit smaller than the ones I flew when I was in the Air Force, but they're fun. My husband is my co pilot. We came down here a couple of years ago, and plan to stay awhile."

Paul asked Kathy to take a picture of them in front of the plane, and when it was done, they got aboard to find they were the only passengers. Moments later, the plane soared into the sky. When they approached the mountains, Brandy looked at Paul's hands, which had a death grip on the arm rests. His knuckles were white, and his face was completely colorless. She thought, *Gosh, he's terrified! I should never have talked him into coming along. I have to calm him down, or he'll have a stroke!*

"Hey, look out the window! The mountains are beautiful, and the sun is just starting to set. You can see the rainforest on your side, and there are rolling fields and mountains on mine."

As she spoke, the plane was ascending to the mid-point of the nearest mountain, when a dense cloud cover obliterated everything in sight. From the look of horror which rose up in his eyes, it was clear that Paul was thinking that the plane could not have possibly risen over the mountain top. Brandy was frantically trying to calm her friend down, when the plane dropped six or seven feet, then began bouncing and swaying from side to side, losing, then regaining altitude. Brandy laughed and said, "Kathy just hitched her seat belt up a notch or two. Isn't this fun?"

Paul was not amused, and answered,

"Hell no, it's not fun! You must be nuts! We're going to die up here!"

"Oh, don't be silly; just pretend you're on the bus. If you were, you would feel we were going to die every time we went around a curve, and that would be for several hours! Up here, if we aren't dead in the next half hour or so, we'll be in San Jose. Besides, if we die, we won't be in the air; we'll be on the ground, or splattered over the side of a mountain!"

She decided to let Paul sweat it out, and hope he would forgive her for bringing him along. She thought, *I don't blame the poor guy, I fly in helos and light planes all the time, and this is the worst ride I've ever had for turbulence! We may go splat on the mountain any minute and die. It's scary, but it's the most breathtakingly beautiful flight I've ever experienced. There is something incredible about flying so low, close to the mountains and the ocean. If we were only in a helo! I'm definitely going to fly some more before I leave here.*

She looked at Paul, and said, "We made it! That's San Jose down there. Now, aren't you glad we flew? Nora left long before us, and she's probably bouncing over the mountains."

"We're not on the ground, yet! When we land, I'll feel safe. But not until we land! By the way, thanks for trying to calm me down! You are very special, even if you are crazy!"

"You're welcome, and thanks for coming along. You're a neat guy, even if you are a wuss!"

He kissed her lightly on the cheek. During the taxi ride from the airport, neither of them spoke, but Brandy began to feel she had bonded with her classmate, and hoped they would travel together again before he left, though she was certain it would not be in an airplane.

Chapter 16

Confusing Conversations and a Disaster at Daycare

Back in San Jose, Brandy found Rosita and Guido sitting in the parlor, and told them of her weekend adventures. They had dinner together, and then she retired to her room to prepare for her classes. On Monday morning, when she was walking to school with Paul and the Sullivans, she learned that Kerry had returned to the states suddenly without telling anyone se was leaving.

After they had walked for a few more minutes, Mikasa moved to Brandy's side, and said, we're going to go to a bar after dinner tonight, and thought you might like to join us."

"I'm not sure I want to go drinking this early in the week, but I'm still stiff and sore from surfing over the weekend, and couple of margaritas before bedtime might be good therapy. Count me in! I'll meet you on the corner at about seven."

That evening, in Magdalena's Bar, Brandy sat at a table with Terry, Mikasa, and Paul, sipping a margarita, and trying to follow the conversation, which was complicated by the fact that Terry spoke English as well as Japanese and Chinese, and a little bit of Spanish. His wife spoke Japanese, and some English, but wanted to practice her Spanish, and the alcohol was affecting their speech with every swallow. Brandy was further perplexed because for some reason, she had been designated as spokesperson for the table when the waiter came to take orders for drinks. Terry would ask Mikasa what she wished to order in Japanese, and she would start to answer in Spanish, then drift into Japanese. The talk at the table began to get further confused when Terry, with his pronounced Aussie accent, droned on about the bloody politicians in the "Estado Unidos," often interrupting Paul in Japanese, then translating into English. In the midst of all of the confusion, one thought was racing through Brandy's mind: *I'm going to have a hell of a time dealing with the paperwork involved in reporting my contacts with foreign nationals when I get home! I can't handle this on one drink!*

When they finally called it a night, she went home, and dreamt about the nation's economy in Spanish, English, Japanese, and a word or two of Chinese. The next morning, her class went to the market to learn about the various kinds of fruit grown in Costa Rica. While she was surrounded by an abundance of exotic fruits, she thought, *I had no idea that most of these morsels even existed, and will have to sample one of each before I leave.*

Brandy went to the daycare center in the afternoon, to teach and play with the children. When the chaos of welcoming her ceased, they played games, then decided to dance. At first, she was amused by their antics, and grateful that she could be a small part of their lives. However, after bouncing around the room for several minutes, the tykes decided that they wanted to paint. Not long after that activity began, however, Daniel and Marissa began fighting over brushes, and screaming at each other in Spanish. Brandy began to feel frustrated because she could not understand what they were saying, or control the nightmarish scenario which she was witnessing. She thought, *They won't listen, and I have no idea what they're saying! They might as well be speaking Hebrew! I don't understand them; they don't understand me, and they have no respect for me! I'm doing a horrible job, and I might as well be drinking after class like Paul and the others!*

When she left the children, she went directly to the gym, where she listened to her walkman in English, feeling defeated and close to tears. She began to wish she was back home with Chuck and her friends. After her workout, she walked home, where her hostess greeted her at the door.

"I saw you coming up the walk, and you look like your best friend has passed away. What's wrong?"

"The children were so wild, and I couldn't control them! They don't respect me, and I wish I was back home!"

"Children can be that way, sometimes, but they mean no harm, and I know you love them. You are here now, so you must put that aside. I have a surprise for you.

"We're having guests for dinner tonight. They're family, and you're part of the family now, so it is time you got to know them!"

Chapter 17

Dinner with the Family

Brandy followed Rosita into the dining room, where the table was set with china plates, wine glasses, and highly polished silverware. After she had taken a shower, she put on a lace trimmed white blouse and a short denim skirt. She returned to the kitchen to assist Rosita. They placed on the table an enormous bowl of pasta, a platter of filet mignon the size of the bed of a pickup truck, bread, salad and asparagus. When Brandy had set down the last of her burden, the doorbell rang. Rosita rushed into the foyer and opened the door. Eight lively people flooded the room, and began hugging Brandy, Rosita, and Guido. Brandy knew Rosita's sister, Gina, and her cousin, Alberto, but the other faces were unfamiliar to her. A diminutive woman with silver tresses giggled as she squeezed Brandy, and whispered, "I'm Lorena, Rosa's cousin! I've heard so much about you, and how lovely you are! Has Guido pinched your bottom, yet?"

Brandy smiled mischievously, and said, "He's a perfect gentleman!" Then she winked, and added, "When Rosa is around!"

They laughed as they walked together into the parlor with the others, who were jabbering loudly in Italian. Soon they were seated at the table, and Guido popped the cork on a bottle of Targano Russo Riserva wine; the boisterous group began eating and drinking as if they were celebrating a major holiday, the end of a war, or some other momentous occasion. Between bites of food, and gulps of the potent beverage, they yelled at each other in Italian, telling stories of the escapades of various family members, with an occasional off color story to add spice to the verbal exchanges, until Brandy spoke out in Spanish,

"I love all of you, and this is really fun, but I can't understand a word you're saying!"

Everyone laughed, and Guido scolded them, "Shame on all of you, we are here to honor this beautiful Senorita, and she has no idea what any of you has said, because you are speaking Italian!"

The stories became more outrageous with each bottle of wine, and the teller of each spoke several decibels louder than the person who had just finished speaking. Rosita left the table, and returned with a tray of dishes filled with melon slices topped by scoops of chocolate ice cream. One female at the table had enjoyed the wine so much that she was scooping her ice cream from her plate with her melon slice. The revelry continued, and soon Tuffy appeared on the scene, sitting in the classic begging position, but Rosita quickly chastised him in Italian, and then in Spanish. After he meekly departed, Brandy, speaking as much to herself as anyone else, said aloud, "How great is that? Dogs are supposed to be dumb, but Tuffy understands two languages, and I have trouble with both of them!"

Alberto, on hearing the remark, laughed so loudly that the china on the table rattled. Soon the men followed Guido into the parlor. Brandy joined the ladies in clearing the table and washing the dishes. Lorena, whose speech was so slurred by the wine that she could no longer master Brandy's name, said, "Beany, you are now a member of our family, and we all love you!"

Rosita, who had heard the remark, said, "Yes, you are family now, and we want you to join us this Sunday on a picnic at a country club.! Will you come with us?"

"Of course I will! It sounds like great fun!"

Chapter 18

Paul Makes a Decision and Pleads His Case

On Wednesday, Brandy attended her classes, went running, and prepared for her Thursday classes. After dinner, she watched a movie with Rosita and Guido, while sitting on the floor with Tuffy's massive head resting on her knee. She was preparing to go to bed when Paul called on the telephone. "Hello, Brandy, I know it's late, but I was hoping we could walk to the corner bar for a drink. You must be bored hanging out with those old people."

"Actually, I'm not bored at all. They're my family while I'm here. You're very sweet to call me, and I could stand a margarita, but I'm all ready for bed. I'll see you tomorrow. We can walk to school like we always do."

"Okay, I'll se you then, but I won't be around much longer, because I'm going back to Texas on Saturday."

"You're leaving school? I thought you were going to be here two more weeks! I'll miss you. Maybe we can have dinner Friday night."

"That sounds great! I'll see you tomorrow. Goodnight"

"Good night Paul."

She hung up the phone, said goodnight to Rosita and Guido, and went to her room. The next morning, when she left the house, Paul was waiting outside the gate.

"Buenos dias! The others have gone ahead, because I asked them to give me some time with you. I wanted to explain why I'm leaving, because I really feel we've made a connection. I've told you how I feel about you, and I know you like me, but you won't give it a chance."

"Paul, you're someone who wants things I can't give you! If I were ready to settle down, and give up my dreams, I probably would be married to Chuck by now. Right now, I'm a student, but long range, I plan to apply to be a Federal agent, and they can't really settle in one place, and that's especially true for a woman! Most agents are married to their jobs. We're going out tomorrow night. I promise that I'll be a fun date, and then it will be goodbye, because I'm not the girl you're looking for."

"Well, you're the girl I want, and I think we could be happy together!"

Brandy paused, then replied, "I'm sorry, but that's not going to happen! You'll always be a very special friend, but that's all! Do you still want to go to dinner on Friday?"

"Sure, but I warn you, I'm going to keep trying until I'm out of here!"

They finished walking to school in silence. When the school day ended, as she headed for the daycare center, she saw Paul walk into a bar.

Chapter 19

Contented Kids, a Smiling Sloth, and a Language Lesson

When Brandy arrived at the daycare center, the children rushed up to her. They dragged her to the tiny tables and chairs, yelling and screaming her name, she decided to just sit down, and be herself. She picked up a lump of playdough, and fashioned a snake, then she made a big sombrero, and put it on his head. Daniel yelped, "Senor Serpente! He is Senor Serpente!"

The other children joined in, "Maestra Brandy has made a snake, and his name is Senor Serpente! Ole!"

When the gleeful chanting subsided, Brandy created a river of popsicle sticks and began speaking for the snake in a very deep voice, "I think I will go for a swim in the river, and then I will take a siesta!"

The moppets squealed with delight when Senor Serpente's sombrero fell into the river, and soon they were all making snakes and other animals. As Brandy watched, she thought, *I'm onto something, here! I've been trying so hard to understand them, and their language that I forgot how easy it is to be a child. From now on, I'll keep it simple!*

On Friday afternoon, she and Vicki had lunch together, before they went to the University to attend a health fair. Senor Sloth was also in attendance, and, to Brandy's surprise, he was awake. She was impressed by the size of his nails and teeth, and ruminated, *He always seems to have a smile on his face! But, what the heck, if all I had to do was lie on my butt all day, eat and sleep I wouldn't have much to frown about!*

After leaving the University, she went home to pick up her gym bag, and then went to the gym. While she was exercising, one of the trainers, expressed his curiosity about the meaning of the phrase, "hang loose." He told her that he had seen the hand gestures on television, and said that he was "very loose." When she attempted to explain that he should not say it that way, his face reddened. Brandy, roared with laughter, and commented, "Hey, dude, your face is redder than a Costa Rican taxicab! I'm sorry I embarrassed you, but we gringos have trouble with your language, too! Today one of my classmates was trying to describe his love of mangoes. He chose the wrong words, and told the instructor that he became sexually aroused when he saw a mango. She laughed for five minutes before she could go back to teaching. We all have problems with different languages! Once you convince yourself that it's no big deal, it's almost fun! Hang loose!"

Chapter 20

Paul's Last Night

When Brandy returned from the gym, she started to get ready for her dinner dater with Paul. As she stepped into the shower, she began to wonder what Chuck's weekend plans might be. Her first instinct was to try to look as plain as possible, for fear that she might build false hopes in Paul's mind, since he had made it clear that he had strong feelings for her. Then she began thinking, *I'm about to go out a date for the first time since I came down here! I like Paul, and I'll never see him again. I'll miss him when he's not around, at least until I get back home with Chuck, if he hasn't met a lady cop by now, and decided that I'm history!*

After she had showered, she dried her hair, then carefully brushed it to frame her face. When she was satisfied with her coiffure, she donned a short white skirt, a turquoise blouse, a pearl necklace with matching earrings and white stilettos. Finally, she applied her lipstick, and picked her clutch bag up from the dresser, before she walked outside to find a taxi.

Fifteen minutes later, she alighted from the cab in front of the La Divina Comida Restaurant, where Paul was anxiously waiting outside the front door. When he saw her getting out of the cab, he whistled, and said, "Wow, do you look gorgeous! You're always beautiful, but I'm used to seeing you in blue jeans or running shorts."

"You look pretty hot yourself, and you deserve a classy dinner date your last night in town, especially since we will never see each other again!"

"I'll never forget you anyway, but having seen you when you're all cleaned up, I might just stick around. Let's have dinner, and then maybe we can look for some excitement."

He eagerly took her by the hand. "We're on a date, tonight, and I don't want you to forget it!"

She smiled demurely, and said, "Okay, Boss, just keep in mind that this is one time only. Let's start with dinner. We'll discuss the excitement part after that."

Soon after they were seated in the restaurant, a waiter arrived, and Paul ordered Jack Daniels and water, and a margarita for Brandy. Then he said, "We'll have a bottle of wine with our dinner, but don't be in a hurry, we'll probably have a drink or two before we order."

After Brandy had almost finished her second margarita, she looked at her menu, and said, "I'm not always lucky with fish, but I think I'll try the salmon al dijon, a small salad with vinegar and oil, and scalloped potatoes."

"I'm going for a New York sirloin, baked potato, and a Caesar salad."

When the waiter returned, Paul placed the food order and asked him what wine he would recommend. He replied, "The lady ordered fish, and you've ordered steak. I would recommended Pinot Noir, which will go well with either of your choices."

"Thanks! We'll have a bottle of Pinot Noir.."

Brandy said, "By the time the food arrives, I'll have put down two margaritas, then we're having wine. If I didn't trust you, I'd think you're working on that one night stand you keep saying you don't want!"

Paul' reply was, "Trust me!"

'You sound like the guy who sold me my first car!"

While they were eating, Brandy couldn't resist teasing Paul about the flight over the mountains."

"Are you flying home, or will you go by boat? That might take awhile."

"I'm not afraid to fly in a big jet, but bouncing up and down over mountains that can't be seen scares the poop out of me. I can't help it if I'm not certifiable like you!"

Brandy began to relax, and realize that she had become uncomfortably fond of Paul. *He's cute, and a very nice guy. I wish Chuck was here. I miss him so much! I'd better pass on any more booze, and split after we finish eating.*

Paul paid the check, and as they were leaving the restaurant, Brandy said, "I'm going to find a cab, and go home now, Paul. Thank you for a wonderful evening!"

"Forget that! We're supposed be on a date! There's a Cervecheria down the street which has live music and great suds, and it's not even nine-thirty yet! I let you hang out with those old people you're staying with when you could have been drinking with me, and I won't be cheated now!"

"You're right; I promised you a real date, so I'll have a couple of beers. Remember, you're flying out in the morning, I don't have to get up early, but I usually do!"

"I'll have plenty of time to sleep on the plane and my bags are already packed."

He took her hand again, and they walked down the street looking like young lovers. Within minutes, they entered Christiforo's Cervercia, where they were escorted to a table near the bandstand by the comely hostess, who had been furtively given a generous tip by Paul , while Brandy was admiring the ambiance. Paul ordered a pitcher of American Lager, just as four young Tico males, wearing Levi's and jeans jackets began playing U-2's smash hit, "I Will Follow You," and singing the words phonetically in English."

During the entire performance, clouds of dry ice generated smoke filled the air around them. For the next two-and-one-half hours, Paul and Brandy drank beer and listened as the four musicians played and sang several songs made famous by U-2 and Depeche Mode. After the last set, Brandy said, "Paul, this has been a special night. Those kids, and their ripped off music almost made me forget I was in Costa Rica. You've touched my life in an awesome way, and I'll never forget you! It is getting late, though! We'd better find a cab and head back to our homes away from home."

"You don't have to be in a hurry! Tomorrow is Saturday. Besides that, I moved out this afternoon, and have a room at the Marriott Courtyard. My bags are there, and I'm all ready to go. Why don't you come back and check out my suite? I have VIP privileges because my partner and I travel a lot to promote the restaurant. Some great perks go with the deal, not counting the special rates. What do you say? We can walk there in a few minutes. I'll be a real gentleman. Scout's honor!"

Brandy thought, *I'd better leave now, or I might regret it! I'd better get the heck away, now!* She looked straight into his eyes, and said, "I've had a wonderful time, and, as I just said, the past few hours, when we were drinking beer and listening to that music, I felt like I was back in the states, but our date is over, now! Good bye! You're a great guy, and I know you'll find that girl you're looking for! Kerry was really interested in you, and I think she would have stuck around awhile, if you had given her a chance. I kidded a lot about her, but she was actually very nice!"

A look of pain appeared on Paul's face; he shrugged his shoulders, but said nothing. She hailed a passing taxi, and the driver pulled to a stop in front of them. She put her arms around Paul's neck, and kissed him. "I'm going to miss you, coach! Goodbye!"

She quickly climbed into the cab, and closed the door. When she reached home, she put on her pajamas, and slipped between the sheets. To her dismay, she was wide awake at six-thirty, thinking about the past several hours. *Well, that was close! If I can just keep on hanging out with old people until I get back to Chuck, I'll be okay..*

Since she was awake, she decided to consult her travel guide for ideas for weekend junkets during the remainder of her time in Central America, with Nicaragua, Panama and Cuba in mind. She quickly narrowed her choices to two, because she was certain her agency would reject Cuba as a security risk. Soon, the aroma from Rosita's kitchen reached her nostrils, and she quickly dressed to go have her breakfast. When she entered the kitchen Rosita said, "Good morning did you and your friend have a nice evening?"

"Yes, it was very nice. We had dinner, and then went to a Cervercia to listen to music."

Her hostess smiled a knowing smile, then placed a bowl of fruit on the table, and began making toast. The rest of their conversation was about the weather. After she had eaten, Brandy walked to the gym, where she was greeted by Manuel. When she had first gone to the gym, she was distracted because either Manny and his side-kick, Edmundo would be competing for her attention. Manuel was eager to speak English with her, and Edmundo was always dancing or clowning for her benefit. Soon, however, she began to enjoy the antics of the two handsome young Latino males, although it extended her time in the gym. She had learned early in life that she had no problem attracting men and working in a male-dominated environment with the government had enhanced her ability to communicate with them effectively, which occasionally annoyed some of her female associates.

"Ole! Our beautiful gringo lady has come to teach me the English! Buenos dias, Seniorita Brandy!"

"Good morning Eddie, will you spot for me after I finish stretching?"

Manuel, who had been silently waiting for an opportunity to vie for her attention, laughed and said, "Do the howler monkeys like bananas? He has been hoping you would come in today, but when you are ready, I will teach you how to dance."

"I'd like that, Manny, but I went dancing last night!"

Ninety minutes later, she returned home, where Guido was chasing Tuffy around the garden, and Rosita was polishing silverware in the dining room. "Rosa, I'm going sightseeing today, but I have your phone number in my wallet, and I'll call you if I get into any trouble."

"Be careful, young lady, and don't carry a lot of money with you! There are thieves out there."

"I have lunch money, bus fare, and enough money to get into the museum. Don't worry about me, I love you and Guido! I should be back by suppertime! If I'm not, it will mean I got on the wrong bus, and will be on my way to Nicaragua!"

Rosita giggled, and said. "Trust me, child, you do not want to go to Nicaragua!"

Chapter 21

El Nerdo

When she got to the Plaza Cristal, Brandy climbed onto the first bus that came along. One stop later, a small man wearing thick horned rim glasses boarded the bus, and sat down next to her. She smiled, and said, "How are you today?"

The young man grinned nervously, and replied, "I'm fine, how are you?"

"Very well, thank you! Isn't it a lovely day?"

"Yes it is! You are from the United States, no?"

"Yes, I am. Do you live in San Jose?"

"I am from Las Juntas, but I'm a student at the University of Costa Rica. Are you as tourist?"

"Only on weekends; I'm studying your language."

"And I would like to learn to speak English. So we can talk!"

"That's fine, but let's speaks Spanish, because I need the practice."

"Okay, but will you be on the bus very long?"

"Actually, I'm just riding around the city. Today I'm a tourist. When I got on this bus, I had no idea where it was going. I 'm going to get off soon and walk around."

"So you are--how you say? Killing time? Can I walk around with you? I will be your guide! I know this city well. I am killing time, too! I work at the Pizza Hut, and have eight hours before I have to go back."

Brandy did not answer right away, but thought, *Like every Tico I've met so far, I'm several inches taller than this guy, and he can't weigh much over one hundred pounds! His glasses are thicker than the bullet proof glass at my office. If he pulls any crap. I can knock his glasses off, and break him in half!*

"Please let me go with you. My name is Ernesto. Here is a coupon from the Pizza Hut. With it you can get a Combo One, with a free liter of Coca Cola!"

Brandy accepted the coupon, and said, "That's so s sweet of you! Thank you! I would like to have somebody to talk to! Let's get off at the next stop."

They started walking, and Ernesto told Brady that his classmates teased him. "They call me the 'Library mouse,' because I spend most of my time there. The girls also make fun of me. They call me El Nerdo. It bothers me, but I work and study very hard and someday will be muy importante!"

"You shouldn't worry about what those girls say! I saw a motto in the Museum de Oro. It goes like this, 'No todo lo que es oro,' or, in English, 'All that shines is not gold.' It is a line from Shakespeare's play, 'The Merchant of Venice,' but he wrote, 'All that glitters is not gold.' I wrote it down on this paper." She removed a slip of paper from her wallet, and handed it to him. "You can have this, and I think you've got the right idea; work hard and study. Someday you can have it all, and that includes girls, too!"

Ernesto eagerly accepted the paper, carefully refolded it, and tucked it securely into his wallet.

Brandy stopped at the National Theatre to pick up a schedule of future events, then they walked to the National Museum, where Ernesto seemed to know everything there was worth knowing about the artifacts, and the history of his country. As they descended the steps, Brandy said,

"Ernesto, I am very happy that you came with me. You're a wonderful guide. Thanks for the tour!"

"But you are welcome! Brandy, I know we just me a short time ago, but I love you! You are so beautiful! My mother and sister are coming here tomorrow to visit me, and I want you to meet them. We can meet somewhere. Please?"

"No, Ernesto, you're very sweet, and those girls who call you El Nerdo don't know how wrong they are, but I have someone back home, and I plan to marry him! Thank you very much for being so nice today. I will stop by the Pizza Hut sometime and say hello. I have to leave now. Goodbye!"

She started to walk away, and then began running. When she was sure that she had not been followed, she went to a nearby park, where she sat under a tree with bright orange flowers to listen to a band play marches, and watch little children chasing pigeons. She began thinking about her recent encounter with Ernesto. *He said I was beautiful, but I'm not sure if that's a compliment, considering that his glasses were very thick, coated with grease from the Pizza Hut, and the prescription probably hasn't changed since the Costa Rican Civil War! Still, he was very sweet, and doesn't seem to have a very happy life, but who knows? He might be President of thus country some day!*

She left the park, and began walking aimlessly through the streets, watching shoppers dashing from store to store and from street stall to street stall looking for bargains. When a bus stopped near her, she then jumped aboard, and rode around until she realized she was very close to home. She left the bus and walked home, where she was greeted by Rosita, who seemed to be relieved that she had survived. When she realized that her hostess had been worried about her, she smiled sweetly, and said, "I appreciate your concern, but I was in no danger, because I was carrying my knife, and had my emergency contact number fastened to my bra!"

Rosita shook her head in the manner of a perplexed parent, and went back to her chores. Brandy retired to her room, where she spent the next hour studying Spanish, then decided to take a siesta. She fell asleep immediately, but was awakened by the sounds of a series of explosions, which shook the house. Thinking that a hostile force was attacking her peaceful paradise, she jumped out of her bed, and rushed into the kitchen, where Guido was sitting in chair petting Tuffy, and Rosita was chopping vegetables. When they saw the terrified look on Brandy's face, they laughed boisterously, and Tuffy's huge eyes gave her the impression that he was also amused.

"Tranquilo, child, the churches and other fiestas do that every week. You've been traveling on the weekends. There is nothing to worry about; this country doesn't even have a military!"

Brandy thought, *Tranquilo? No military! I wonder if she has ever thought that means Costa Rica cannot defend itself! An aggressive country could bomb the hell out of this place, and they could only throw rocks, or spit at the planes! I don't have the heart to tell her that!*

Guido and Tuffy went to the parlor to watch a soccer match and Rosita said, "Gina is coming over in a short while to make pizza. Would you like to help us?"

"Yes, I would! That sounds like fun, but I'd better take a quick shower and change clothes!"

Chapter 22

A Pizza Party and a Picnic

When Brandy returned to the kitchen, Gina was holding a ball of pizza dough which appeared to be the size of a small horse. Rosita was stirring a large bowl of tomato sauce, adding spices as she sloshed the contents around with a wooden paddle. Soon Brandy was chopping onions, and mushrooms. When she finished, she sliced up a long stick if pepperoni, while the other ladies ran the dough through a rolling machine to flatten it. Then the dough was spread onto four large circular pizza pans, the sauce, sausage, and other ingredients were spread over it, and the pans were placed in the oven by Rosita. Thirty minutes later, three different kinds of cheese were added, before the pizzas and a bowl of salad were set on the dining table, where Guido was pouring Chianti wine from a basket bottle larger than Tuffy's head.

While the four hungry people ate pizza and drank wine, they watched the remainder of the soccer match. Brandy began wondering if she could possibly get her host family interested in the NCAA basketball tournament, and her choice to win it, Duke University. As the game went into the final minutes, Rosita served Tiramasu, which she explained was Italian for "pick me up," and, after her first bite, Brandy thought, *This is loaded with cheese and sugar spread over lady fingers! By the time I leave here, the only way anyone will be able to pick me up will be with a top loader! Who cares? I will just have to settle for being fat!*

When dinner was finished, Brady helped with the dishes, then went to her room to read a book assigned by her teacher before she went to bed. She awoke in time for breakfast. When she reached the kitchen, her breakfast was on the table, and Rosita was giving orders to Guido and Gina, who were carrying bottles of wine, picnic baskets loaded with uncooked chicken, steak, sausage, and other food to Gina's car, which was parked in the driveway. She wolfed down all that had been set before her, and then joined the others in the frantic travel preparations. Although she was shocked and apprehensive about the obvious disdain her hosts had for ice, despite the 80 degree temperature, she convinced herself that if she drank enough wine, she would not care if everything she consumed was filled with bacteria.

The rest of the party arrived just as the last basket was loaded, and the caravan of three little cars, packed with fourteen sweating people set out for the Country Club at Heredia. Brandy was riding shotgun in Gina's convertible Tracker, acutely aware that if they encountered a bus on the wrong side of the road, it would mean instant death. After stopping once to buy strawberries from a boy at a roadside stand, the convoy reached the mountains and entered El Castillo Country Club, an immense park overlooking San Jose.

Rosita, acting with the precision of a drill sergeant, guided her underlings to her favorite picnic spot in the shadow of a palatial building with an ornate balcony, which circumvented the upper level. She directed them to the shade of a gigantic oak tree, under which there were a dozen picnic tables. She quickly commandeered two of the sturdiest, which were adjacent to a stone grill. Within minutes her well trained subordinates had carried everything from the parked vehicles, and a charcoal fire was soon raging in the fireplace. When the situation was under obvious control, Brandy and Alberto decided to explore the building which dominated the skyline behind them.

As she stood on the balcony she gaped in wonder at the sights below. There was a huge swimming pool, a cluster of tennis courts, and scores of ponds, on which she saw ducks, swans, and other aquatic birds swimming about. In the background she could see part of the Central Valley, with more mountains in the distance. Flowers bloomed everywhere, and a band was playing tunes like "Colonel Bogey", and "When the Saints Go Matching In." She turned to Alberto, and remarked, "What a lovely park this is! I wonder how big it is."

"I have heard that it covers over fifteen acres, but I'm not certain."

"It's gorgeous, and being here with your family makes it special. I'll never forget you people, and the hospitality you've shown."

"Well, you're by far the best house guest Rosita has ever had, and we'll remember you fondly when you're gone!"

They strolled back to the party, where the grill was loaded with sizzling steaks, sausages and chicken. The tables were draped with checkered cloths, and laden with bowls of salad and homemade bread. Guido was diligently pouring wine into plastics glasses, and Alberto's wife, Lucretia was busily setting the table, assisted by Giovanna, who was married to Guido's cousin, Guissepe. Brandy went over to the grill to help Guiseppe's daughter, Anna turn the meat. Rosita was supervising the entire operation. When the meat was cooked, and placed on platters, the screaming throng of hungry people scrambled to their places at the table. Guido said the blessing in a manner which would have made the Pope envious, and everyone began eating, laughing and drinking wine as if it was grape juice.

Within a very short time, most of the food had disappeared, and everyone began to drift into the mellow state which generally results from good food and wine. Alberto suggested a tour of the grounds, and the others eagerly joined him. When they passed the bandstand, Brandy noticed that he had shaken the conductor's hand and whispered something in his ear, which produced a mischievous grin. He hurried back to his self appointed task as leader of the raucous gaggle of merrymakers, while pointing out peacocks, toucans, and a mother duck, waddling happily in front of her six tiny offspring, heading towards a nearby pond. Brandy made the group laugh by saying, "Alberto, you and the momma duck are doing the same thing! You were born to lead!"

He laughed and said, "We have in common that we look out for our families!"

At that moment, the bandleader announced that he wanted to welcome a beautiful senorita from the United States by playing a tune in her honor. Then he pointed his baton directly at Brandy, and the band began playing, "Carry Me Back to Old Virginia." She smiled appreciatively, and waved to the cheering crowd.

When the tour was over, Alberto led his charges back to the tables, and Rosita served strawberries, scattered on top of slices of Tress Leches, a butter cake covered with creamy white icing, for dessert. Guido never wavered from his chosen duty to see that no one's wine glass was ever empty. When the cake pan was barren, and the strawberries were gone, Rosita spread a large blanket on the ground, and the assemblage of merry makers, wine glasses in hand, sat or reclined on it, and each attempted to outdo the others with stories of the past escapades of various relations, some of whom were present, and many who were not. After Guido had finished a long tale about how he had won Rosa's heart, he turned to Brandy and said, "Our newest family member has not yet been heard from!"

"Okay, if I must tell a story, I'll try to entertain you. When I was in high school my dad hated my boyfriend, Chuck, and he used to sometimes follow us around on dates. One night, Chuck talked his best friend, Jimmy, who was about the same size as he, into wearing his baseball cap and driving his van, while we sneaked off in Jimmy's car. Dad followed Jimmy and his girlfriend around for two hours, until he pulled alongside them at a traffic light. He was so mad that I got grounded for a week!"

The jocularity continued until late in the afternoon, when the trio of cars began the journey back to San Jose. Brandy was in awe of the wonders before her, as they sped past fields of coffee plants and banana trees, with the bright orange sun sinking slowly over the volcano in the distance, and began to realize how much she would miss when her hiatus ended.

Chapter 23

A Berkeley Belle, a Cowboy and a "Kid Brother"

On Monday, at the end of her final class of the day, Glenna advised her students that she was open for suggestions for the topic of Tuesday's conversation class. Brandy said, "We could read the newspaper tonight as a homework assignment, and discuss the articles we've read."

"That's an excellent idea! Does anyone have any objections?" When she got no response, she dismissed the class, saying, "I'll see everybody tomorrow! Don't forget to read the paper tonight!"

The next morning, five minutes after class had started, Beverly Givens, a hair stylist from Berkley, California, announced that she had read an article about the war in Iraq. "George Bush has gotten us into a war, and war is wrong! We should never interfere with other countries! He is a blatant Imperialist!"

Brandy, whose father had made listening to Rush Limbaugh a part of the family's daily agenda, spoke up.

"He's trying to do something about people who fly airplanes full of women and children into buildings full of people! I'd hope that you would understand that! Another thing which you should interest you is that women have no rights in the countries you're talking about!"

Glenna quickly changed the subject by calling on Jethro Bates, a retired postal worker whose hobby was bird watching, and his interest in an article he had read about Cockatoos. Soon, however, Ms. Givens, whose massive, obviously implanted breasts were trying extremely hard to escape the low cut sweat soaked sun dress she had draped over her otherwise unimpressive body, began a campaign to legalize marijuana, admitting she smoked it on occasion.

Brandy thought *What a piece of work she is! She probably smoked at least one joint before class, her toenails haven't been trimmed in at least six months and those tacky sandals must stink like a dead piranha! There's one thing I like about her, though! The way she bumbles through her words has convinced me that my mastery of Spanish is better than at least one of my classmates!* She spent the remainder of her time in class looking at the mountains, content that she now knew what was on the other side, thanks to Rosita and her family.

Before she departed from the school, she went to make arrangements with Savannah to go to Tortuguero on the weekend. When she finished, she went to visit the children, who greeted her with their usual enthusiasm, climbing on her and begging her to pick them up. They started a game of hide and go seek, designating Brandy as a huge rock to hide behind. She was uncertain whether the role they had chosen for her could be considered a compliment considering her food intake over the weekend. She went directly from the daycare center to her step class, where she was unsuccessful in an attempt to hide in the back row because she towered over the petite Latino ladies in front of her. Wednesday went by without incident, and she returned to the daycare center on Thursday.

That evening she helped Rosita prepare dinner, spent an hour preparing for the next day's classes, watched an opera on television with her family, and went to her room to shower before going to bed. To her chagrin, she was awakened at four o'clock by the neighborhood security guard, whose duty mainly consisted of walking around all night carry a club, and blowing a whistle. Once awake, she was further taunted by the shrieking of a strange bird, whose shrill calls sounded to her as if a child was being murdered. At breakfast, she mentioned the bird to Rosita, who said, "Yes, they are terrible creatures, and they are not native to Costa Rica. They come from Nicaragua!"

Guido, who was sitting at the table sipping his morning coffee, laughed, and said, "Ah yes, but she thinks everything that she doesn't like comes from Nicaragua!"

When Brandy reached school, Savannah was waiting for her with two young men. One was a tall muscular man with a serious acne problem; the other was short, stocky, and barely out of adolescence. She had seen them both at the school in the past few weeks, but had not been in any classes with either of them.

"Brandy, I want you to meet the two other students who are going to Tortuguero with you. This is James Kelly, who is a law student from Oklahoma, and Terry Martin, a college student from Kansas City, Missouri. Why don't you go out to the break area and get acquainted, then I will fill you in on the details of your package."

Terry held the door so Brandy could step outside, and pulled out a chair for her when they reached a table. Kelly, who was wearing a white straw Stetson, faded skin tight Levi's, cowboy boots, and a tee shirt which said, "Cowboys

Do It In The Saddle," said, "Whoooee! This dude is a perfect little gentleman!"

Brandy ignored him, and smiled at Terry, "Well, I'm a lady, and I know the difference between a gentleman and a jerk, but I want to set you guys straight. If I'm going to travel with you, you need to know that I can take care of myself." Then she looked at Terry, and said, "I have a brother who's about your age, and my dad has always made him open doors and pull out chairs for me and my little sister. It really pissed him off, but he did it. Thank you for being sweet, but on this trip, I'm just one of the guys!"

Jim scowled at first, and then pushed his hat back on his head. "Boy, honey, you just cut my water off! I'll play it your way, but you don't know what you're missing!"

"I think I can live with that! I came here to be immersed in the culture and the language, like the hype on the net recommends, and I don't care to be immersed in bullshit, so let's just be friends. I have a boyfriend back home, and I'm not looking for action!"

She walked back into the building to retrieve her back pack, and duffel bag. After Savannah gave the them their itinerary, the three young people took a taxi to the depot of the Wild Rider Travel Bureau in San Jose, where they joined Joe and Mary Wilson, a middle aged couple from Denver. After a wait of several minutes, a 1998 Ford 4x 4 screeched to a stop, and a burly Costa Rican male in his early forties stepped out.

"Hola! My name is Gilberto Munoz, but you may call me Gil. I will be your guide and driver for the next three days. After I load your baggage on top, we will be on our way."

Glancing at Brandy, he said, this Senorita will ride shotgun, the cowboy and his side-kick can ride in the rear seat, and the young lovers will sit in the middle."

Brandy smiled, and immediately climbed into the right front seat. Kelly and Martin crawled towards the rear, and the other passengers got into the truck. Munoz started the motor, and began talking. "We soon will be traveling through the Braulio Camillo National Park on the Guapiles Highway."

Minutes later, it began to rain as the vehicle began climbing the mountain. When it reached the top, mountains and rainforests could be seen everywhere. Brandy counted five tall peaks, and steam arose from the multitude of rainforests in the distance. When the van rounded a curve, a waterfall appeared which began at the midpoint of one mountain, and fell almost two hundred feet before it was out of view. Brandy gasped, and exclaimed, "This isawesome!"

Gilberto said, "Much of what you will see in the next two days will be awesome, so be prepared!"

As they descended from the mountain, he said, "That wide streak of Amarillo is the Rio Sucio. It runs from the volcano, and the orangeish yellow color is caused by sulfur. In a few minutes, we will be where it merges with another stream in which the water is blue, so that it will be half blue, and half orange!" Then he announced, "We will be stopping for breakfast in a few minutes, then will continue our journey."

While they were eating, the climate changed abruptly. The sun was shining. and it was not only hot, but also very humid. When the group left the restaurant, they were no longer in the mountains, but speeding through a flat expanse of land abundant with flowers of every color of the spectrum, with rows of palm trees, a scattering of roadside stands, an occasional open air market. They eventually reached Siguirres, where they turned onto a dirt road, and spent the next hour bouncing in and out of crater like potholes at an average of thirty miles per hour, passing through several tiny villages, and then swerving through kilometer after kilometer of banana plantations. As they did, Gilberto explained, "Each tree only produces one bunch of bananas and has a life cycle of only nine months. Workers place blue plastic bags over the trees to raise the temperature of the bunch, and to protect it from insects. We will soon be stopping at the Del Monte plantation to watch the workers."

Five minutes later, he was leading the group through a large open air facility, past workers sorting bunches of bananas, selecting only the top quality for export, and putting the rejected fruit on trucks to be sold locally, or fed to animals. At the next station, workers were placing the selected bunches in bins, where they were soaked in water to remove sap or other impurities, then transferring them to trays for spraying to prevent premature ripening.

When the group reached the next stop, where stickers were being placed on each bunch, the plantation foreman told them that the stickers had to be placed on an exact spot, and a worker who failed to do that could lose his or her job. The final venue was the weighing station, where the bunches were crated and loaded on tractor trailers to be shipped out of the country. Brandy asked Gilberto how much the workers were paid, and he said, "They work hard for an average of twelve hours a day, and the average wage is about fifteen dollars a day. Brandy was somewhat distressed by that information, thinking, *Those poor people! I will never look at a banana the same way! How ungrateful and spoiled I feel for throwing away the bruised part of a banana before I eat it! If I can eat meat which has baked all day in the sun without getting sick, a black banana won't kill me!*

When the tour was over, an employee brought out a tray of paper cups, filled with a chalky liquid. "Who would like to sample Aqua de Pipa?"

Jim asked, "What is it?"

"It is the juice of a Pipa."

"Okay, but what's a Pipa?"

"A Pipa is a coconut before it turns brown. If you're out of water somewhere where there are Pipas, you can cut one open, and quench your thirst!"

Brandy picked a cup from the tray, and sipped the contents, and then she gasped, groaning, "That tastes like spoiled skim milk with sugar in it! If I had to choose between that, and dying of thirst, I'd be dead."

The others, including Terry, made similar comments, but Jim quickly chugged a full cup, then drank another.

"Hey, that's good stuff! I think I'll take a case or two homes when I leave! Hot damn!" He picked up another cup, and downed the contents

Brandy smiled, and said, "Now there is a real man! Of course a woman wouldn't do anything that stupid. Good luck on the bus, cowboy!"

The other members of the party laughed. Jim grinned at Brandy, and then stuck his tongue out at her. After the van returned to the dirt road, it passed through hamlets named Maryland, and Nuevo Virginia. The poverty of the occupants was apparent. Many of the dwellings were made of weathered boards and had grass roofs, and Brandy thought, *Appalachia would look like Beverly Hills compared to either of those two tiny towns.*

The faces of the filthy little children who looked into the van as it bounced along had such an impact on Brandy that she could not look into their eyes, which reflected the sadness of their lives. She thought, *This is terrible! I have so much, and these poor kids have so little that it breaks my heart to look at them!*

She had just closed her eyes to feign sleep, in order to avoid eye contact with the hapless urchins on the roadside, when Gilbert exclaimed, "We have reached the Rio Pacuare, and our boat is waiting. I have to park the van, but will join you in a few minutes. He lifted the passenger's luggage down from the roof rack, and Brandy claimed her belongings.

Chapter 24

Swimming with Frogs, and Kayaking with Crocodiles

While Gilbeto was in the office, Brandy and Mary found the restroom, and the males went in search of the men's facility. When they were reunited, Terry had a grin on his face, and Jim seemed slightly in anguish. Terry reached Brandy first, and whispered, "John Wayne has the shits, but don't say anything. He's playing 'tough guy' and threatened to kick my butt if I told you."

Though secretly pleased, she promised to remain silent, and scrambled aboard the wooden boat with the others. When she sat down, Kelly moved in beside her. "Hey, sweet thing, I'm sorry we got off on the wrong foot back at school. I just think you're hot, and I reckon you'd like me if we get to know each other."

She said, "Hey, we're traveling together, and there's no reason we have to hassle each other. I'm just not here looking for action. I came down here while the guy I might marry someday is away for three months to immerse myself in the language and the culture, like I told you earlier. We'll get along if you don't give me any shit! If you do, I'll give it back!"

"That's cool, let's just enjoy the ride, but I don't see any rings on your fingers!"

Brandy did not reply, and began to watch as the captain of the unwieldy craft tried to start the motor, which gasped for breath several times, then sputtered to life. The boat began heading up the muddy river, passing palm trees and grazing cattle on both banks. Jim began explaining that they were Brahma cows, which were relatives of the Texas long horns he tended on his father's spread in Oklahoma. Brandy tried to act like she cared, but her seatmate did not seem concerned if anyone was listening to him. Ten minutes into the journey, the captain asked everyone to move towards the bow of the vessel, which had gotten mired in the mud in a shallow part of the stream.

The engine coughed and choked, but finally thrust itself out of the shallowest part of the river. No sooner than it was in the clear, a dredge came by which was loaded with workers whose responsibility it was to keep the stream navigable. Brandy noticed that every man in view was either drinking beer, or taking a siesta. She made her fellow adventurers laugh when she said, "Does anyone want to place a bet on whether the river gets any deeper any time soon?"

When the old tub reached the mouth of the river, and turned to enter Canal de Tortuguerro, Brandy could see the crashing waves of the Caribbean where the river flowed into its glistening turquoise waters. As they sped through the surrounding rainforest, Brandy was captivated by the lush scenery spread out along the waterway. The captain slowed occasionally as they sloshed past crocodiles sunning themselves, or swimming along as if they were hoping one of the riders might fall into the water, and provide a tasty snack.

After an hour had passed, the sightseers reached the Rainforest Cabins, and Brandy carried her gear into a wooden cabin with huge screen windows, on the edge of the rainforest, and facing the ocean, which was no more than six hundred meters from her door. She opted to use the bathroom before she started to unpack, and when she reached the door, she was confronted by an enormous bug, which appeared to be some strange species of beetle. She speculated that he apparently had checked in before her, and thought, *Thank God for all the Tiramasu and all the Italian food I've been scafing down! Otherwise, he might carry me off in the middle of the night!*

When she had finished unpacking, she walked to the beach with the Wilsons, Jim, Terry, and Gilberto. She was surprised that the waters of the Caribbean, which she had previously surmised to be calm, were raging ashore, with a crushing impact, and not coming in as sets. There was wave on top of wave, and it was clear that rip tides were skimming violently across the water. An array of warning signs cautioned that entering the water was forbidden and dangerous. Other than Brandy and her companions, there was not another soul on the black volcanic sand. Jim, who apparently could not read, said, "Look at those waves, how come there ain't no surfers out there?"

Gilberto shook his head, and said, "Because there are sharks and barracuda out there, and the rip tides alone can kill without the help of the fish!" Then he said, "There is a boat waiting to take us up the river to Refugio Doctor Archie Carr."

When they reached the refuge, Jim stayed by Brandy's side the entire time they were there, but had little to say, which caused her to be grateful, albeit curious. They watched a movie about Carr's efforts to save the turtles, toured the Refuge, and searched in vain for turtles.

Back at the lodge, she surprised Jim by asking if he and Terry would like to go kayaking on the river. Jim seemed apprehensive, which amused Brandy, considering his earlier displays of bravado and attempts at acting macho for her benefit.

"What's wrong, cowboy? Are you afraid I'll feed your butt to the crocodiles?"

Before he could answer, Terry said, "I'll go! I go! I kayak on white water back home."

Jim, seemingly having regained his composure, announced, "If this dipshit can do it, it can't be hard. I know how to paddle a canoe, so I'm sure I can handle a kayak! You're on, baby cakes!"

Gilberto offered to go along, but after Brandy declined the offer, he cautioned them to return before sunset. The trio, led by Brandy, paddled up the river for forty minutes, passing scores of crocodiles lurking on the bank or swimming in the murky black water, until Terry commented that the sun was beginning to sink down into the forest. They turned around immediately, and began furiously paddling downstream, aided by the swift current behind them, shouting frequent warnings of "crock at three o'clock, twelve o'clock, or any other number that came to mind, because it had become apparent that each of them had forgotten how to tell time. Soon the setting sun, which had reflected off the black surface of the stream, sank into the rainforest, and was replaced by billions of incredibly bright stars, and the moon, which had begun to admire its image on the inky liquid ahead, outlining the trees of the forest, where frogs, monkeys, and birds made their presence known in an uncommonly eerie manner.

Back at the lodge, they joined Gilberto and the others for dinner at a table on the riverbank, and listened to the sounds emanating from the rainforest while they ate. When they had finished eating, Gilberto excused himself, and left to visit friends who lived close by. Brandy decided to go swimming, and was not surprised that Jim, wearing an extremely tight Speedo, was already at the pool by the time she got there. When he saw her, he lifted his beer bottle in a mock toast, and shouted, "Hey sweet cheeks, I'll take off my suit, if you want to go skinny dipping!"

She pretended not to hear, and jumped into the water. When she surfaced, a man with an unmistakably Australian accent swam over to her.

"Mam', is that bloke a friend of yours? If you wish, I' ll advise him to mind his manners!"

She tuned towards the voice, and saw a husky, handsome male with curly yellow hair, who appeared to be about thirty years old.

"Yes, I know him, and he's harmless! We're students at a language school in San Jose, and are on the same tour. I appreciate your concern, but I can take care of myself."

"I had that figured out as soon as I saw you, but I figured it was a good excuse to talk to you. My name is Rodger O'Rourke, and I come from Melbourne, Australia."

"It's nice meeting you, I'm Brandy, and I live in Virginia."

They paddled about making small talk, then began to notice that they were sharing the pool with a multitude of brightly colored frogs, and Roger asked, "I beg your pardon, but is there a toad sitting on my arse?"

Brandy looked, laughed, and said, "There certainly is!"

Soon frogs were jumping on their heads and shoulders, which made it impossible to swim. Brandy started to swim towards the side of the pool to get out, but was confronted by a large yellow snake inches from her face. She cried out in Spanish that there was a snake in the water, and began frantically swimming at a pace which would have put the Iguanaphobic German from her earlier adventure to shame. The people who understood Spanish began to flee in terror, but were soon overtaken by those who did not, but had reacted to the obvious panic. Gilberto later told Brandy that her adversary was a harmless vine snake, but she found little solace in that bit of information. When he realized this, the guide added that there were many varieties of very deadly serpents in the country, and that it was wise to be cautious.

When Brandy reached her cabin she searched every crevice she could find for snakes, and used the spare roll of toilet paper to plug a gaping hole in the door. After that, she checked her bed, then lay down and pulled a sheet up around her ears, closed her eyes, and listened to the sounds of the rainforest in the hopes she could drift off to sleep. She began thinking of Chuck, and how secure she felt when she was curled up in his arms. *I miss him so much! Here I am, all alone in a shack in the middle of a rainforest, with only a beetle the size of a linebacker standing guard in my bathroom, and I'm not sure whose side he's on!"*

Despite her efforts, Brandy could not stop thinking about snakes, and did not sleep well.

Chapter 25

Brandy Dumps a Drunk

Brandy had just finished dressing when Gilberto knocked d
on her door in the morning. When he saw the toilet paper
in the door, he asked, "What is that for?"

"I put it there to keep the snakes out!"

He scratched his head, but did not comment further,
which Brandy interpreted as meaning that he did not
consider toilet paper a formidable defense against venomous
reptiles. When she followed him outside; they joined
the others and walked to the dock, where a battered old
wooden boat was moored. She turned to Terry and said, "I
thought the crate that brought us here was bad, but I think
Christopher Columbus must haves handcrafted this one all
by himself!"

The captain began guiding the tired old barge through
the intricate canal system which wound its way through the
rainforest. When it entered one stretch of the system, the
canopy formed a tall tunnel of lush vegetation, with rays
of light cascading down from the treetops above, reflecting
off the jet black surface of the canal, mirroring every
tree in sight. Parrots, Toucans and many other brilliantly

colored birds were perched in tress, or fluttering about, and kingfishers stood along the banks. Hordes of monkeys chattered and fought high in the treetops. An aggregation of white faced monkeys seemed to be having a meeting of some importance, and a gang of spider monkeys, including a mother carrying her baby on her back, gawked curiously at the creatures on the boat. Gilbert pointed to a lizard who was skimming across the canal, saying, "That is a Jesus Cristo lizard! He's called that because he can walk on water!" Butterflies fluttered around the crowds of elegant flowers which peeked out from the foliage, and sloths were loitering in the trees at every turn. Hundreds of crocodile crawled along the banks or swam around the boat.

They returned to the lodge two hours later, and Brandy ate breakfast with Terry, Jim, and Gilberto, then excused herself, and went to her cabin for her bathing suit. She spent the next hour splashing around the pool, looking for snakes, and trying to avoid inhaling errant multicolored frogs when she was taking in air. As she was returning from the pool, she met Gilberto outside her cabin. "I came to tell you that I will be leading a hike trough the rainforest in fifteen minutes, if you'd care to join us"

"I have to change clothes, but I want to go along."

"Okay! We will be waiting at the lodge."

The hike was an encore of the morning's boat ride, with frequent encounters with a variety of the inhabitants of the dense foliage which surrounded them. Gilberto called out the names of the vividly colored blossoms which enveloped the trail as they strolled along. At one point he stopped at a flower which vaguely resembled a large pinkish dandelion. "This is a Mimosa. If you touch the leaves, they will wilt. When the sun goes down it will shrink, and close. When it sees the sun again, it pops open!"

He started walking again, but stopped suddenly and said, "There is an eyelash viper!"

Brandy looked, and saw a tiny, bright yellow snake, curled up on a reed. "He's not very big, and such a pretty color!"

Gilbero said, "He may be pretty, but he's very deadly! There are many poisonous snakes in the rainforest, and you must be careful at all times!"

In the early afternoon, Brandy went walking alone on the beach, and when she returned to her cabin, she began to feel the effects of her sleepless night, combined with her very active morning, so she decided to take a nap in the hammock outside her cabin. Soon after she had positioned herself comfortably, she began to think about her experience with the snake in the pool, and the viper on the trail. *I hope snakes don't like hammocks! If they do, I'll die in my sleep, anyway, and I'm too exhausted to care!* She quickly drifted into a deep sleep, and did not awaken until the sun began sinking slowly in the sky. After she was fully awake, she alighted from the sling, and went into her cabin, where she consulted briefly with the vigilant bug in her bathroom, while she freshened up. Feeling refreshed, she headed for the dining area to watch the sunset while sharing the evening meal with her guide and her fellow travelers. While she was eating, she thought, *How beautiful! It's almost like watching a rerun on television! The scene is always spectacular!* Her mind went back to the many times she had watched the sunset in the mountains or at the beach with Chuck. She thought, *I wish he was with me now, but here I am, sharing a romantic setting with a very nice middle-aged Tico, a sweet kid my brother's age, and one of the biggest dufuses I've ever met!*

When Jim noticed that she was seemingly lost in her thoughts he chortled, "Hey honey bunch, you seem to be somewhere in outer space! Come back to earth. Why don't you and me go out on the town?"

Gilberto saw the look of annoyance on Brandy's face, and, having become aware of the tension between the two from the outset, spoke before she had a chance to respond.

"It's a beautiful night. We could walk along the beach to Tortuguerro. It is not much of a town, but there's a little place there where we can have a beer."

Brandy started to make an excuse, but decided that the suggestion seemed better than swimming in a frog-infested pool while dodging snakes, or sitting in her cabin trying to converse with Senor Beetle.

"That sounds like fun! Maybe I'll get lucky and meet a handsome boat captain who will sweep me off my feet!"

With Gilberto in the lead, the foursome set out along the edge of the water. Brandy began to concentrate on the beauty of the sky, with the laser bright stars dancing above the Palm Trees. Suddenly, in a place where the ocean and the rainforest came together, she got one of her flip-flops caught in a fallen branch, and shifted her weight to the other foot, causing the rubber sandal to begin floating out to sea. Jim roared with laughter, Terry said nothing, and Gilberto threw himself into a very large wave to retrieve the escaping footgear. Brandy started to say, "Nice save, Gil. Bravo!" However, when she realized that her hero's trousers were soaked with sea water, and that he would have to go into town wearing wet pants because he had risked his life to save an item which had purchased in a Dollar Store, she remained silent. She had to bite her tongue to avoid laughing and telling him that she would have been content to go barefoot, or possibly hop on one foot. She managed to restrain herself, even though the thought of an extremely Macho Latino male walking the rest of the way into town wearing wet shoes and pantalones which appeared to be painted on, made it nearly impossible.

Shortly after Gilberto's heroics, the ocean disappeared, and the rest of the way the hikers were making their way through the rainforest, Brandy's gratitude for her guide's feat of daring intensified, because, while her thongs were little protection against snakes, she would be more at risk without them. When they emerged from the rainforest, and entered the village, they heard the raucous sound of loud Reggae music, and soon found that it was coming from a bar. When they entered, everyone was dancing, including a full figured waitress, who was carrying a tray on which a half dozen bottles of beer were swaying precariously in time with the music. From there they followed Gilberto to a shack in which there was a large screen television set, picnic tables and a bar. Several men sat at one of the tables playing dominoes, and every one of them momentarily lost interest in their game when they caught sight of Brandy in her cut off jeans and tank top.

She began wishing that she might convince Gilberto to leave with her, but he had ordered a beer the moment they reached the bar, and it was apparent that he was trying to forget that his pants were still dripping water from the ocean. Jim, who had started drinking beer, seemed annoyed when Brandy ordered a bottle of water, and his ire increased when Terry asked for a coke.

"I guess I'm going to have to settle for one of the local chicks tonight." Then he put his arm on Terry's shoulder, and said, "Why don't you pour that soda pop on the floor, and have a beer, then, after we get drunk, we can ditch goody two shoes, here, and find us some real women!"

Brandy smiled, and purred, "I'd tell you to kiss my ass, but you'd jump at the chance, then I'd have to cut your balls off, if you have any!"

His face reddened slightly, and he silently sat down at the bar, and began chugging his beer. Within a short time it was apparent that Gilberto had consumed enough beer that he didn't even care if he was wearing any pants, and that Jim was about to return to being a pain in the ass in a very short time. She was relieved when Terry asked her if she wanted to go back to the resort with him, and they slipped out the door without saying goodbye to the others. When they reached the edge of the village, Brandy and her young companion discovered that it was high tide, so that they would have to return to the lodge by boat. At the dock, a local opportunist offered to take them back for five dollars. They accepted, though it was higher than the usual rate. They began to regret their decision seconds after the engine stared and the Boston Whaler charged violently away from the dock. The skipper stated yelling above the sound of the motor, telling a wild story about his day, which he had spent taking a party of Japanese businessmen on a fishing expedition. Terry muttered, "Oh, my gosh! This dude is smashed!"

Brandy nodded her head, then, in an attempt to reassure her friend, said, "That's obvious, but he knows how to drive this thing, and in this rough water, it isn't easy!"

Within minutes, the wobbly seaman was skillfully maneuvering up to the boat dock at the lodge, and his passengers gratefully jumped ashore. Brandy said goodnight to Terry, then went to her cabin, where she quickly showered and washed her hair. She was sitting at her dresser blow drying it, when someone knocked on her door. Thinking it was a maid delivering some extra towels she had requested, she opened the door, and Jim burst into the room.

"Where did you guys go? When I noticed you were gone, I bought a six pack and went looking for you. I was only messing with your head back there, and don't want you to be pissed off. I was looking for you, and a Tico in a boat told me he had taken you back here. He looked like he was about on his ass, and I conned him into bringing me home too. I really screwed him! He wanted ten bucks, but I got him down to eight. Can I use your John?"

"Yes, if you promise to get the hell out of here so I can get some sleep."

The uninvited guest staggered into the bathroom, and after he flushed the toilet, he yelled, "Hey, Sugar, there's the biggest damn cockroach I ever did see peeking at me from behind your commode! Want me to squash it for you?"

"No, that's my guard beetle!"

"Honey, I'm from Oklahoma, and I played football at Old Miss! That critter is a good old southern style cockroach, if I've ever seen one!"

"It's a beetle, and he told me he'll keep the snakes out! You've finished peeing; now get the hell out of here. !"

He stumbled back into the room, and sat down on the bed. "Aw, come on babe, let me stick around. I'll protect you from snakes, and we can have some fun! You'll be smiling' in the morning. I promise!"

When he removed his hat and set it beside him, Brandy pretended that she was going to sit down next to him, grasped his right hand, and twisted his arm behind his back. After she had pulled him upright, she dragged him to the door, turned the knob with her free hand, and threw him out onto the grass. While he lay groaning on the ground, she picked up his hat, and tossed it out after him.

"Go back to your cabin and sleep it off. I know you're drunk, and I've done a few dumb assed things when I was drinking! I'm going to cut you a break, and forget it happened, but don't ever pull any crap like that on me again!"

When she was sure that Jim had gone, she finished packing for the journey home, then turned out the lights and got into bed, thinking, *Maybe my beetle is really a cockroach, but if he is, he must have survived Chernobyl and migrated to Costa Rica! I'd better check my baggage to be sure that his family hasn't moved in. Rosa will never forgive me if I bring bugs into her home, especially if they're mutant cockroaches who might have relatives living in Nicaragua!*

She finally fell asleep, but was soon awakened by the sound of rain cascading down on the roof of her cabin, which was shaking as if a curious giant had picked it up, and was trying to figure out what was incise. The rain continued for several hours, and Brandy began thinking of a newscast she had watched with Rosita the previous week. They had seen graphic photos of flooding in the port of Limon, which was only fifty kilometers down the coast from Tortuguero. Because her cabin was on the river, and a mere six hundred meters from the ocean, she wondered if it might be carried out to sea, and float all the way to Cuba. She managed to go to sleep again, despite the turmoil. When she woke up and left the cabin it was still raining, but there was a beautiful rainbow in the sky, which extended from one edge of the rainforest to the other.

After breakfast, she carried her bags to the boat, and the journey back to San Pedro began. Gilberto appeared none the worse for wear. Jim was silent, and Terry was more talkative than usual. He sat next to Brandy, and when he was certain that Jim, who was sitting alone at a safe distance, could not hear, he said, "I saw you throw my buddy out of your cabin last night, and laughed my ass off. You are some kind of cool!"

By the time the touring party was on the road back, Jim began making small talk and acting as if nothing had happened, and Brandy decided that she would do the same. The return trip was uneventful, and that evening at dinner, Brandy regaled Rosita and Guido with tales of her weekend adventure, but carefully avoided any reference to any of her traveling companions except Gilberto. Rosita seemed to take particular pleasure in Brandy's account of how the guide had rescued her shoe, and gently chided Guido about the macho attitude of all males.

Chapter 26

A Lady from London

When Brandy entered the school on Monday morning, Jim was sitting in the break area drinking a coke. As she passed him, he silently tipped his hat, and she responded with a syrupy smile. She began walking up the stairs behind a slender woman who appeared to be about the same age as she. "Good morning, I've never seen you before. Are you a new student?"

The attractive raven haired girl stopped momentarily, then turned, and cast her immense mahogany eyes in Brandy's direction. "Yes, my name is Kitty Kent."

"Are you in Amanda Ruiz's class?"

"Yes, I just met her, she seems nice. Do you know where her classroom is?"

After noticing a distinct British accent, she answered, "We're almost there. I'm in that class, too." She reached out and shook hands, "Nice meeting you! My name is Brandy Barton." Then she asked, "What part of England are you from?"

"I was born in Watford, about twenty kilometers north London, but I live in the city, now. I'm a student at the

University of the Arts. I'll be here for two weeks, and then I'm going back. Which part of the United States are you from?"

Brandy smiled, and then said, "I guess my accent gave me away, too! I'm from Virginia, but I worked across the river, in the District of Columbia, until I came here to improve my Spanish!"

When she had finished speaking, they had reached the top of the stairs, and Brandy said, "Our classroom is just across the hall, follow me."

At the end of the lesson, Brandy invited her new friend to join her for lunch, and, while they were eating, Kitty asked Brandy if she had seen much of the country during her stay in Costa Rica.

"I've been here a month, and have taken three weekend trips. The first was to Arenal volcano and Tabacon. The second was to Manuel Antonio Playa. I stayed in town on the third weekend, and last weekend I was in Tortuguero, looking for turtles, but didn't see any."

"Well it sounds like you've been making the most of your time here! Have you done this all on your own?"

"The first two trip I went with an Iranian woman and a guy, and last weekend I was with a Tico guide, a young kid, and that idiot in the cowboy hat who was staring at you when you came in. He's a real jerk, though there was a girl here the first couple of weeks who would have thought he was really hot, but she left before he got here. Nobody stays very long."

"Well what are you doing this weekend? Maybe we can travel together."

"Actually, I was thinking about going to Monteverde, and if you want to go with me, you're welcome. Traveling with guys has been bad news for me. The first one wanted me to marry him, and that cowboy really was a pain!"

"Righto, then, it's on to Monteverde we'll go!"

By the time they left the café, they had formed the kind of bond which often is forged by people in shared short term situations. Brandy asked, "Where are you staying?"

"With a host family about seven blocks from here."

They soon discovered that Kitty's hosts lived one block from Rosita's house. They walked back together, and when they reached Rosita's gate, Brandy invited Kitty to go pothole dodging with her."

"Pothole dodging? What in heaven's name is that?"

Brandy chuckled. "Some people call it jogging, but here it's a life threatening experience! Want to join me?"

"Yes, I try to run every day. But it's not always possible. When do you want to start?"

"Meet me back here in an hour, and be prepared to run with your head down!"

During the next three days, the two girls ran daily, and Brandy brought her new friend to step class on Tuesday. When class ended, she introduced Kitty to the Valdez twins, Maria and Melissa. Maria, who was several minutes older than her twenty year old sister said, "Would you girls like to go to El Pueblo with us on Friday night? It's Ladies' Night at El Vaquero."

Kitty said, "That sounds like it might be fun. What do you think, Brandy?"

"Sure! Why not? We're leaving for Monterverde early on Saturday, but we can sleep on the bus. We'll meet you outside the bar on Friday might."

O n Wednesday, Brandy brought her new friend to the gym, where they were greeted by Manuel, who had picked up two ten kilo dumbbells and began doing curls as soon as he noticed Kitty. He grinned widely, and then said, "Hola, Brandy, who is your beautiful amiga?"

"Hi, Manny! Kitty, this is Manuel, and he's posing for you! Are you impressed?"

Kitty smiled flirtatiously. "Why of course! He's gorgeous!"

Without saying anything more, she hefted a fifteen kilo dumbbell with her right hand, sat down on a weight bench, and slowly started doing concentration curls. Edmundo had stepped out of the locker room just before Manny had started to show off. He watched silently, and then almost went into hysterics, and screamed, "Bravo! Bravo!" He looked at Brandy, and said, "I like your friend. Who is she?"

"This is Kitty, and if you guys want to put any serious moves on her, you won't have much time. She's going back to London very soon."

When they had finished working out while the two trainers tried to out do one another with wild dance moves, and other outrageous antics, Kitty thanked Brandy for bringing her along. "I really enjoyed those guys. They seem very nice, but men are all pretty much alike. All a girl needs to do is wiggle her bottom, and they'll make perfect asses of themselves!"

When Brandy and Kitty went to lunch on Thursday, they shared a booth with Shari Reed, a policewoman from Arizona Kitty had met at the airport when she arrived. "Kitty said, "What are you doing tomorrow night?"

"I have no plans, but I'll probably study, and then go to bed early. Why do you ask?"

"Well, Brandy and two girls from her step class are going to Ladies' Night at a place called El Vaquero. Would you like to come along?"

"Yes, I'd love to! What time, and what should I wear?"

Brandy, in a serious tone of voice said, "I think clothes would be appropriate. We're not going hunting, at least I'm not, but we are going out on the town."

"I get your drift. I do have a getup I wear when I'm undercover as a hooker in Phoenix, but I probably won't wear that!"

"Why not wear it? You'll take the pressure off the rest of us. We'll see you tomorrow night."

Because it was the beginning of the Easter holidays, known as Semanta Santa, it appeared that everything and everyone seemed to begin moving a bit faster than usual. Also, Friday marked the end of the work week, and it seemed that every body was preparing to celebrate the holidays or had already begum to celebrate. When the morning classes ended, Brandy and Kitty traveled by bus to the Intercity Terminal to purchase tickers to Monteverde a day in advance.

That evening, Brandy met Kitty in front of Rosita's house, and then the two of them walked to the corner to meet Shari, and find a taxi. When the petite twenty three year old blonde arrived, she was wearing tight white jeans, a scarlet tank top, and matching high heel shoes. Don't say it! This is not my hooker outfit!"

Kitty said, "You look fantastic! It's a good thing Brandy and I aren't hunting! We would have to settle for your leavings!"

"I don't know about that! Those skirts you girls have on don't hide a hell of a lot! Brandy, I love your hair, who did the highlights for you?"

"Nobody believes me, but it's from the sun!"

Kitty interrupted at that moment. "If we stand around here much longer the twins will wonder if we're coming. Let's find a hack."

When the cab pulled up to the curb, the twins were waiting near the door where a bouncer was admitting a few mostly female customers at a time. Shari started to fish in her purse for identification; Brandy smiled, and then said, "Relax! They don't do IDs here. I think that guy is collecting phone numbers. Everyone laughed as they stood in line, and soon the bouncer motioned the twins through the door, then Kitty, and Shari. Brandy started to follow, but the muscular bald man firmly grasped her wrist. I'm sorry, angel face, but this act is for grown ups, and you'll have to wait here with me until they leave the stage. From where she stood, she could look through the window and see a half dozen very short, muscular men without shirts, and well lubricated with baby oil, gyrating on the stage. Brandy said, "I'm older than any of those ladies I'm with, and you let them all in there!"

When the man smiled in a condescending manner, Brandy acted as though she was about to cry, and pretended to be trying to scratch her way through the wall. "Oh, please mister, let me in! Short guys wearing tight jeans, cowboy hats and baby oil really turn me on! Please-- let me go in!"

It was apparent that the stone faced guardian of the portals did not appreciate Bandy's sarcasm. Seconds later, the men filed off the stage, and he said, "Okay, Nina, you can go join your amigas!"

When the others saw Brandy, they began teasing her, and when she told them about her dialogue with the bouncer, they squealed with delight. By the time she had ordered a drink, a man with hair that obviously was not growing on his head was singing and dancing on the stage, doing a very bad impersonation of Bruce Springsteen. Brandy began dancing along with the crowd, which was gradually pushing her and her group closer to the bandstand. Suddenly, while she was attempting to gracefully perform her best salsa moves, someone grabbed her by the arm, and began dragging her up the stairs to the stage. Kitty, Shari, and the twins began shouting, "Shake it, Brandy, show them what you've got!"

Brandy was not happy with her cheering section, and less pleased that the singer now had her firmly in his grasp on a stage in front of a large crowd of screaming people who were at various levels of intoxication. She was tempted to laugh or spit in his face, but decided to play along to amuse her friends. *I can't believe that I'm on stage with this complete loser, and I hope no one is filming thus! If they are, the next time the agency makes me take a polygraph, I'll flunk when I'm asked if I could be the subject of blackmail! The worst part is that he's singing to me in Spanish, and I have no idea what he's saying! That is never good!*

The song finally ended, and Brandy gratefully rejoined her friends. When they left the club shortly after midnight, the twins were dancing with two middle aged American men.

Chapter 27

Battling Arachnoids and Careening Through the Canopy

On Saturday morning at five, Brandy and Kitty boarded the bus to Monteverde. The first two and one half hours were spent on a winding paved road, and during the next two and one half hours, the bus crawled over hills and mountains on a steep dirt road with many curves and sharp turns, which caused the vehicle to stall, then drift backwards, within a short distance from a ravine with a two-hundred foot drop. In order to take her mind off her predicament, Brandy checked her guidebook and learned that local authorities had refused to pave the road to restrict tourism. The situation was exacerbated because the bus was not air conditioned, and the passengers were inhaling dust throughout the journey. When they got off the bus in the dusty little town of Montverde, a mud covered ten year old 4x4 truck stooped abruptly in front of them, barely missing Brandy's left foot. The driver said, "Do the two senoritas need a taxi?"

Brandy replied, "Yes, we do, we're going to Ignacio's Rainforest Lodge." The driver jumped out of his truck, opened the door, helped the two women into the middle seat, and loaded their bags in the back. He climbed behind the wheel, put the battered conveyance into low gear, and started bouncing past souvenir stands, shops, tour offices, cafes, and tiny markets. The truck bounded into and out of several sizeable potholes along the way, and climbed a hill at an angle of nearly forty-five degrees. The driver turned off the main road into a pasture, drove a short distance, and stopped in front of a small square white house next to a long one story white structure with seven doors. While she was paying the driver, Brandy said, "This the Rainforest Lodge? It isn't in the rainforest and it's not a lodge! It reminds me of the stables at the state fairgrounds, and it's sitting on top of a rock pile!"

Kitty nodded in agreement before she commented, "Well. We knew it was a one star accommodation, and you can't expect much for twenty-three dollars a nigh, even in Costa Rica! We aren't planning to spend much time in our room, anyway!"

They carried their bags to the front of the house, where they were greeted by a friendly little woman who reminded Brandy of a miniature version of Anthony Perkins in drag, when he was masquerading as his mother in the movie, "Psycho," which she had watched many times with Chuck on television. The lady gave Brandy a key, and then said,

"You are in room four. That's the middle one! I hope your stay is a pleasant one!"

Brandy unlocked the door, and looked inside. She turned to Kitty and warned, "Watch your step, the floor is wood, and it's elevated. Once inside the small room, Brandy placed her bag on one of the twin beds. After Kitty had placed her luggage on the other bed, she put her hands to her mouth, and exclaimed, "Crikey! The walls are full of holes!"

"All of them aren't holes. The ones which are moving are spiders! She looked up at the ceiling, and noticed that it sagged. "Maybe this is a wildlife reservation! I wonder what species live up there. Maybe we ought to hope that we never find out!"

Kitty started to lean on the wall, and when it bent inward, Brandy said, "Careful, whatever is in there might not want to be disturbed! Look at the bright side, we have four large windows, and each one is broken, so we will have plenty of fresh air!"

She pushed the bathroom door open. "Hey there's a shower, a basin and a potty, so we apparently have indoor plumbing, but I wouldn't bet that that thing doesn't flush straight down under our beds. This place is a dump, and if I weren't so rugged and manly, I'd suggest that we find another place to stay."

Kitty shrugged her shoulders. "It's really not that bad. I stayed in a place in Kenya last year when I was back packing with my boyfriend, Reggie, which would make this place look like the Dorchester in London! Let's freshen up, change clothes, and get out of here!"

One half-hour later, they were climbing up steep hills, over large rocks, and around gaping holes in the ground, while the ever present dust assailed their nostrils. By the time they reached Monteverde, Brandy could barely speak when a guide approached them, and asked, "How can I help you ladies?"

"We'd like to go to the Santa Elena Cloud Forest Resort. I found a hike in my guide book to a tower which overlooks the Arenal volcano. I've been in this country over a month, and haven't seen it erupt yet!"

"I've lived here my whole life and have seen it many times! It's spectacular to watch, but it's very cloudy today. I'd suggest that you return here early tomorrow. That way, even if it is cloudy, the animals will be active, so you will have something to do, even if you can't see the volcano. Are you interested in a canopy tour?"

"Kitty answered, "That sounds intriguing. Brandy, what do you think?"

"Sure, we might as well."

They soon were riding in another old 4x4, in which they bounced for twenty minutes until they reached the Canopy Tour Center. As she approached the rigging area, Brandy looked up at the ladder leading to the first platform high in the treetops, and began to think. *That is really a long way up, but if I don't get over my fear of heights, I'll never be able to rappel out of a helicopter! Being high off the ground doesn't really bother me, but dangling from ropes or crawling up things which might break almost makes me poop! The idea of falling doesn't scare me, but the thought of landing is the problem!*

"Now, how does that feel?" The rigger's voice brought her back to reality, as she realized she was wearing a harness.

"I'm not sure. Maybe you'd better check it again."

She repeated the request two more times, before she finally approved the perplexed guide's work, and followed Kitty up the ladder to the first platform. When she reached the top, another guide attached her harness to a pulley which he then attached to a steel cable, and gave her a shove. She zoomed above the trees on a zip line until she reached a tower, then another. By the time she was at the second tower, she was shaking, and holding her security line in a death grip.

The second cable was longer and higher than the first, and as she was again flying over the trees, she began to think, *I've already violated the second rule of nature, which is, never show fear, and, if I'm going to die, I should at least enjoy myself!* She was no longer in panic as she looked around, sometimes soaring above the canopy, sometimes dipping below the treetops and through the trees, often within inches of flowers and vines. She had just begun to relax, when she reached a platform from which she had to rappel to the ground. The guide said, "You can control your speed by your grip on the rope. Just step off the platform backwards."

When Brandy heard the instruction, she was terrified. *He's got to be kidding! My legs have gone numb! I can't walk backwards off a tree one hundred and ten feet in the air!* When she finally found her courage, she closed her eyes tightly, and did her best impression of Michael Jackson's moonwalk. When she did, she dropped seventy-five feet straight down, screaming so loudly that she was sure Rosita could hear her back in San Pedro. The guide at the other end eclipsed the loudest howler monkey in the country with his laughter. When she was on the ground facing him, she recognized him as the guide who had noticed how terrified she was when he helped her into her harness at the first platform, and asked, "Why do you think this is so funny?"

"Because I was controlling your fall from down here. Did you have fun?"

When she responded, she was sure that the rest of her trip through the trees would be pure torture, and, in jest, she said, "Well, if you were counting on a tip, forget it!"

She ascended with the others to the next platform. As her journey continued over half a dozen more cables, each view seemed higher and more beautiful than the preceding one. Her complacent feeling was soon to end, however, when she reached the Tarzan swing. She watched in horror when Kitty, whose harness was attached to a rope which extended several hundred feet in the air to another tree, stepped off the platform, dropped abbot ten feet before the rope caught her, and then began swinging through the treetops towards the tree on the other side.

The guide beckoned her forward, and while he was securing her harness to the swing, she looked straight down, which increased her terror. She began to look directly ahead, and concentrate on the beauty of the forest. She was lost in her thoughts until she heard the guide say,

"If you don't jump, I'll pick you up, and throw you off the platform!"

She closed her eyes and felt a rush of adrenalin, which caused her to jump up, rather than out, which made her free fall fifteen feet. She screamed until she lost her voice, which sent all who were present into fits of laughter. After she had stopped falling, she swung high into the trees brushing several branches with her feet. When she was reunited with Kitty on the ground, she said, "I don't understand this, because I was terrified, and now my legs are wobbly, but I'd like to go back up there and do that again!"

At the final station, the guide informed the group that the ride would be over 600 meters at a height of 416 feet, and cautioned them not to brake until they were at the end. Brandy tapped Kitty on the shoulder, and whispered, "I don't like the sound of that! It's a miracle that I haven't peed in my pants at least once already. I'd bet cross my legs on this one!"

Soon she was zooming along, trying to concentrate on the splendor of the rainforest, when her pulley started to wobble, and make a distressed sound. She thought of the opening scene from 'Cliff Hanger,' and grabbed the cable above her, determined not to drop to her death without a fight, with the result that she was no longer moving. She began trying to pull herself towards the platform, when a guide, who was laughing like a monkey, came sliding towards her at high speed while hanging upside down in his harness. She screamed, "What in the hell are you doing? Get off my cable! We'll both be killed!"

With tears in his eyes, he chortled, "Mam', this cable will hold 37,000 pounds!" Her first thought was, *Little man, if you knew how much I've been eating, you wouldn't be so damned arrogant!*

The guide continued laughing as he hooked his legs around Brandy's knees, and dragged her three-hundred meters to the platform. Back on the ground, she and Kitty started to hike back to their hotel, just as darkness began to envelope the rainforest and the tree tunnel over the road blocked out the moonlight. Suddenly they were surrounded by flying insects with glowing eyes, at first Brandy thought they were fireflies, but later learned they were flying cockroaches. Kitty said, "I wish we had an electric torch!"

"What's an electric torch?"

"You would call it a flashlight."

"I have one in my bag but it's back at the hotel, but if I push the button on my camera down part way, the flash will stay on."

"That is ingenious! How clever you are!"

"If I was a genius, I'd have thought to bring my flashlight, but at least we have some light."

They soon were out of the forest, and walking in the moonlight. When they reached their lodgings, they could see the moon reflecting off Lake Arenal. They were hungry, as well as exhausted, and decided to order pizza. While they were waiting for the deliveryman, Kitty told Brandy that she was afraid of the spiders which were crawling everywhere. Brandy said, "We can decrease their population if we kill as many as we can before our food gets here." She picked up a shoe, and started towards the wall.

"That won't do, because if you kill one, it will mean six years of bad luck!"

"Well, they're too big to chase outside, and besides, they outnumber us, so I'll take my chances."

Kitty watched in mock horror while Brandy methodically stalked her prey. When the pizza arrived, she announced that by her calculations she had accumulated 120 years of bad luck. Kitty laughed when, with her shoe raised triumphantly in the air, Brandy said, "The bright side is that if I die tomorrow the spider's curse will be wasted!"

When the last sliver of cold pizza had been consumed, Brandy inspected her bed for spiders, and for snakes which might be coiled under the covers or beneath her pillow, and then she collapsed on top of the bedspread without undressing, and went to sleep.

Chapter 28

Mutant Spiders, a Lizard, and an Earthquake

Kitty's alarm clock went off at five o'clock the next morning, and Brandy was barely awake as she stumbled into the shower, where she was shocked into consciousness because the water was icy cold. After she got out to get dressed, Kitty stepped into the shower, and when she emerged, her teeth were chattering.

Brandy asked, "Do they put ice water in the showers at the Dorchester?"

"I wouldn't know! I've never been in the Dorchester, but our lodging in Kenya didn't have inside plumbing at all!"

They finished dressing just as their driver arrived to take them to Santa Elena Cloud Forest. By six o'clock, they were rolling along the dusty roadway, and soon were hiking through the rainforest, surrounded by wild creatures, and gazing at the mist from the clouds as it drifted through the canopy. As they walked, they heard a three stage bird call which ended with a loud bonk sound, which the guide book said was distinctive of a three wattle bell bird, but they searched the area in vain hopes of seeing, and possibly photographing, it. After they had been on the trail for over one hour, Brandy froze in her tracks when she heard a loud snort behind her. "Kitty, I'm fairly certain that wasn't you! Do wild boars live in the rainforest?"

"I live in London, and I've not seen any around Piccadilly, or in Soho, but I had one boyfriend who was pretty much like a pig!"

"Well, I would be really embarrassed if, after surviving those horrendous bus rides, and dangling 400 feet in the air, I got mauled by a wild boar in the rainforest!"

After hearing two more snorts, Brandy saw a brown, furry animal with a big nose, small ears, a long, straight tail, striped like a raccoon's, dart out the bushes behind Kitty. "It's not a boar, it's a coati. I saw them in the forest at Tortoguerro. He doesn't seem interested in us!"

They resumed walking, and thirty minutes later, Kitty let out a blood curdling scream. When Brandy reaches her, she pointed to a branch, and said, "I just saw a spider the size of the Queen's white horse!"

When Brandy looked, she saw a huge red and black insect. "I thought you were overreacting when I heard you, but that appears to be a tarantula on steroids!"

While they were gawking at the bug, a guide came down the trail. "I heard you scream, and it sounded as though someone was in bad trouble! That guy looks scary, but he won't bother you! He's a male red knee tarantula, and he's looking for ladies, but you are not his type. All the males come out in search of a mate this time of year."

Twenty minutes later they saw another male with romance on his mind, which made the first one look small.

Brandy said, "Wonderful. It's just out lucky day! We're walking through the woods, surrounded by horny mutant insects!"

Because they had reached the end of the trail forty-five minutes before their truck was due to pick them up, they headed for the observation tower. When they got to the top, the wind was shaking their perch so violently that they were forced to drop to their knees on the rusty steel deck. Dark clouds drifted by, restricting their field of vision to less than ten feet in any direction. Frustrated, they descended from the tower, and set out to join their driver.

When they reached the town, they signed up for the skywalk, and then hiked six kilometers to the art galleries. From there they went to the Monreverde Cheese Factory, where they sampled cheese and ice cream, and learned that the area and the factory were developed by a Quaker sect which had migrated from Alabama in 1951.

When they joined the skywalk tour, Brandy was frightened at first because the winds were howling, and she had to climb 120 feet up a steel ladder, and then walk halfway across a swaying bridge when she began to fear that the wind was going to throw her into the trees. On the second of the five bridges, suspended above and below the trees, she began to enjoy the natural wonders of the panorama before her. When the tour ended, they remained determined to see the volcano, and asked their driver to take them to a mountaintop restaurant Brandy had found in her guide book. Clouds were swirling around Brandy when she and Kitty got out of the truck. The driver was laughing, and in a good-natured manner, he said, "I hope you enjoy the volcano! The view from here is amazing, if you can see it."

Unperturbed, she retorted, "Marco, you're very funny, but I'm no quitter. I'm sure we'll love the view! We'll see you in about an hour and tell you all about it!"

"I'll be waiting here when you come out, if I can see you!"

He was still laughing as they walked into the café, in which there were no other patrons. They sat next to a large picture window.

Kitty said, "If we pretend the clouds are smoke from Arenal, maybe we can convince ourselves that we're seeing it erupt."

"That isn't a bad idea, but we can't even see the truck, and it's parked right outside!"

They soon became aware that the only light was coming from the window and the candles in the tables. Moments later they heard the sounds of a generator starting, and the lights flickered to life. A waiter came to the table and they ordered chicken fajitas. Then, after ten minutes of life, the generator sputtered to a halt. While they were waiting for their food, they could hear two women making jokes about the gringo ladies staring at the clouds. Brandy began to get impatient. "We can't see the volcano, and whoever is out back murdering our food is certainly in no hurry!"

"Not to worry, here comes our waiter."

The waiter placed two plates of food on the table, and walked away. Brandy stared incredulously at her plate.

"What is this stuff, anyway? The French fries look green, and the chicken is probably iguana!"

They stirred the contents of their plates to make it look like they had consumed portions of it, then paid the check and made a hasty exit, to try to find the truck in the clouds.

Soon they heard Marco laughing, and when he came into view, he taunted, "What is wrong, Senorita Brandy?

Did you enjoy the volcano?"

"It was the most beautiful volcano I've ever seen! Now you can get us the hell out of here!"

When Marco started the motor, he asked, "Should I take you back to your hotel, now?"

"Actually, no, I'm so thrilled at the magnificence of the volcano we just saw, that I feel the need to celebrate. Do you know where we can get a mojito?"

"There's a Cuban restaurant about a mile from your hotel which features the mojito."

"All right, then you can take us there, and we will walk back to the hotel."

When Marco stopped in front of a long white building with a red tile roof, he winked at Brandy, and said, "This is a very nice place. I hope you enjoy your mojitos, and if you're still hungry, the food is very good, too!"

Brandy winked back, then said, "We just finished a delicious meal, but thanks for the information, you have been a big help! Adios!"

There was a crowd of people at the bar when they entered the restaurant, so they went to a table, and sat down. When the waitress came to take their order, they ordered mojitos. When the server headed to the bar, Kitty picked up a menu. "I'm famished, but I don't want to risk another meal like we just abandoned!"

"Neither would I! What kind of appetizers do they have?"

Kitty handed her the menu, and she scanned the top of the page. "Why don't we order some Papas Rellenas?"

"What are they?"

"They're seasoned mashed potatoes with ground beef, but the seasoning is all you can taste, so even if the meat is iguana, it won't matter!"

When the drinks arrived, Brandy ordered the appetizers. She then sipped slowly from the tall Collins glass on the table and remarked, "This is delicious, and the bartender must have noticed how pissed off I looked when we came in! He didn't spare the rum. Things are looking up! Three plates of Pappas Rellenas, and two mojitos later, Brandy gave her check card to the waitress, but when she ran it through the register the electricity went out. The manager was called to try to cancel the transaction, and after a few frantic minutes, he told Brandy that everything had been taken care of. They walked outside, and then skipped back to their hotel, despite the rough terrain they had to cross.

Back in the hotel room, the two girls began looking for spiders. Brandy resumed stalking insects with her shoe, and after a short period, she announced, "I'm going to have another sixty-years of bad luck, but maybe I can get it to run concurrently with yesterday's sentence!"

In order to assure herself that a snake had not checked unto her bed, Brandy threw back the covers. "What a lovely surprise! I just found the remains of a spider I squashed last night!"

After she had repositioned the sheet, she got into bed. "I'm going to try to go to sleep before I find a dead viper in my pillow case, I'm covered with dust, and I smell like Tom Brady's jersey after the Super Bowl, but I'm not going to freeze my butt off in that shower, and then try to go to sleep!"

Kitty giggled, and said, "I agree with you there, but I'm going to make sure there are no snakes under our beds before we turn out the lights." She quickly glanced under each bed, and then lay down after fluffing her pillow, and switching the light off.

Brandy closed her eyes to try to go to sleep, and from her silence, it was apparent that Kitty was making a similar effort, until she heard sounds coming from the front of the room. She opened her eyes just in time to see a creature crawling through the crack under the door. "Kitty, we have a visitor, and since your fear of spiders has convinced me that I am the male in our relationship, I'm going to squash it before it can attack!"

She got out of bed, and saw a very docile lizard. "Relax! It's just a little lizard. Maybe he'll eat some of the spiders I missed with my shoe, so I don't mind sharing the room with him. I'm going to use my track training, and triple jump to the bathroom, then I'm going to try to sleep."

When she returned to bed, Kitty started to tell her stories about the ghosts who haunted almost every building in the United Kingdom over one hundred years old, and Brandy reciprocated with tales about the most wanted criminals in America. Finally they got up, and repositioned their beds, so each could look under the other's bed for unwanted visitors. Brandy put her knife, flashlight and shoe next to her pillow, and fell asleep.

She soon drifted deeply into dreamland, where she found herself in Chuck's arms, making the kind of love that only people who really care for one another can experience, when a violent wind came rushing through the broken windows. Her bed shook with such fury that she thought that the incredible hulk of the tarantula clan was bench pressing her bed, hoping to avenge his kinfolk who had been the victim of her shoe. When she looked across the room, she was astonished that Kitty was still sound asleep, and she began to think, *I'm a mature, intelligent, twenty-five year old woman, but I'm so terrified that my only thought is to pull the covers up over my head, and hope God will have mercy on my sorry butt!*

She soon returned to her dreams, and when the two females woke up, they each managed to tolerate a final frigid shower, before they packed their things. At seven o'clock; they boarded the bus, and returned to San Jose. Back at the bus depot, Brandy told Kitty that she needed to stoop at an ATM.

"I want to be sure our friends back at the bar canceled that charge."

The machine refused the card, and she went to a teller to cash some traveler's checks. She signed three checks, then handed them to the teller, who, to her astonishment, said, "I am sorry, Senorita, but those signatures do not match!"

On hearing what the young man in the plaid bow tie had said, she thought, *Look, you bozo, I just signed these damned checks in front of you! If your country wasn't infested large spiders, and glowing cockroaches; if my bed hadn't bounced across the floor last night, and if it hadn't taken five hours to travel sixty-kilometers this morning, my signature would not be showing sighs of stress!* Then she smiled, and signed the checks again. After the teller counted out several bills and handed them to her, she tucked the money in her wallet, and said, "I hope you have a lovely day!"

When Brandy arrived at Rosita's house, she immediately phoned her bank, and a representative advised, "Access to your card was denied because someone tried to charge $21,000 to it, and then cancelled the transaction!"

"I was in a restaurant yesterday, and the cashier must have confused colones with dollars, by accident! Thank you for looking out for me."

She hung up the phone, then hugged Rosita, then Guido, then accepted Tuffy's extended right paw. "I love you all, and it's good to be home!"

Rosita wiped her hands on her apron, and said, "It is time for lunch, and I want to hear all about your trip!"

Brandy followed her hostess into the kitchen, and Guido returned to the parlor to watch his soccer match with Tuffy at his side. While they were eating, Rosita said, "We had some excitement in the middle of last might. It was an earthquake and it was a lot stronger than the last one!"

Brandy burst out laughing. "Thank you for telling me that! Now I know why my bed almost bounced back here last night! 'Estoy como los vacas!' "

Chapter 29

Kitty goes home

Early the next morning Brandy and Kitty caught the bus to Sarchi, a town slightly over twenty kilometers from San José.

"This might be the last time we travel together, and we've really had fun. I'm going to miss you, but maybe someday I can show you around London."

"And maybe I'll get a chance to show you Virginia, and our Capitol!"

They were soon rolling past farms and pastures which reminded Brandy of the Shenandoah Valley. Soon a huge red church came into view. Brandy consulted her guidebook.

"That must be the Cathedral de la Mercedes, They call it the 'red metal church' because it was made with metal pieces imported from Belgium in the late nineteenth century. I wouldn't mind seeing that, but the other big attraction here is the 'World of Snakes' serpentarium. They have fifty species of snakes from all over the world.

Kitty laughed, and said, "Well, I don't mind missing that!"

When they climbed off the bus in Sarchi, Brandy said, "It looks like all there is in this town are shops a restaurants, and my stomach is voting for a restaurant!"

They found a small cafe, where they drank coffee and ate sandwiches before they began their tour of the tiny village, walking in and out of shops which sold furniture, jewelry and a large variety of hand carved items, including ornate bowls and kitchen utensils. Brandy purchased a hand painted bowl for Rosita, and wooden spoon with an intricate figure of a chef carved into the handle for her brother.

"Tyler is going to culinary school. He loves to cook, and some of his stuff is actually edible!"

When they reached the cooperative, they watched artisans crafting ornate wooden bowls and trays. On the way back to the bus stop, they saw a red tile roofed canopy, under which there was an ox cart with carved wheels, and painted with brightly colored decorations. A placard said that it symbolized the town's past history as maker of the ox carts which hauled coffee and other products all over the country in the late nineteenth and early twentieth century. Brandy tipped a local boy to take their picture, and promised to e-mail it to Kitty.

After the bus ride back to San Jose, they hailed a taxi. As the driver began weaving through five lanes of heavy traffic at high speed, Brady commented, "This guy is doing the dance of death, and if I appear to be in a trance, it will be because I'm terrified! My seat belt is missing, but I'm too tired to care! She started to doze off when her head suddenly crashed into the seat in front of her. She looked up, then exclaimed," My gosh! Our cab is rolled up like a tube of toothpaste!" Then she looked at Kitty. "Are you okay?"

"Yes, my seat belt saved me, but what about you?"

Before she could answer, the driver spoke in a very calm tone of voice. "I am sorry, but we have been in an accident. Will you please get out of the cab?"

Brandy thought, *Great, here we are in the center of five lanes of heavy traffic, this guy just totaled his cab, and he wants us to disappear!* They complied, and in an instant, another cabbie, who had witnessed the crash, picked them up, and began driving away. Brandy rubbed her head, and then started laughing. "Kitty you told me not to kill those spiders last weekend, but I didn't listen, and I still have over a hundred years of bad luck coming up!"

Kitty snickered. "I'm flying to London on Saturday, and I'm going to miss you, but I'd best part company with you before your hex rubs off!"

Chapter 30

The Children's Hospital

The next morning after breakfast, Brandy went running. When she returned, she showered, put on clean clothes, and started out the door.

"Rosa, I start volunteering at the hospital today, but I'll be back for dinner."

"All right, but that place is in a pretty bad neighborhood. You must be very careful."

"I've been working the streets in Washington for a long time now! I can take care of myself, and I'm very eager to work with the children. Besides, I have my Dollar Store umbrella, and I'll clock anyone who messes with me! I've enjoyed the daycare kids, but from what I've been told, those at the hospital are in much worse shape, and they need someone who cares! Back home, I worked in the pediatrics ward, and a lot of the kids there were dying of cancer. I'll be fine!"

After a thirteen block walk from the bus stop, Brandy reached a five story concrete structure which had been painted beige, and was surrounded by a chain link fence. Each of the large windows was covered by an iron gate. A sign on the lawn said, "El Hospital Nacional de Ninos." She stopped at the gate, where she presented the authorization slip proved by CASA, and entered the building, where she was greeted by the head nurse. "Are you Senorita Barton?"

"Yes!"

"I'm Lily Guzman, and I am very happy to meet you! The people at daycare have said very nice things about you. They tell me the children love you! However, the children you will meet here might not be like the ones you met there, or at the hospital in the United States. Most of the ones you will be working with here are very ill. Some have AIDS, some have cancer, and others have psychiatric problems. Many have no one who cares enough to visit them. It will sometimes be very difficult for you to communicate with them, but they all have one thing in common. They are in desperate need of love and understanding. All you can do is talk to them, or color pictures with them, or read stories,"

"Well, I'll do my best, but I was wondering about one thing. The hospital in the states had all kinds of toys and games. I don't see any toys."

"We have no toys. If we did, the parents who do visit their children here would take them home to their other children. If a child here has a toy of a coloring book, a parent brought it here, and they disappear quickly! I'll take you to meet the children now. Come with me!"

When they entered the ward, a little boy was standing near the door. "Lucio, this is Brandy, and she has come here to play with you and the other children."

The boy smiled, and grasped Brandy's hand, but did not speak.

"Lucio is seven years old and he is very shy. No one ever comes to visit him. He is a very lovable child, like the other children here. I must leave you now, and I'll talk to you before you leave. One little girl, named Elena has AIDS and is confined to her bed. She is on a respirator, and has IVs in both arms. She could die at any time."

Brandy, with Lucio still clinging to her hand, began walking from bed to bed, speaking to each child in turn. "Hello, my name is Brandy, and I've come to play with you!"

When she reached Elena, she asked the other children to gather by her bed. Ten year old Vincente, and nine year old Tomas helped Brandy push Teresa, who was six, seven year old Anna Maria, and five year old Sadie, who were in wheelchairs and hooked up to IVs, into a circle, around seven year old Elena's bed. One of the boys found a Bingo game, and Brandy became the caller, using Elena's tray as a table. While they were playing a nurse entered the room to administer shots or to inject medication into some of the IV's, and Anna Marie and Teresa became upset. To distract them, and comfort Elena, Brandy held her hand, and began to tell a story.

"My family has the funniest little dog in the world. His name is Buddito, and he has very short legs, a very long body, and a pointed tail. When he walks, he waddles like a duck, and is always tripping over sticks. One time he carried a frog into our house, and put it in my sister's bed."

Elena smiled weakly through her tears, and Tomas also smiled, and said, "Buddito is a sausage dog!"

The other children began to laugh, and say, "A sausage dog!"

When Brandy looked at the children's eyes, she thought, *I wonder what they think Buddy looks like. I'm going to bring some crayons and paper next time, and have them draw him.*

While they were laughing, a doctor began performing some sort of procedure on a little boy on the other side of the room, and he began crying, then screaming that it hurt. Brandy began to wish that she had never learned the Spanish word for pain. She began asking the children questions and telling stores about her family and friends back home. About two hours after she had arrived, she started to say goodbye. Lucio, who had never left her side, but had not spoken, looked into her eyes, and whispered, "Please come back to see me! I love you, Brandy!"

She said, "I'll be back tomorrow," but as she began to walk towards the door, the metal beds began to shake, and roll against the walls. To Brandy's surprise, the children all began to laugh, and none seemed to be frightened. The excitement was soon over, and when Brandy stopped to say goodbye to Lily, she learned that the tremors, as she had surmised, were from another earthquake.

The next morning, she returned to the hospital, and remained there for five hours, telling stories, playing games, and pretending to be a number of different animals, until, while she was reclining with her arms and legs in the air in the role of Senor Sloth, she thought, *I'm going to have to learn more about the local wildlife if I'm going to do this! I'm exhausted! I can't keep pretending to be a bear, a dog, a horse, or a crab, and this sloth act is making me sleepy! I'm going to have to find a toy store!*

She went directly to the mall from the hospital, and found that the stores were closed for Viene Santa (Holy Thursday). A security guard told her of one store which was still open. She ran there as fast as she could, and purchased paper, crayons, coloring books, and playdough for the children. Then she saw a little Teddy Bear, which she decided to give to Elena.

She had started toward the checkout counter, when she remembered that Rosita had asked her to get some mangoes for Sunday. She pushed her shopping cart to the produce department. When she arrived there, she not only put mangoes in the cart, but also loaded it with three melons, two cartons of strawberries, and two pineapples. It was not until she was outside the store that she realized that she was not in the states, and had no car. By the time she had struggled the half mile to Rosita's house, both of her arms had gone numb.

Brandy took a taxi to the hospital the next day, and when she entered the ward with the things she had bought for the children to play with, they were overjoyed, and began screaming and laughing with excitement. "Brandy has toys! Brandy has crayons! Brandy has playdough!"

"Calm down, please? I want to give something to Elena, and then we we'll play!"

She removed the Teddy Bear from the bag, and gave it to the little girl. She took it from her hands, and, smiling weakly, she groaned, and her eyes seemed to say, "Gracias, Brandy, I love you!"

During the next six hours, Brandy and the children made playdough animals, including images of a long dog with a pointed tail. One little boy drew a portrait of Brandy with purple hair and orange eyes. Then, as she prepared to leave, the mother of one of the boys approached her. "My friend and I want to know if we can take the playthings you brought today home with us."

Brandy, who was shocked and surprised that a parent would ask her such a question, said, "I bought these things for the children in the hospital, and they're not to be taken from the hospital."

"Well, will you buy some toys for us to rake home?"

Shaking her head, Brandy said, "No, you should buy your own toys!"

She left the ward quickly, and when she reached home, she told Rosita that the apparent greed of the Costa Rican people was very difficult for her to accept. Rosita gathered her apron up in her hands, and said, "I agree, many of the Ticos seem to think only of money. Every day I thank God that I am Italian! Of course, some people here seem greedy because they have so little, and do not understand!"

On Friday, when she returned to the hospital to play with the children, Elena was clutching the toy bear. When she saw Brandy, she smiled weakly. For the next three hours, the children drew pictures, colored pages, and made up stories. When Brady arrived home that afternoon, she became congested, and soon discovered that her temperature was slightly elevated. She decided not to go to the hospital on Saturday, so she spent the morning resting and reviewing her lessons. In the afternoon, she felt better, and decided to help Rosita prepare for the family's Easter celebration. After supper, she watched television with her hosts, and then went to bed early.

Chapter 31

Praising the Lord

Brandy woke up on Sunday morning just as the first rays of sunrise flickered through the blinds on her bedroom window. She arose immediately, and went to the bathroom to brush her teeth. When she finished, she looked out the window at the flowers in the garden. *What a gorgeous day! I think I'll go for a run before breakfast, and then I'll look for a church that has an Easter service.* She slipped into a pair of shorts, pulled a tee-shirt over her head, put on her socks and running shoes, and headed for the street. When she was five blocks from home, she passed a small white church with a sign in front. She stopped to read it, while jogging in place. "Semana Santa Service Today! 9:00 am."

She thought, *Christ must have read my mind! I'll finish my run, then change clothes and walk back here. I may even have time for breakfast.* When she got back to Rosita's, her breakfast waiting. At 8:45 am, she reached the church, where a handsome middle-aged man in clerical attire and a little girl were greeting the congregation. When he saw Brandy, he smiled, and said, "Welcome to our church! I am Pastor Aguilar, and this is my daughter, Christina. I saw you earlier, when you were out for your morning run. Our visitors from the Estado Unidos are always welcome!"

Brandy smiled, and said, "How did you know I was Gringo?"

"You were wearing a Duke University tee-shirt! Did you go to school there? I'm a fan of your Coach 'K'! I love 'March Madness'! I went to college at Evangel University in Springfield, Missouri, but I'm sure that you never heard of it!"

"You are right about that! I've never heard of your school, but I went to a college I'm sure that you never heard of. I went to Mary Hays McCauley College in Fredericksburg. She was better known as Molly Pitcher! I've never even been to the Duke campus. I'm just a Coach 'K' fan, like you! My name is Brandy Barton."

"Well, Seniorita Barton, you are most welcome, whether you went to Duke or not! Why don't you sit with Christina during the service? She will take good care of you!"

Christina took Brandy's hand, and led her through the door. The minister returned to greeting his parishioners. While Brandy was following her petite guide towards the front of the church, members of the congregation stopped her from time to time to introduce themselves, and extend their welcome. Christina led Brandy to a pew facing the pulpit, and then sat down. Brandy joined her, and an attractive, wide-eyed middle-aged woman wearing an embroidered white dress sat down beside her.

"Hello! I am Acacia Garza, and I have been a member of this church for several years now. I see that Christina is looking after you! You are in good hands, but I thought you might like to learn more about our church!"

During the next ten minutes, Brandy learned the history of the parish and most of the regular parishioners. She also answered numerous questions about her life, including a few of a somewhat personal nature. When the service started, the congregation began rapidly clapping and singing Gospel songs in Spanish. Brandy recognized the tunes, but though the words were projected on a screen, was uncertain as to exactly what she was singing about. She thought, *I feel like Forrest Gump, when he was singing with the choir in Bubba's church! I'm butchering the words, and only God knows whether I'm singing to him in words my mom taught me to never use in public!*

Acacia apparently read her eyes, and whispered, "Don't worry child, God only cares what is in your heart, not what language you speak."

During the three hour service, the more excited the preacher became as he spoke of Christ rising from the dead, the faster the words sprang from his mouth. Then he paused for a moment, and shocked Brandy by asking her to stand. "We are honored today to have a visitor from the United States! This is Seniorita Brandy Barton, from the state of Virginia."

The people began clapping, and Brandy began to think, *Great! I don't really like to speak in public using English, but I'm about to speak to a church full of Hispanics in their native tongue! I just hope I don't wind up announcing that I like to get drunk and run naked through the streets!*

She stood up and said, "I'm Brandy, and I love your country!"

She quickly sat down, and then stood up again, to acknowledge the applause of the crowd. After church, the head of the women's bible study class invited her to join them for tea at their weekly meeting.

Chapter 32

Another Angel

Back at Rosita's, the entire family was there to dine and celebrate. Despite Brandy's protests, Rosita kept piling food onto her plate. When the meal was over, she felt the skin over her stomach tighten. She had avoided drinking because she was expected at the hospital. She said goodbye to Rosita and her guests, and began the walk to the hospital. When she arrived there, she was concerned that she was out of breath, which, as a conditioned athlete, was an unaccustomed phenomenon.

On the way to the front entrance, as she passed the Emergency department, she thought, *I wonder if I could get my stomach pumped! After all, I am giving them my time!* When she reached the ward, her concern about her obesity was replaced by anger. The visiting parents had taken every toy, crayon and sheet of paper that she had bought for the children. One of the mothers, whose child was in the bed next to Elena's, had pilfered the Teddy bear from the dying girl's bed while she slept. After Brandy confronted the parents, who had not yet left, the missing items, including the bear, were retrieved from under mattresses, cabinet drawers, and suitcases. She returned the bear to Elena, who was considerably weakened from the time she had last visited. When Brandy placed the toy beside her, she smiled. Brandy, whose anger had been replaced by compassion, asked the nurse if she could rock her in her arms.

"I want her to know she's with someone who cares about her!"

She sat on the bed, lifted the frail body onto her lap, and began to sing in Spanish, making up the lyrics as she sang. She thought, *I have no idea what I'm saying! My voice is just coming back; this could be the last day this poor child has on earth, and she is being sung to by someone who could make Macy Gray sound like a soprano!* Eventually, Elena fell asleep, and Brandy tried to make her comfortable in bed. She placed the bear under her right arm, and left the room.

That evening, she watched "Titanic" on television with Guido, Rosita, and Tuffino. On Monday, she followed her usual daily routine, attending her classes, running in the streets, and spending an hour at the gym. She ate dinner at home, spent an hour preparing for her classes, and then watched television with her host family, which she had treated as surrogate grandparents almost from the day she first entered their home.

On Tuesday after class, she went directly to the hospital, and when she entered the building, a staff Doctor said that Lily wanted to see her. "Do you know what it is about?"

"Yes, but I think it best if she tells you what she wants to say!"

She began to think, *What did I do now? I hope I haven't done something to jeopardize the health of the children!* At that moment, Lily appeared in the hallway, and said, "Good afternoon, Brandy! I have some sad news. Last night, shortly after midnight, little Elena went into respiratory arrest, then cardiac arrest. She is now at peace!"

Brandy fought to hold back her tears. "How sad! Of course, I knew when I was with her on Sunday that she was going to die, but at least she will not suffer anymore, and I know that God will see that she can talk, run, play, and be happy forever!"

"Si! Un angel mas!" Then, in English, she said, "One more angel!"

Brandy said, "Now I wish I had come here yesterday."

She started to leave the office when Lily said, "She was not alone, because of this." As she spoke, the nurse pointed to her desk, on top of which was the toy bear that Brandy had given Elena, sealed in a plastic bag. "She was holding it tightly in her arms when se died! The mother of the child in the room with her wanted to take it home, but I thought you might like to have it." She handed the package to Brandy. "

"Yes, I would like that very much, and thank you!"

She put the bear into her back pack, and then went directly to see the other children.

Chapter 33

The Rest of the Day

When Brandy passed Elena's empty bed, she felt very sad, and struggled to keep from crying. When the other children saw her, they seemed to sense her distress, and eagerly rushed to her side. She said, "It is so nice to be here with all of you, and I have a surprise. She reached in her back pack, and removed a bowling set, with ten colored plastic pins, and two black bowling balls.

"I'm going to teach you how to bowl!"

During the next two hours, the delighted tots enthusiastically played, and the first time one of them was lucky enough to knock down all of the pins on the first effort, Brandy yelled, "Jorge got a strike!"

From that moment, whenever one of them duplicated the feat, he or she would scream "Strike!" As she watched, Brandy thought, *When they say that word with a Spanish accent, it sounds so cute! It's amazing how such a simple thing can amuse them so much! I bought that game at the Dollar Store, but it's priceless to them!"*

During the first hour of the game, Brandy noticed that a very frail little girl named Lucia, who was always alone, and who had steadfastly resisted any efforts to get her to play, had crept to the fringe of the crowd, and seemed very interested in the activity of the others. Brandy knew that her mother had died of AIDS, and her father had abandoned her. A few minutes later, Brandy felt someone tapping her shoulder, and when she turned, she saw Lucia, with one hand tightly gripping her IV pole. The emaciated little girl whispered, "Brandy, will you play with me?"\

Brandy helped the fragile child sit beside her on the floor, and put her arm around her tiny body. Lucia placed one of her paper thin hands on Brandy's knee, and let her stroke her sleek, coal black hair, which seemed to be her only healthy feature. When the game was finished, Jorge, who had scored the first strike, and took great delight in screaming the words, had suddenly become very silent, and seemed to be very sad.

"Jorge, what's wrong?"

"I'm leaving the hospital tomorrow. They are discharging me."

"Why, that is wonderful news! I'm so happy for you! I'll miss you, though, because you have helped me very much! When I haven't understood what the others were saying, you've repeated their words, and explained what they've tried to say. You've even acted out their meaning when I still didn't get it! "

"Well, I don't want to leave here! It makes me very sad."

"Are you sad because you'll miss the other children, and the nurses?"

"No, I'll miss them, but that is not why I'm sad."

"Well, you are always so full of energy, and you are always laughing. Do you want to talk about it?"

"No, I don't want to talk about it!" Having said his piece, he walked slowly away.

Brandy went to see Lucia again, and later in the evening, one of the nurses asked her to help Jorge call his mother to arrange for her to take him home. They walked together to the pay phone, and, to assure his privacy, she stood where she could watch him without monitoring his conversation. After he hung up the phone, he seemed even more distraught than before.

"Jorge are you okay? What did your mom say?"

"I didn't talk to her. A man I don't know answered the phone. He said she was busy, and couldn't come to the phone! I don't know who he was, and I don't know what to do!"

"I'm sure it'll work out. I'll tell Lily, and she'll know what to do! Don't worry, sweetie."

As she spoke, she thought, *This is so sad! I'm not sure how I would comfort this poor kid in English, and I sure don't know how to do it in Spanish.* Then she said the first thing that came to mind which might cheer him up. "Strike!"

His eyes seemed to light up, and he began to laugh.

"That's better! You're going to be all right. Just think about that word when you feel bad, and I'll be thinking about you for the rest of my life."

He smiled, and then walked away without saying anything more. She told Lily what had happened before she left the hospital. She had started to walk to the bus station when she noticed an elderly woman who was carrying a shopping bag.

"Excuse me, but are you on your way to the bus station?"

"Si, yo soy!"

"Would you like some company?"

"Yes, I would like that! You are from the United States, aren't you?"

"Yes, and I came here to learn your language, but I don't speak it very well!"

The woman smiled, and said, "Oh, you can speak Spanish, but you have a gringo accent!"

When they arrived at the station, they parted company, and, as Brandy waited for her bus, she thought, *That lady was very nice, and she was probably right. If I ever learn Spanish, I will have to find a way to lose my Gringo accent!*

Rosita was waiting at the door when Brandy entered the house. "I was worried about you! That hospital is in a very bad neighborhood, and you are late, but I have your dinner waiting for you."

"Thank you for worrying, but I can take care of myself. The little girl I mentioned to you died, as was expected, but it was very sad news. I stayed later than usual, because one of my favorite children is being discharged. He is very sad because he wants to stay there. He tried to call his mother, but a strange man answered the phone, and said she wasn't available. It is so sad!"

"Well, I was worried about you. There are many people who don't deserve children, and it's sometimes heartbreaking. Now, come eat your dinner."

That night, while she was lying in bed, her mind began to wander. *Poor Jorge! He's such a nice kid, and many people would be proud to call him their son, but his mom seems to be the kind of person who doesn't deserve to live, let alone have kids. If I weren't too tired to get out if bed, I'd try to say 'Shazam', or some other magic word and turn into a superhero so I could make things right for Jorge and kids like him!*

Chapter 34

Paul Returns

The next morning, when Brandy arrived at the school, she was shocked to see Paul sitting in the break area.

"Surprise, sunshine, I'm back! I decided to take a few more lessons. Are you still traveling on weekends?"

"Yes, in fact, I've signed up for a day trip on Saturday. It's called a 'Highlights' tour. It leaves at six o'clock in the morning, and includes plantations, coffee factories, volcanoes, and a whitewater raft trip. Want to come along?"

She desperately tried to hide her surprise that Paul had returned.

"Hey, that sounds cool! Why don't we have a few drinks after class and talk about it? I'm at the Marriott, again. I'm not sure how long I'll be staying."

"You know I don't like to drink in the afternoon! Besides, I'm going right to the gym, then I'm going for my usual run. You can join me, if you'd like. We can catch a bus to the mountains and run there. I've explored every inch of concrete in the city, and it isn't safe to run alone in the boonies!"

"No thanks! I'll see you later. I've not enrolled yet, and I think I'll only do private lessons this trip, if I decide to hang around. I really need to talk to you. Let's grab something to eat before you go to the gym."

"All right, I'll meet you at the café across the street after class."

When she entered the building, she thought, *I like this guy, but I have a feeling that he might be a problem! I'd better set him straight real fast.* At noon, she strolled to the café, where Paul was seated in a booth in the corner. When the waitress came, she ordered a sandwich and a bottle of water. Paul ordered a beer. Before she could speak, he reached into his pocket, then set his hand on the table, palm down.

"I was hoping I could do this in a more suitable ambiance, but this dump will have to serve the purpose. Ever since the night I left, I've been unable to forget you. I told you some time ago that I was looking for someone to spend the rest of my life with! The restaurant has done very well, and my partner and I are about to close a deal to sell franchises! I can give you things that your boyfriend will never be able to afford."

He then knelt beside the booth, and displayed a ring with a very large diamond in the center. "Will you marry me?"

Brandy was taken aback when everyone close enough to see and hear, began staring at the spectacle before them. She stood up and said, "Isn't he cute? We've been rehearsing for a play, and my leading man wanted to see if he is as good an actor as he thinks he is!"

She kissed Paul on the lips. Then, in a very dramatic tone, she screamed, "I cannot marry you because mother would never approve! Now I must run!"

She picked up her backpack, and sprinted out the door without looking back. Paul did not show up at the school the next day, and Vicky later told her that he had cancelled his request for private lessons, saying that he had been called back to the United States on an urgent business matter, and did not plan to return.

Brandy thought, *He's really very nice, and I hope he finds the girl he's looking for. What I did was pretty crappy, but he took me by surprise. I'm not looking for someone to give me things, or take care of me! If I ever get married, it will be to someone I'm sure I can share the rest of my life with as an equal partner! Chuck and I have a great relationship, but I'm not sure that I'm ready for "till death we do part, even with him!"*

Chapter 35

The Twelve Hour Tour

Brandy got out of bed at 4:45 am on Saturday morning, dressed quickly, and picked up her travel brochure. Because it was a cool day, she put a sweatshirt and a pair of long pants into her backpack. As she headed for the street to find a taxi, she glanced at the brochure. After reading that she was about to see, "All that is natural, fresh, and spectacular of Costa Rica in 12 hours," she thought, *Wow! Paul has no idea as to what he will miss! I really feel sorry about the way I handled that, but he blindsided me, and I panicked. I hope he's okay, because he is a nice guy, but I have a nicer one back home, and I'm not ready to marry him!*

A half hour later, while she was in the city waiting for her minibus, she began talking to a huge man, who resembled the death row inmate in the movie, The Green Mile, who was standing near by. When he noticed the brochure in her hand, he said, "I see that you're going on the twelve hour tour! I did that last week. It's worthwhile, but the river trip was so wild that I screamed like a little girl the whole way! The rapids are terrifying, and when I left the boat, I ached all over from bracing myself for death, and banging into very large rocks."

"Sounds like you had fun, but what was the scariest, the river trip, or the bus ride?"

The man laughed, and then said, "Definitely the bus ride! I'm a very strong swimmer!"

The minibus screeched to a stop in front of them,, and tie big man bid her farewell. She mused, *What a nice guy! If what he says is true, and I survive the river, maybe Chuck and I'll reconsider doing the Galley River next time we go to West Virginia!*

After the tour group had climbed onto the bus, the guide began asking his passengers where they were from. Brandy soon learned that she would spend the day with four young Swiss women, six elderly men from California, a man from Mexico, a married couple from Panama, and two middle aged men from New Jersey. The bus began speeding through country villages, past dairy farms, and highlands forests, before it stopped at a coffee plantation, where Brandy's brochure boasted that there was a "breathtaking view." As she stood with the others in a chilling downpour, she whispered to one of the men from New Jersey, as she pointed to the words. "Whoever wrote that was either here on a sunny day, or delusional enough to think that a cow peeing on a flat rock was breathtaking!"

Before they returned to the bus, she went to the restroom and donned her warmer clothes. When the tour stopped at the Poas Volcano National Park, the guide told them that the temperature was 50 degrees on the "cool summit," where the elevation was 87,000 feet. When they alighted from the bus in the raging torrent, an opportunistic Tico was selling ponchos, and each member of the party was elated to purchase one. As she donned the camouflaged garment, which was undoubtedly bought at a fraction of the sale price at a surplus store, or quite possibly stolen, she muttered, "We look like a mini militia on a secret mission!"

The guide, who had brought his own poncho, began leading his group through the primeval cloud forest, abundant with vegetation, including giant leaves, epiphytes, ferns, elfin forests, and colorful blossoms. A few minutes after they had started, one of the senior citizens from California asked the guide if he could go back to the bus to get out of the rain. "I am sorry, Senor, but that is not possible because the driver has been awake for twenty-four hours, and is taking a siesta!"

On hearing this, the old man said, "Wonderful! I can hardly wait to get back on the bus and ride through the mountains with him!"

When they reached the summit where the brochure said they would see "One of the largest, most active craters in the world," the deluge continued, and, though they were standing by a sign which indicated that the volcano was behind it, the rain, mixed with sulfur, limited visibility to a few inches. Brandy had just taken a picture of the sign, when she got an idea which she felt would show her frustration. She handed her camera to the man from Mexico, then held up her right hand with the middle finger pointing skyward, "flipping off" the volcano. Her cohorts decided to follow her example, and soon the volcano had been properly punished a total of sixteen times for hiding in the rain, before the wet, cold and miserable assemblage hiked back to continue their adventure. Back at the bus, they discovered that the driver had gone for coffee, and the Mexican man said, "Hop aboard! I'll drive, and if I cannot find a volcano, I'll find a good bar!"

The group did not have a chance to find out whether the man was joking, because the driver had wisely taken the keys with him. When he returned, he drove for twenty minutes before he pulled into an outdoor restaurant, where he announced, "We will be having a traditional Costa Rican breakfast called Gallo Pinto. It's beans with rice, seasoned with spices such as cilantro, pepper, and onions."

While they sat eating, and sipping strawberry juice, with the wind and rain blowing sideways, one of the men from New Jersey commented, "This stuff doesn't taste bad, but it looks like something that came from a cow that ate confetti!"

The group buttoned their ponchos and dashed back to the bus through the torrential rain. As they boarded, one of the men groaned, "I wonder why the guides never tell us where the bathrooms are. I didn't see one back there, and I'm damn sure not going out there again to look!"

Brady smiled in sympathy. "Well, if you can't hold out until we stop again, nobody will know the difference, because we brought plenty of water onto the bus on our designer rainwear! The floor is flooded!"

During the next forty minutes, the mini-bus rumbled along, as the guide spoke of the high volcanic edifices, deep jungle growth, canyons and sparkling streams. The Mexican gentleman whispered loudly. "What is he talking about? All I can see is the rain!"

Brandy muttered, "Oh, I'm sure it would be lovely, if we could see it!"

Their comments seemed to have infected the other members of the group, causing them to be giddy with sarcasm. Regardless of their demeanor, the guide was not dissuaded, and continued his commentary, until the vehicle stopped again at the La Paz Waterfall Garden, where he led them first to the butterfly garden, where the butterflies were not able to fly because their wings were wet. Brandy noted that the prettiest butterflies were pinned to a corkboard at the entrance. When they reached the hummingbird garden, Brandy took several photos, then stopped, and thought, *My mom will think I'm nuts! There are hummingbirds in Grandma's backyard in Virginia. I'm only taking these stupid pictures now because I'm a tourist!*

Soon they were once again hiking through the rain along a path past the Templo, Magica Blanca, Encantada, Escondida and La Paz Waterfalls. As she marched along, shivering in her wet poncho, Brandy began wondering why all waterfalls look the same in the rain. Eventually, the wet, cold, and miserable troupe reboarded the bus, and traveled to another open-air restaurant. While they were waiting to be seated, a dark, distinguished looking gray haired man asked Brandy if she was an American. "Is it that obvious?"

"As soon as I heard you speak, I recognized your accent! My name is Sirhan Singh, and I was born in India, but my father was a diplomat, and I've lived in many countries. I'm currently working near here, and I eat lunch here every day. The food is good, but I also like it because it gives me a chance to meet interesting people. I would like very much to talk with you. I don't often get the chance to speak English these days!"

"I would like that, but I'm with that bunch of people in these ugly ponchos!"

"We can sit near them; it's not often that I meet such a lovely lady!"

"That's very nice of you! How could I refuse? The people on the bus are fun, but I'm going to be with them until midnight!"

Once they were seated, Sirhan asked, "Where are you from in the United States?"

"I'm from Virginia. I'm here to learn to speak Spanish. I hope to become fluent some day, but can't seem to master it!"

Sirhan smiled gently. "I can relate to that! I have lived all over the world, and have learned to speak Chinese, Japanese, Arabic, German and Swahili. I had to learn in order to survive! One thing I know is that the most difficult problem is to speak without an accent!"

Brandy listened intently to her new acquaintance. She found his background impressive, especially when he told her that he had been a professor at Harvard, and the University of London. As he spoke, she thought, *My catch phrase, 'Estoy como las vacas,' really comes to mind just listening to this guy, who has been to places I can only dream of visiting! The problem is that he's from a country where cows are sacred animals. He'd probably think I was flattering myself!*

When the group began to leave, Brandy said goodbye to Sirhan. The bus was soon rolling through the Caribbean lowlands. The next stop was the boat dock at the Sarapiqui Jungle River, where the group was confronted with a long line of very steep stone steps, which were an ominous sight, especially because of the pouring rain which was cascading down to the dock. After Brandy had descend part way, the man behind her screamed, then slid toward her in his wet poncho, in a manner which reminded her of a "Slip and Slide" at a water park. When she turned as he careened toward her, she thought of what Kitty had said about killing spiders and bad luck, until he stopped inches short of taking her feet out from under her. Two of his friends rushed to help him back on his feet, and Brandy felt ashamed that it had taken all of her strength to keep from laughing. Everyone was relieved that, though he was obviously shaken, the man was not seriously injured.

When the party reached the boat and climbed aboard, the driver rearranged the seating order of the passengers to distribute the weight, and prevent the rickety craft from flopping over. Brandy smiled as she thought of the calories she had ingested during her stay at Rosita's. *At least he didn't*

counter balance my body with that fat guy from California!
Maybe her Tiramizu isn't getting the best of my thighs.

The motor began to sputter when boat reached the middle of the river, and the driver yelled to a man on the shore. "El propellor es muy feo!"

On hearing this, one of the Californians yelled, "Want in the hell does that mean in English? Send out the alcohol, or, We are going to sink and die?"

Brandy said, "Actually, I think it means, "The propeller is nasty. But the way we're fighting the current, we're probably all going to die before they have time to send out the alcohol!"

The driver's battle with the rushing waters continued as the antiquated vessel tipped each time the passengers on one side leaned to look at iguanas, monkeys, and exotic birds on the other side, with the result that he kept spinning the boat around to keep it from capsizing. After more than an hour of spinning slowly up and down the river, the boat retuned to shore, where the survivors were rewarded for their bravery with carrot juice and crackers, before they boarded the bus to return to San Jose.

On the return trip, the mini-bus stopped at a small store, and Preston Phipps, a retired Navy Captain from San Diego, bought three cases of cold canned beer for all to share. Brandy was fearful that she might be faced with a crisis if she imbibed on a bus without a bathroom, but found the remainder of the trip very entertaining, because the geezers in the back were more afraid that they would spill their beer than they were of dying, as the bus swerved wildly up and down the mountains in the fog.

Twelve hours after they had departed, the group arrived back at the depot, and Brandy returned to Rosita's house by taxi. When she arrived, the entire family was there to greet her. She spent the next forty minutes eating pizza, and regaling all present with a detailed account of her adventure, before she excused herself, by saying, "I don't want to seem rude but I'm exhausted from seeing all that is natural, fresh, and spectacular in only twelve hours, so I'm going to go to bed now! Goodnight!"

Chapter 36

Brandy Makes
Two New Friends

On Sunday morning after breakfast, Brandy and Rosita's sister, Gina, went to the farmer's market to buy fruits and vegetables. When they left the house, she was thinking, *I'm so simple that I am actually excited about going to a market to buy produce!* After two-and-one-half- hours, and five trips to the car with such bargains as ten pounds of potatoes for a dollar, the thrill was gone. The two women stopped at a bakery to buy bread, then were held up by a parade of ox carts and dancers, before they got back to Rosita's, in time for lunch.

Shortly after 1:00 pm, Brandy excused herself, and went to the hospital. She was very happy to see the children, but sad to discover that all of the toys, paper and crayons she had bought for them had disappeared, except for some finger-paints which had been hidden under a mattress. The nurses gave them some chart paper, and while they were playing, the children surprised Brandy by asking questions about life in the United States, and such topics as the World Trade

Center. One little boy made a paper airplane, and smashed it into a chair. The children began chattering incessantly, asking questions about perfume, skyscrapers, cell phones, and cartoon characters like Scooby Doo. Brandy became increasingly perplexed, thinking of how horrible she felt, hearing some of their remarks, as she described life in the United States to them, and hearing them each tell her how much they wanted to live there.

Finally, she said, "Your country has much to offer! It's beautiful, even though my country is a bit more modern." As she spoke, she thought, *Who am I kidding! None of these kids get enough to eat when they're home, and Diego doesn't have his own shoes! Why should they buy into my bullshit! I wonder if Chuck would still want me if I adopted a bunch of little ticos and ticas?*

After she had returned home she went for her daily run, but could not get the children out of her mind, thinking how every night on the news she saw stories about children like Diego, who lived in shacks without running water, and had no shoes or toys. *The worst part is that I feel powerless to help! Money only goes so far, and buying books and crayons is a frustrating effort with the result that some children have them, but some don't. Then the parents rip them off and take them home, so we're back to square one! I'm not even sure I can blame the parents, because they're very poor, which would go a long way towards explaining their apparent greed!*

On Monday morning at school, Brandy arrived in the classroom just as a beautiful white-haired woman who appeared to be in her early sixties, was introducing herself to the class. Her hair was neatly styled, and she was wearing a light blue pants suit. An antique gold locket dangled from her neck. In a sultry, very feminine voice, she said "My name is Ingrid Dietrich. I was born in Germany. My parents were both doctors, and during the war, Hitler separated my sister and me from them. We did not see them again until it ended. I'm a psychiatrist, and have practiced in Utah for the past several years. I speak English, German and Italian and am here to improve my command of Spanish. I sometimes confuse the languages, but probably don't have to tell you that, because I've been drifting from one tongue to the other for the past several minutes!"

Brandy was very impressed by this fascinating, elegant woman, whose stories were not only incredible, but very amusing. On Tuesday, Brandy had a taste of déjà vu, because no sooner than she had entered the room, a tall very handsome man with flecks of grey around his temples, and in his mustache rose to his feet, and began to speak

"My name is Andro Kovacevic. I was born in Croatia in 1959, but my mother was from Lebanon, and I moved there with her when my parents separated in 1969. She was a nurse in a clinic in an impoverished area which had been ravaged by war for many years. I decided to become a doctor when I was fourteen years old."

Brandy found his stories almost as captivating as those told by Ingrid, who seemed to be listening intently, although she was knitting a sweater and did not miss a stitch during the entire morning. As they were leaving, Brandy asked her why she knitted in class, and she explained, "I have a tendency to fall asleep if I'm not active, and it actually helps me concentrate."

"How do you stay awake when you're with a patient? It seems to me some of them would freak out if you were knitting."

"No, I never knit during therapy, but I do jumping jacks if I'm getting drowsy!"

When the day's classes came to an end, Brandy asked Ingrid and Andro to go to dinner. She had wanted to return to La Guaga since the night she had eaten there with Paul.

"My host and hostess are entertaining a friend from Italy tonight. The whole family will be there. I was invited, but I don't want to make Guido and Rosita translate from Italian all evening! Anyway, I'm in the mood for Cuban food, and my craving for mojitos is almost constant! Would you two care to join me?"

That evening they met and shared a cab. Since the hour was early, the threesome ordered mojitos, and engaged in conversation for an hour before they ordered dinner Halfway through the meal, when Brandy had just finished her third mojito, a television crew began interviewing a local soccer star at the adjoining table. She set down her drink, and began waving at the camera. When the interview ended, the young Latino athlete approached Brandy and offered to pay for her dinner, if she would join him afterward. Ingrid and Andro were laughing at the predicament she had gotten into, and good naturedly urged her to accept the young man's offer. She smiled, and said. "Some other time, maybe, but I'm having dinner with my mom and my uncle. Thank you, anyway, it is really nice of you to offer!"

Although the youth seemed slightly perturbed that any woman would not have fallen gratefully in his arms, he sauntered away with his entourage and left the restaurant A short time later, when Brandy asked for the check, the waitress said, "Your bill has been paid by Renaldo Sanchez. He is one of the best futbol players in Costa Rica, and he loves the beautiful senoritas. Then she handed Brandy a carefully folded sheet of paper and returned to her station. Brandy unfolded the message, and read, "If you change your mind, I will be in suite 651 alone for the next two hours. Do not bother to knock; the door will be unlocked. Renaldo."

Brandy laughed, and as she handed the note to Ingrid, she said, "I wonder how he'd feel if all three of us walked into his room. After all, he did buy our dinner and drinks!"

When Brandy got back to Rosita's, her family descended upon her like a contingent of drones on a queen bee. They fought to hug and kiss her and welcomed her with salutations in rapid-fire Italian. After they had calmed down, the group went into the parlor to watch a Pavarotti concert. Soon, everyone in the room was singing along in Italian, and when Brandy began laughing, the others asked her to explain why. She said, "His eyebrows are fake! They are painted on!"

They all rushed forward for a closer look, and then Guido announced, "She is right, his brows are pencil marks!"

When the concert ended, the guests left, and Brandy went to bed. She slept fitfully, however, because she found herself dreaming that she was backstage with the great Pavarotti, speaking Italian, and discussing the fact that her eyebrows had been completely waxed off, and seeking his advice as to how to draw them back on her face.

Chapter 37

Ingrid Extends
a Tempting Invitation

On Wednesday, Brandy was chosen to tell a story in Spanish, and although she was somewhat disconcerted, she began speaking. Unfortunately, after less than a minute, she was interrupted by the teacher, who was obviously trying not to laugh.

"Excuse me Brady, but many of the words you have used are Italian!"

In response, she blunted out, "But I don't know any Italian!" She paused, and thought, *Damn you, Mister Pavarotti! My little chick pea-sized brain is on overload, and might spontaneously combust any moment! I wonder if my insurance will cover that!* After she regained her composure, she continued speaking slowly, and managed to finish her story.

That afternoon, while studying at home, she arranged a large stack of flashcards on the desk, but soon fell asleep When she awoke, she realized that the power had gone off. She went to the living room, where Rosita, Guido and Tuffy were sitting, and Rosita said, "You were very lucky that you didn't wake up, because there was a terrible storm! Come join us, the electricity should be on soon, but we're in no hurry. We can pass the time telling stories. When we were young we had no television, and we relied on conversation, but people don't do that anymore."

Right after Brandy sat down, Guido fell asleep, and Tuffy did the same. The two women sat in the dark for about an hour, laughing, and joking, until Rosita said, "The power may be off for quite a while, so we will probably have to eat sandwiches, but we have no bread."

Brandy said, "I'll go to the market and get some, and you can spend your time listening to Guido and Tuffy snore until I get back."

Twenty minutes later, when she returned, the electricity was again functioning, and when Rosita greeted her at the door, she began laughing.

"What's so funny?"

"You've aged during the storm! There are lines all over your face!"

Brandy walked into the foyer and glanced in the mirror. To her surprise, she discovered that her flash cards had left their mark while she was taking her impromptu nap. She thought, *I'd like to explain that by saying that all else having failed, I decided to try learning by osmosis, but I don't know the right Spanish words to do that!*

They woke Guido up, and ate sandwiches in front of the television set, while watching the news. During the sportscast, Brandy was surprised to see the interview she had witnessed the night before, and her smiling face as she waved at the camera from background. Guido and Rosita began clapping and yelling, and Tuffy began barking after he had been rudely awakened by the commotion. Guido said, "My lovely princess is a television star!"

She thought about telling her adopted kinfolk that Guido's futbol hero had made a pass at her, but decided to keep it to herself. When she went out to join her classmates for the walk to school the next morning, several who had seen her on the news began teasing her about her newfound celebrity. To patronize them, she donned her sunglasses despite the fact that it was an overcast day.

That morning in class, the students played a game similar to Trivial Pursuit. A statement was made that Vitamin C would help for constipada, and Brandy remarked, "I didn't know that Vitamin C relieved constipation!"

The instructor began to laugh, and tears filled her eyes.

"No, Brandy, constipada is congestion from a cold! It has nothing to do with the bowels."

Andro commented, "No wonder my Spanish patients don't come back! They can breathe, but they have difficulty pooping!"

As they were leaving the classroom, Ingrid approached Brandy and Andro and said, "Tomorrow is my last day of class, and I'll be going home on Sunday, but I want to see Pueblo Atiguo before I go. It's a recreation of Sa Jose in the early Nineteenth century. Have you been there?"

Brandy replied, "No, but why don't the three if us go tomorrow evening?"

After they agreed to take the tour, Brandy headed for the daycare center. After an enthusiastic session of hugging and screaming, the group played and colored until it was time for Brandy to leave. When she got home, she went running through the streets, had dinner, and then went to bed. She had just placed her head on the pillow when the sounds of her German neighbors, who were obviously chugging large quantities of beer, began singing La Bamba to the accompaniment of a poorly tuned guitar. Despite the noise, she eventually drifted off into dreamland, and slept through the night.

Because Friday was Ingrid's last day at the school, Brandy, Andro, the instructor, and she went to lunch together. While they were eating, Brandy thought, *Ingrid leaves on Sunday, and Andro goes home next week! I wonder why all of the nice, really interesting people that I meet leave so quickly, but some, like Jin, the jerk who knows everything, will probably still be here when I leave!*

That afternoon, as Brandy headed for the gym, a violent thunderstorm erupted, and she fell back on her skill as a sprinter to arrive quickly. As she ran, she mused, *These storms come out of nowhere! I've been told that the rainy season starts early during leap year, which worries me about the trips to the beach I've planned before I leave here, but they say it doesn't rain much on the Pacific side. Gracias a Dios!*

After an hour's workout, Brandy left the gym, and set out to meet her friends. At five o'clock, the trio boarded the bus to Pueblo Antiguo, where they was met by a guide in nineteenth century attire who began leading them through the town.

When the tour ended, they watched a show featuring dances from different time periods, and various locales in Costa Rica. After that, they had dinner together, and then returned to town. When they parted, Ingrid said, "I'll miss you both very much, and want you to know you have an open invitation to visit me in Utah any time you wish! I live very close to the ski slopes, and you can use my car. You can also get to know my two chocolate Labradors."

Brandy said, "I grew up near ski slopes, and I love Labradors, so I'm going to buy my ticket tomorrow morning! I'll miss you very much."

The two women hugged and when Ingrid left, Brandy turned to Andro, and said, "I'll really miss her. She's a very special person, and, by the way, so are you! I wish you weren't leaving next week."

Andro kissed her on the cheek, and said, "I'll see you in class on Monday. Enjoy your weekend." He turned and walked briskly away.

Chapter 38

A Quiet Weekend

Brandy spent Saturday morning in the school's computer lab, checking her e-mail, and responding to her friends. She was pleased to receive a message from her college suite mate, Carolyn Duckworth, who was called Ducky by most of her friends. The message confirmed her pending arrival at the International Airport on Friday for their planned trip to the beach. Brandy spent the rest of the day at her usual routine, studying, running, and working out at the gym. That evening Rosita's entire family came for dinner, and engaged in their usual raucous behavior, assisted by copious quantities of alcoholic beverages.

On Sunday morning, Brandy was delighted to discover that the torrid weather to which she had become accustomed had returned. When she stepped out of her room, she noticed that Guido was sitting at the kitchen table eating his breakfast. When he saw her, he said, "Good morning, Brandy, come and join me! Rosa and her sister have gone to the market. You were sleeping soundly, and they didn't want to disturb you, but, as you can see breakfast is on the table. Brandy walked to the table, filled a small plate with fruit, and sat down, munching on melon slices, and sipping orange juice.

"I'm going running, but I'll be back in about an hour"

When she returned, Guido was in the garden throwing a ball for Tuffy to catch. She walked out the door to join them, and sat on a small stone bench under the mango tree. Tuffy ran up to her with the ball, and dropped it at her feet. When she picked it up, and threw it, Guido sat down beside her, and began telling stories about his early life with Rosita. She found the stories to be amusing, even though she had heard many of then several times, and half the conversation was in Spanish, and half in Italian. A short time later, the ladies drove into the driveway with enough fruits and vegetable to sustain a small army for the winter, and Brandy went out to help unload the car.

Brandy, Guido, Rosita and Gina had lunch together, and then she left for the hospital. As she approached her destination, she saw hordes of soccer fans coming towards her, accompanied by police in riot gear on foot, and two busloads of police reinforcements rolling along beside them on Paseo Colon. She thought, *Gosh, I'm the only person walking towards that mob, but I'm not going to move, because this is my sidewalk, and I use it twice a week! They can yield to me! Besides, I doubt my chances of making the news twice in two weeks!*

She met the oncoming crowd, and pushed her way through. Soon she was standing in front of the hospital, looking up to the windows. She became excited when she saw the children smiling down, at her, and frantically waving. She began to feel sad, and thought of how painful it would be when she left the building for the last time, realizing how they had touched her life. Once she was inside, she sat with the children while they colored, and read books, and then brought out the Dollar Store bowling game.

When the children began to play, Eloy, an eight-year -old boy who had frequently displayed serious behavior problems in the past, began kicking down the pins, and trying to get the ball away from the others. Brandy tried for several minutes to calm him down, and convince him to wait his turn. When she failed, she called Amanda Salazar, a huge nurse who always wore a cervical collar, and reminded her of a character in an old movie about a woman's prison she had seen on television, the name of which, she could not recall.

The nurse motioned to the boy, and he approached her cautiously, like a small trapped animal hoping to placate a hungry much larger predator without being eaten alive. When he reached her, she leaned down, placed her hand gently on his frail shoulder, and whispered softly into his ear. He paused briefly, nodded his head, and scampered off to the corner of the room. Brandy thought, *I wish I hadn't had to do that! The poor little guy has problems, but if I didn't know how sweet Amanda is, I would have to change my underwear if she called me out for anything!* After five minutes, Eloy crept slowly to Brandy's side, and she had no further problems with him that day.

When the children finished bowling, they gathered around a table with Brandy, and she started teaching them English. Each of them was very timid when asked to pronounce words. Brady said, "Don't be so shy, there is no reason for fear. I mispronounce every Spanish word I speak, but I won't give up, because I know that if I practice I will get it right, but if I quit, I never will!" They began to gain confidence, and by the time the lesson ended, they were shouting the English words when it was their turn to speak. Brady spent that evening with her adopted family, watching television, and talking about the weather.

Chapter 39

A Nasty Fall

On Monday morning, the rain began to pour down just as Brandy entered the school building, and the temperature had gone down to 70 degrees. She complained that she was freezing, and to the delight of the class, her teacher told her that she had become a Costa Rican, because a foreigner would never think that a temperature any temperature below 85 degrees was cold!

That afternoon, at the hospital, she followed her usual agenda of drawing, coloring and playing with the children, and then began teaching English. Two parents who had been observing the lesson began calling her "Maestra," and asked if she would teach them English. She laughed, and said. "I'm not a teacher; I have no idea how to teach!" The women looked stunned, and one asked, "Are you a doctor?"

She laughed, again, and said, "No, I'm not a doctor, either!"

When the two women continued to appear shocked, she thought, *I'd like to tell them I'm a rocket scientist, but they might ask too many questions, so I couldn't get away with that. I could never use rocket scientist as a cover!*

She said, 'I'm a volunteer; I come here to be with the children. I'm in your country to learn Spanish, and want to do all that I can to brighten the lives of these children. They deserve whatever I can do for them. I'm not paid. I come here to help!"

One of the women shook her head, and said, "You get no money, and you just come here to be with sick children? That is so sad!"

Brandy walked to the bus station, boarded the bus, and greeted the night driver. When she sat down, she thought *I may be weird, but I enjoy this bus ride! I know half the people who ride at this time, where they work, and where they live. Simple things amuse me! The driver is crazy; he doesn't like to yield to other vehicles, and I think he'd like to paint strike marks on the side of his bus for every pedestrian he takes out in traffic! He acts like he is in combat, and anything in his path is the enemy! He slows to 40 miles per hour when making a sharp turn, and I especially like hitting my head on the top of the bus when he hits a pothole!*

She recalled one night when the bus encountered a pothole with such impact that a little man bounced up and hit his head on the stop button, causing the driver to stop abruptly, and wait for someone to exit. When the bus began moving, the riders laughed, as if it might have been their last chance to laugh before they met the grim reaper.

Because it had recently stormed frequently in the evening, Brandy went home after her Tuesday classes, so she could go running before it rained. She started to sprint a run which usually took an hour, and quickly reached the top of a very large hill. Her plan was to cruise the rest of the way down the next hill, which was also very precipitous, but took her eyes off the road surface for a split second. When she did, her right foot found a sizeable pothole which had not been there the day before. Her ankle rolled all the way to the side, her left knee skidded across the pavement and her right elbow then made contact, until she was able to stop sliding.

While she was lying face down on the pavement, her first thought was that she had broken her ankle. *I don' think my medical plan will cover surgical repair, so the cost of this junket just went up! Even worse, I just slid through dog poop and garbage, which is rushing through my veins, so it is very likely that I'll go home wearing a peg leg like Long John Silver. Anyway, I'd better find a way to get up out of this hole!* She struggled to her feet, and began limping away, delighted that her ankle was apparently intact. She was bleeding from her right elbow, left knee, and right hand. As he stood on the corner, she thought, *I hate being a grown-up at times like this! I wish I could cry for my mommy, so she could make it all better like she always has!*

When she reached home, she slipped silently inside, to avoid alarming her host and hostess, tip-toed to her room, took a shower, and applied antiseptic to her wounds. She put on a pair of long pants and a long sleeve shirt to go to dinner, to conceal her injuries. However, Rosita noticed that she was limping, and asked, "Did you hurt yourself?"

"No, I fell into a small crater while I was running, but I'm okay!"

"Well, I can call the Doctor if you want me to. He'll come here."

"That's reassuring. Back home doctors do not make house calls, even if you're dying! Don't worry, though. I'm fine."

After dinner, she filled a plastic bag with ice, elevated her ankle on a pillow, took two Ibuprofen tablets, and iced her ankle. Before she fell asleep, she watched as her ankle swelled to the size of a large grapefruit. By morning, she estimated that it was the size of a cantaloupe. She limped to school, and went to her morning class. When the lunch break came, she headed for the gym and worked out, which resulted in further swelling. She returned to school, where she met Andro at the front door. "Hello, Brandy, I missed you at lunch. Why are you limping?"

"I fell into a pothole the size of a volcanic crater while I was running yesterday. I just tried to work out at the gym, and now my ankle is more swollen than before."

Andro shook his head, and asked, "Do you mind if I look at it?"

She hesitated, and then pulled up her pant leg. The doctor squatted, and then felt the swollen area. "Well. It isn't broken, but you have a serious sprain, and walking around on it doesn't help. You shouldn't go running for at least a week. I'll wrap it for you tomorrow, and maybe you can ride a bike, if you love pain, and feel that you must exercise. My recommendation would be that you don't put weight on it for several days! I haven't known you for very long, but I know you well enough to know that you won't stay off of it!"

When her class ended, she decided to walk to the hospital. By the time she reached her destination, her ankle resembled a small watermelon. She began playing with the children, who were bowling. Soon one of the them said,

"Brandy, why are you moving so slowly?"

"I fell in a hole yesterday when I went for my daily run."

Half of the children expressed their sympathy, and hugged her affectionately. The other half, mostly little boys, laughed hysterically. She tried to be as silly as possible while telling her story, feeling that the little tykes dealt with more serious problems every day than she would ever encounter in her lifetime, and, as a result, she felt their reaction gratifying. One of the boys almost wet his pajamas when she reenacted the scene of falling in a hole and sliding through dog poop. At this point, the head nurse, who had heard the commotion, entered the room to investigate. When she heard that Brandy had injured her leg, she insisted on seeing it. Brandy pulled up her pant leg, and when she did, the room was filled with gasps of "Grande!" She decided to diffuse the situation by joking that she would teach her charges colors in English, and began pointing to her swollen area, and saying, "Amarillo. Roja, Negro, Azura, Verde and Moreno," before translating each word into English. The nurse smiled, and went back to her rounds, shaking her head

When it was time to leave, Brandy called a taxi, and the driver told her he would discount her fare if she would help him learn English. She agreed, though she was thinking that she had to be careful in the event that he was a serial rapist or killer, perhaps both. She accepted his business card when she had him drop her off at the shopping mall a block from her house to prevent him from knowing where she lived. The next morning, she met Andro before class, and accompanied him to the medical office where he taped her swollen ankle.

Chapter 40

A Tender Parting

On Monday afternoon, because Andro was leaving at the end of the week, Brandy invited him to go to lunch at her favorite Japanese restaurant, and invited their teacher, Vicki, to join them. Vickie had never eaten Japanese food, and Brandy became amused at the expressions on her face as she sampled various types of Sushi.

"Why don't you order a Sake Bomb? That will make those tasty morsels slide right down!"

"What's a Sake Bomb?"

"You fill a shot glass with Sake, and then drop it into a glass of beer. They're really potent!"

"Sounds wonderful, but since I'm driving, I don't believe that's a very good idea."

Brandy expressed her agreement with a smile, and thought, *She's right, and she's a good driver, but she would probably still be safer drunk than most of the people who drive in this country!*

After lunch, Brandy spent the afternoon at the daycare center. That evening she and Andro went to a dance performance at the National Theater. The theme of the presentation was violence against women, a major problem in Costa Rica, and the first act featured traditional dances. The second act was ballet, and the finale was modern dance. After the show they dined together at La Guaga. As they sat making quiet conversation while sipping mojitos in the candle light, Brandy thought of the night she had bid farewell to Paul, when she had partaken of too much alcohol, thinking, *I got wasted when I was here with Paul, but left in time to avoid making a mistake! Andro is close to Dad's age and I wouldn't need nearly as much booze to get a little carried away, if it weren't for Chuck! A lot of older men are very sexy, and if he asked me to marry him, if I didn't have a special guy back home, I might give it serious consideration.* She began nursing her drink, and when they had finished eating, despite Andro's protests, she called for the check.

"This is my treat. You're leaving on Saturday, and I want to buy your dinner. You're a very special friend. They rode a taxi back to town, and when she got out in front of Rosita's house, she kissed the handsome doctor on the cheek. "I'll see you tomorrow morning, and I wish you a safe trip home. I'm going to miss you!"

"I'll also miss you, and I hope that your ankle heals quickly!"

When they were out of the taxi, he looked into her eyes, took hold of her hand, and, in a low voice, said, "Adios mi querida y joven amiga. Siempre tendras un lugar en mi corazon!"

He kissed her on the forehead, returned to his seat in the taxi, and closed the door. Tears welled up in Brandy's eyes as the cab disappeared into the night. When she awakened on Friday morning, she thought of Andro, and his last words to her. *He said there will always be a place in his heart for me! That's so cool! Sometimes I wish I could be more than one person, but I can't, and Chuck will probably be stuck with me for the rest of his life!*

She showered, and then she packed her bags for her trip to the beach. After breakfast, she went to her classes, but wasn't able to concentrate, because she was elated that she would soon see her college friend, Ducky, and share an adventure at the beach. She called Oscar, the taxi driver who had offered discount fares in exchange for English lessens, and asked him to pick her up to take her to the airport. During the trip, she became concerned because while they were practicing English, Oscar was continuously turning his head so he could he could watch her mouth as she spoke, while traveling at high speed on the highway.

Chapter 41

The Beach Odyssey Begins

Brandy was greatly relieved when the taxi reached the airport without a mishap. After asking Oscar to wait, she went to the arrival area to meet Ducky. While she watched people excitedly greeting their friends and family members, she began to think of military families whose loved ones were away for extended periods of time, and sometimes never returned. *When I think about that, I almost want to cry. I've only been away from home two months, and I can hardly wait to see an old friend I saw several times a year when I was back home!* Then she caught sight of Duck's sleek, shoulder length blonde hair, as she was walking down the ladder from the plane in a manner reminiscent of movies from the 1950s and 60s she had seen on television.

"Hey roomie, do you have me lined up with any cute guys? I'm ready for romance! Do you know any bullfighters?"

"Bullfighters are in Mexico. I did meet a soccer star, but he turned out to be a real jerk!"

The young women hugged and jumped up and down.

"Relax! Just wait till we get to the beach, and meet the totally hot Tico surfer dudes I hung out with the first time I was there."

"We have time to grab some food, and then we're going to anther airport to catch a plane, and fly over the mountains!"

That sounds scary, but the food part sounds good. I'm starving!"

When they left the baggage claim area, they found Oscar, and Brandy told him that they wanted to go to a small private airport to catch a plane to the beach, but wanted to eat before they left San Jose.

"No problem! There is a place very close to the airplanes."

He loaded Ducky's bags into his cab, then started the motor, and peeled rubber on the way out of the parking lot. Minutes later, the taxi stopped in front of a building which resembled a small box built of concrete blocks. Oscar off-loaded their bags, and he drove away after Brandy paid him. As they approached the building, a service window opened, and a stocky man with curly black hair stuck his head out, and said, "Buenas tardes, Senoritas! I am guessing that you're from the Estados Unidos. We have muy delicioso hamburgers and hot dogs!"

Brandy laughed, and turned to her friend. "If I was back home, I'd like nothing better than a huge Eskay dog, smothered with relish, and a cold beer to wash it down, and I'm a gracious enough hostess to allow you to eat what you wish, but I eat Tico food while I'm here."

"I've always trusted your judgment, and it has always gotten me into trouble in the past, but I'll have what you're having."

"Okay, then, we'll have gallo pinto, grilled chicken, salad, grilled plantains, with beets, and yucca!" The man in the window said, "Have a seat at a table, and I will bring your food to you muy pronto!"

They ate their meal while seated at a little concrete table, and then walked the short distance to the airstrip to wait for their flight. While they were boarding the plane, Brandy told her friend about flying back to San Jose with Paul.

"We were bouncing up and down through clouds, and the poor guy I talked into flying with me was terrified. I figured that crashing in the mountains would be an adventure if we lived, and we would make the papers if we died! Besides, when you can see the beauty that surrounds you in the mountains, it's hard to think about things you can't control."

"Well, I hope we make it to the beach, because I can't wait to see those surfers you promised me."

"We'll make it there and back. You won't be disappointed, I promise! There is one problem, though;

The men here are all little guys. You and I are taller than most of the Ticos I've met."

"There's that word again. What exactly is a Tico?

"I'm sorry! I didn't realize you wouldn't know that word! A Tico is a Costa Rican man. A woman is a Tica."

Soon the plane was high above rows of steep pinnacles. To Brandy's surprise, there was very little turbulence as they soared over mountains, banana plantations, the rainforest, and the ocean. When the aircraft touched ground, it was pouring rain. Fortunately, a taxi had just dropped off some tourists headed for a sightseeing flight over the ocean, and Brandy asked the driver to take them to the hotel. They checked in, and then took the elevator up to their room on the top floor. Brandy inserted the electronic keycard, then stepped aside to let Ducky enter, When she did, she exclaimed, "Oh my God! Look at this place!"

Ducky stepped through the portal, and the two girls walked out onto the balcony, which overlooked a huge swimming pool with fountains, and surrounded by hundreds of tropical plants. There was a small table and two chairs just outside the sliding door. A love seat was nestled in one corner, and a hammock large enough for two people stood at the other end of the prodigious overhang. Brandy reentered the room.

"Roomie, you have to see this!" She laughed as she pointed to a heart and swan-shaped creation made with towels, which stood on to the king-size bed, the focal point of the room.

"The management must think we're life partners! This has to be the honeymoon suite! They think we're gay!"

Ducky giggled, "Well, I always thought you were kinda cute, but you're really not my type!"

That night, they had dinner at El Avios Restaurant, and then went to the bar, which was inside a refurbished French cargo plane which was a remnant of the secret war against the Sandanistas in Nicaragua in the 1980s. They sipped margaritas while watching the waves crashing onto the beach.

The next morning, at first light, they were awakened by the screeching of the howler monkeys. Ducky jumped out of bed, and, in a shaky voice, groaned, "What is that? Are we going to be abducted by aliens?"

"No such luck! Those are howler monkeys! Let's go look!"

She led Ducky to the balcony, and pointed to the trees below, which were filed with cavorting primates. As Ducky stared with delight, she said, "How neat! They remind me of the kids back at school, rushing to morning classes!"

"No, they're much better behaved, and we made a lot more noise! Anyway, they woke us up, so we might as well start our day. We'll have breakfast, and then we'll go to the beach."

Chapter 42

Snorkeling With
an Old Salt

As the sun slowly ascended in the cloudless sky, Brandy and Ducky spread their towels on the beach near a cluster of palm trees. They began watching the tourists strolling in the surf, and the activities of those who earned their livelihood by catering to them. Soon Brandy's eyes were confronted by a familiar face, as a huge man wearing a baseball cap with the name of an American ship on it, approached them swinging his burly arms. "Well, well! Hello there, blue eyes, do ya' remember me?"

Brandy thought, *How could I forget a loud mouthed Gringo jerk like you!* Then she smiled, and purred, "Sure, I rode on one of your banana boats when I was here a few weeks ago. It almost flipped over going one hundred miles an hour over the waves! "

"You got it right sweetie pie! I'm Ed Waters, but folks call me 'Salty'. I picked up that nickname when I was in Gator Navy. Who's this little lady you got with you? She looks like my kid's Barbie doll!"

"Her name is Ducky, not Barbie, and we'd both like to know what the Gator Navy is. What country has a Gator Navy?"

"Aw, come on, now, honey, you know that I'm an American. My old lady is a Tica, and I retired from the U.S. Navy, moved here, and bought a couple of boats. Now I own four! The Gator Navy is what we call the Amphibs. I was on LSDs most of my career."

Ducky flipped her shoulder length frosted blonde hair, and said, "You were on LSD most of your career? I tried pot once when I was in college, but I've never tried the hard stuff!"

"Come off it, babe, you're pulling my leg! LSD means Landing Ship Dock. We carried landing craft."

"I know that! I was just teasing you! I used to date a boy who was stationed at Little Creek. He was on the Ashland."

"No kidding? I know the Ashland; I was on couple of her sister ships! Anyway, I didn't come over here to talk about the Navy. How would you two cuties like to go snorkeling today? You'll see lots of purty fish, and it's gonna be a hot day!"

Brandy said. "We were wondering what to do today, and you're so cute! What do you think roomie?"

"Sure, let's do it!"

They gathered their beach gear, and followed Waters to the dock, where he gave them life jackets, and told them to swim out to the boat. After swimming for twenty minutes, fighting waves which pushed them backwards each time they had swum a few meters they arrived on the boat. Several other people were already aboard, including a guide.

Waters began to speak on a bullhorn, "Before we go out, I need to remind you folks to wear your life jackets, going out, and coming back!"

When the boat was several hundred yards off shore, the driver turned off the engine, and dropped anchor. The guide jumped overboard first, and the others followed. The current was strong, and the waves were breaking over the rocks. A large variety of beautiful fish swam about the people in the water. Brandy found it difficult to appreciate the sights before her, because she was constantly spitting out salt water coming through her snorkel from the waves breaking over her head. The problem soon was forgotten when she saw about fifty very large fish swimming rapidly away from the open area of the sea. She soon became convinced that they were attempting to escape from a much larger predator, perhaps a shark with a voracious appetite. Her fears soon disappeared when the "predator" turned out to be a woman who quite possibly would outweigh Orca the Killer Whale. Eventually, the sightseers all returned to the boat, and it headed back to shore.

During the return trip, the large lady complained that she was seasick, and then vomited six times to prove it. Back on the beach, Brandy started to look for Geraldo, her surfing buddy from her prior trip. After a short walk, she saw him standing by his truck. "Hey Geraldo, do remember me?"

He turned, and answered, "Mi amigos and I are still talking about your magnificent wipeout!" Then, after he saw that her ankle was swollen, he said, " Ay, caramba! Your leg is still swollen, that is not good!'

Brandy laughed, "No, no! I got well from that one. This is new. I stepped in a pothole while I was running last week. This is my friend, Ducky, and I want her to learn to surf. Can you go out with us?"

"Sure! How about tomorrow morning?"

"That's perfect! We'll meet you here bright and early. We're staying at the Vista del Oceano Pacifico."

"I know it well; they cater to Gringos on the honeymoons!"

Brandy grinned. "Yes, we found that out after we checked in yesterday! Don't you dare tell them that we're straight! Maybe they'll send us a bottle of Champagne. My boyfriend and I worked that scam when we spent a weekend at a resort before I left the states."

"Don't worry. I won't tell. See you tomorrow, if it doesn't rain. If it does, I'll see you on Monday."

They returned to the hotel, spent an hour swimming in the pool, then went up to their room and ordered pizza. While they waited for it to arrive, they showered, and got dressed. Brandy went to the coke and ice machines in the hallway, then produced a bottle of rum from her luggage, and Ducky lit the candle on the patio table. They ate their pizza by candlelight, then spent the next two hours sipping rum and coke as they watched moonlight dance on the ocean waves while being serenaded by howler monkeys, frogs, and a variety of birds. They talked about their college days, and laughed as they recalled the escapades of their former classmates, until Brandy remarked, "This is so cool! What a romantic ambiance! I don't want to hurt your feelings, but every time I've been in a romantic setting in this country, with one exception, I've either been with another woman or a man I'd feel uncomfortable shaking hands with, and the exception was dad's age!"

"No, I'm not hurt at all. Here we are, two very straight women, in a soap opera setting! Do think maybe we ought to reconsider, and become life partners? After all, we do have the heart shaped towels on the bed, and neither of us snores very loud."

"It sounds good, but neither of us would want to be the female, we're both too butch!"

She lifted her glass in a mock toast, and said, "Let's drink to just being friends." Ducky stood up, clicked her glass against Brandy's and softly said, "Amen!"

When they finished their drinks, Brandy said, "It's only nine-thirty, but we're going surfing in the morning, and I want to rest my ankle, so I'm going to go to bed now. Blow out the candle before you turn in."

Shortly after Brandy had gotten into bed, she fell asleep, but was awakened in the middle of the night by the sound of lightning in the rainforest. Ducky, who was ensconced on the far side of the huge bed, said, "I have a feeling we're not going surfing, tomorrow!'

"Maybe not, but these things don't always last long.' They sat in bed watching the lightning over the ocean, and listening to the rain splatter on the trees, until they went back to sleep.

Chapter 43

Touring the Treetops and Drowning in Daiquiris

When morning came, it was still raining heavily, so Brandy called the desk to arrange for a canopy tour. An hour-and-a-half later, an extended cab Ford pickup truck pulled up in front of the hotel. The driver, who said his name was Horacio, got out, and opened the door. Brandy got into the rear seat, and Ducky climbed in beside her. They rode into town, where Horacio stopped to buy water and fresh fruit, before they began speeding along a slick, muddy road, and into the forest. Moments later, Brandy saw a short, thin man wearing a baseball cap backwards, standing in the rain beside a muddy path, holding harnesses in his folded arms. She began to fear the worst, and her feelings of concern grew when Horacio stopped to pick up the man, who got into the front seat beside him. Horacio said, "Senoritas, this is Junior. Together, we will tour the canopy."

He then drove a short distance further into the forest and stopped to call their attention to a group if squirrel monkeys playing in the treetops, then said, "Now we will climb into the trees!"

The girls followed Junior as he scampered up a ladder to a wooden platform which Brandy suspected had been built by the first Spaniards to explore the country. Horacio was the last to arrive at the top. After the men helped the girls into the harnesses, the four of them began sliding along cables which appeared to be as old as the launching platforms. When the tour ended, they ate watermelon and cantaloupe while sitting on a wooden bench in the rain.

After Horacio deposited Junior back at the muddy path, he drove to the hotel. When he stopped the truck in front, he gave Brandy a card. "I will take you and your friend anywhere in Costa Rica for a very cheap price. You are very pretty ladies, and we can have good times together. Junior likes you, too."

She took the card, and said, "That sounds wonderful! Don't be surprised if we call you soon! Goodbye."

He grinned broadly, displaying a gap made by the absence of his two front teeth, then drove away. When the truck was out of sight, Brandy tore the card into tiny pieces, and threw it into a trash container. Ducky watched approvingly, and then asked, "Are you as glad as I am that the canopy tour is over?"

"I sure am! The high point was seeing the squirrel monkeys play grabass in the trees."

"I agree with you on that, but the monkeys weren't he only ones who played grabass in the trees. Neither one of those creeps missed a chance to cop a feel when they were hooking me up. I thought about kicking Junior off the platform, but was afraid I'd never get down if I did."

"The good news is that we survived, and I'm starving. Let's go to lunch!"

They took a cab to a restaurant overlooking the ocean. It continued to rain while they were eating, and, as she finished chewing the last morsel from her plate, Ducky said, "It is still raining, we don't have a boat, and it's almost noon, so I think we should split a pitcher of daiquiris!"

"My mom would not approve, but I don't want say no to a special guest, my dearest friend, and potential life partner! I'll buy!"

When the pitcher was empty, they went back to the hotel on foot, laughing and dancing in the pouring rain. When they reached the room, they went out on the balcony, where they sat under an umbrella and watched the rain continue to pelt the forest beneath them, until Ducky announced that she was going to take a nap. Brandy remained on the balcony for about five minutes, and when she reentered the room, Ducky was sounding asleep. Brandy yawned, then crawled onto the oversized pallet and lost consciousness immediately. She woke up five hours later. Ducky, who had awakened a few minutes earlier, was preparing to take a shower. While her friend was dressing and applying makeup, Brandy showered quickly, and prepared to go out for the evening.

Chapter 44

The Bora Bora
Reunion Committee

When the bus reached the beach, Brandy said, "The weather is awful, and we slept off the daiquiris, so, why don't we find a bar near the water, and start all over again?"

Ducky replied, "I've always know you were a Brain! That's an awesome idea!"

They began strolling past a row of beachfront shops and restaurants until they reached a restaurant with a balcony on which there was a bar. Brandy said, there are a few people in there, but the name doesn't sound like a Tico operation! 'Casa Hoboken?' Give me a break!"

"It won't hurt to associate with some fellow Gringos for a change. After all, we spent the morning swinging through the trees with a couple of Tico apes who couldn't keep their hands to themselves! Maybe we'll meet some cute mobsters from New Jersey, like the guys in 'The Sopranos'!"

"Boy wouldn't that be fun to explain to the headhunters at the office when I go back to work! Oh, what the heck, let's check it out."

When Brandy reached the top of the steps to the balcony and started to pass the bar, a tall, curly haired man who was leaning on the bar next to three other men, smiled, and said, "Hi, Blondie!"

She smiled back, and then winked playfully. "Hi, yourself, Slim!"

She and Ducky continued to a small table near the railing, sat down, and ordered margaritas. Two other young women were sitting at an adjacent table, and one of them, a shapely platinum blonde, smiled at Brandy, and said, "You'll like this place. We were here last night, and everyone here is very friendly!"

Ducky said, "We noticed that when we came in, He's cute! Do you know him?"

"No, those guys weren't here last night! They came in right after us about a half-hour ago."

Before Ducky and Brandy had finished their first drink, the curly haired man came over to the table.

"My friends and I have decided to move to a table. Would you ladies like to join us? We can watch the rain together."

"Maybe, what do you think, Ducky?"

"Sure! What can we lose? Besides our virginity, of course!"

Brandy turned to the girls at the other table, and said,

"These guys want us to join their party. Would you and you friend like to even things out?"

The men moved swiftly from the bar, and started pushing tables together. When everybody was seated, the tall man said, "Let's get acquainted. I already met Blondie, and she called me Slim, so that's taken care of!"

When the laughter subsided, he said, "My real name is Mike Sweeny, the short guy is Bill Duggins, the big guy is Larry Doyle, and the bald guy with glasses is my big brother, Brad. Brad's a policeman in Newark. The rest of us are detectives in New York City. We came down here to play golf and go fishing, but don't like to be out on the water in bad weather, and every green is like a water hazard in a typhoon! Who are you ladies, and what do you do for a living?"

Brandy said, 'My name is Brandy, I'm unemployed at the moment, and I'm studying Spanish in San Jose. Ducky is a lawyer in Fredericksburg, Virginia, but she's originally from Connecticut. She came here to visit me."

The platinum blonde spoke next, "My name is Linda, and I'm from Atlantic City. I'm a Blackjack dealer. My gorgeous brunette friend, Casey, is from Baltimore, but she works in Quepos as an English teacher."

Mike called the waitress to the table, and ordered a round of drinks. Brandy and Ducky ordered margaritas. The New York detectives were drinking beer, and Brad ordered a banana daiquiri, which caused his brother, Mike, to quip, "He just wants you girls to think he's gay, so you won't come onto him, because he has a girlfriend who would cut off his family jewels if she ever found out he cheated on her!"

Brandy said, "That won't work with me, gay men turn me on, but you should know that Ducky and I are staying in the honeymoon suite at our hotel. When we checked in, there was a heart shaped towel formation on our bed. What the management doesn't know is that we're still straight, but a life partnership is not out of question. Our pad is such a romantic setting!"

When the drinks arrived, a band began playing salsa music. Larry told how he and the others had been talked into eating termites by a guide in the rainforest. Bill said, "They didn't taste bad, but I think a couple of them are still alive, and slowly chewing their way to my groin!"

Mike and Brandy began dancing the Meremge. Soon Ducky and Bill came out to the tiny dance floor, and the others joined them. After four more rounds of drinks, Mike said, "Am I the only one who's hungry? Maybe we can all go some where for dinner. We could eat here, but I'm not in the mood for Tex Mex cooked by some fugitive from Jersey City. We have a mini-van outside. We survived the mountain of death and the road of doom on our journey here."

Bill picked up the check, and the merrymakers walked outside to the parking area. As they approached a blue Daihatsu Terios, Mike said, "This is our ride. It has seats for seven passengers. I'll drive, Brandy can ride shotgun, Linda can sit next to Brad in the middle seat. Casey can sit on Larry's lap, and Ducky can cuddle up with Billy in the back seat. Okay, now everybody get in their assigned seats, and let's rock and roll! We don't have too far to go, so there should be no problem with seat belts. There is a great place near the park entrance where there is something on the menu for everybody. They have Tico chow, and Gringo food."

Brandy said, "I'm a Tica, while I'm here!"

Ducky agreed, "I'm for the local cuisine."

Mike laughed, "Well, Brad likes that crap, too. I'm a steak and potatoes Irishman, myself."

Brandy said, "We don't need to talk about food. Tell us about driving through the mountains. I haven't driven since I've been here, but I've had some hairy experiences as a passenger on busses and in cabs."

"It was like a scene from one of those car chase movies. Brad almost pooped in his pants every time we rounded a curve, and every driver in this country wants to be a stunt man, even some of the women. They drive a hundred miles an hour on roads built for ox carts!!"

Mike slowed down in front of a neon sign which read, "El Hombre Macho", and turned into the parking lot. Brandy said, 'The Macho Man? You're kidding! This is your great place to eat?"

"Yeah, I'm kidding, ever heard of the Barba Roja?"

Brandy spoke up, "Yes, I've eaten there, and they actually serve some Tico dishes, but feature ribs and steak."

"You got it, babe! Meat and potatoes! It has a great view of the ocean!"

Ducky said, "Do they serve termites?"

"No, but we'll sit near the railing outside. Maybe we can find a rotten spot!"

During dinner, Linda said, "This is a fun group, why don't we do this every year?"

"We can exchange e-mail addresses, so we can keep in touch", Casey suggested.

Bill spoke next." Great idea, we can meet next May in Bora Bora!"

Larry chuckled. "With this bunch, we'll probably wind up at the caverns in New York State, but Bora Bora sounds good!"

Brandy stood, and raised her glass. "To Bora Bora next year!"

The others echoed her words, "To Bora Bora next year!"

After dinner, Bill tapped his spoon on his beer glass, and said, "I would like to call the Bora Bora reunion committee to order. Before we adjourn, I make a motion that we conclude this night of debauchery by going to bed with our assigned partners. Everybody seems happy with my pairings, and it looks like Linda might be able convinced Brad that his girlfriend will never know what happens in the next few hours. Do I have a second? "

Brandy smiled, then, in a low, sexy voice said, "Margaritas always make me want to go to bed! I second that motion, but I need to consult with my roommate in private. I have to take a potty break, anyway! "

She headed for the Ladies Room, and Ducky followed her. When she was sure no one else could hear, she said, "I'm ready to go to bed because the booze has made me sleepy! Besides that, these guys are married! They each have little strips of white where a wedding ring is supposed to be! We'll let them take us back to the hotel, and then we'll dump them!"

When they returned to the table, Brandy said, "What do you think, Ducky? Are we ready for bed?"

Ducky did her hair flip, and replied, "I'm ready to do just that! Bill and Mike can take us to our honeymoon suite!"

Linda said, "I need to seduce Brad, and Casey is undecided, but since we're all in one car, lead on! Bora Bora can wait!"

The men started to pick up the tab, but the women insisted on chipping in. When the revelers walked to the car a torrential rain continued to pelt them.

Shortly before eleven o'clock, Brandy and Ducky got out of the van at the front door of their hotel. After Mike got out, and Bill followed, Mike said, "Let's head for the honeymoon suite! Brad, you and Larry take your ladies to our digs, and you can pick us up in the morning!"

Brandy grasped both of Mike's hands, and then she kissed him. Ducky followed her lead, and kissed Bill. Then Brandy said, "You are really nice guys, but you're both married! My boyfriend wouldn't like it if I crawled in bed with you, and I wouldn't like myself in the morning! Tonight really was fun, Ducky and I are going to bed to sleep off the margaritas. When you get to your hotel you can do the same. See you in Bora Bora!"

Ducky followed Brandy as she ran into the hotel. The two men stood in shock as the girls disappeared into the lobby elevator. When they were inside the room, Brandy said, "We'd better turn in, because we're going surfing tomorrow, whether it's raining or not! We're running out of time. We got away from that crowd just in time, one more drink, and I might have lost my virginity!"

Chapter 45

Riding the Waves
With El Gato

The rainforest chorus, led by the howlers, with the birds and other creatures singing doo-wahs in the background, awakened the girls early in the morning, and when Brandy opened her eyes, the sun was shindig onto the balcony.

"Gracias a Dios! Let's have breakfast, and then we'll go for a swim in the pool before we try to find Geraldo."

Later, at the beach, they met Linda and Casey.

Ducky said, "Good morning! Did you ladies shack up with those cops after we left?"

Casey laughed, "No way! Once you guys left, they couldn't wait to unload us at Linda's condo! They were nice guys, but messing with married men is a bit dicey. It was a fun night, though!"

"Sure was! Brandy said that she was one margarita short of losing her cherry!"

"Really? Do they put cherries in margaritas? I hadn't noticed that! By the way, don't go in the water!"

Brandy frowned." Why not? Those waves are incredible, and are begging to be surfed on!"

"I agree, but do you see any surfers out there? They're all standing on the shoreline, or sitting on their surfboards, and some of them are have welts on their bodies. The water is full of jellyfish."

As she spoke, two small boys ran out of the water with sticks filled with the sea creatures. Brandy said, 'I'm convinced! I got nailed by one of those things last year. You couldn't pay me to go out there today! Let's take a walk. We could look for a bar, but it's too nice a day to get wasted. Oh, look! There's Geraldo, and that girl he's with is gorgeous! He told me about her the last time I was here. She's from Florida, but she's working here as an English teacher. Hey Geraldo!"

"Hola, Brandy, the jellyfish have closed down the beach, and I want to hang out with Sally today anyway."

"That's okay, but I really wanted Ducky to learn how much fun it is to get thrown into the air by a giant wave and land on her butt on a rock! I've been bitten by a jellyfish, and it hurt! I don't want any part of that!"

"Maybe you can still surf. I know another beach with no jellyfish. I'll see if a couple of my buddies will take you there. They have a car."

"That sounds be terrific! You're very sweet! Please check it out. We'll be waiting right here."

While Geraldo was gone, Sally said, "Brandy, if you really like surfing, there's an island in Panama with great waves. The people there are very nice, and the beach is beautiful."

"That sounds good, but my visa expires at the end of May, and I might have to find a job here to work that into my travel plans!"

Geraldo came back with two short, very muscular, men, one of whom had a nude woman tattooed on his forearm.

His hair was highlighted, and his baggy purple trunks were decorated with huge yellow flowers. The other man's head was shaved, and he had a tattoo on his right bicep, which read, "El Gato."

Geraldo said, "These are my buddies, Manuel, and Diego. They'll take you surfing, if you still want to go."

"We're game, but we want to have lunch first and I won't swim in water that's infested with jellyfish!"

Diego said, "Not to worry, I don't want welts in my butt, either! I'll show you our car, and we'll meet you there in an hour. Do you mind if we bring a couple of kids along? They can really ride the waves!"

"No, the more the merrier, let's check out those wheels!"

They followed the two men a short distance, and soon were standing beside a bright yellow 1962 Chevrolet Nova with crimson racing stripes from front to back. Donald Duck was strung up from the rear view mirror, and there was a plastic sign in the rear window which read, "F.U.".

Brandi screamed, "These are your wheels? How cool! I can hardly wait to ride in that cute little car!"

Ducky chimed in, "As soon as we eat, we'll be right back! My mom had a Chevy Nova when I was a little kid!"

As they walked away, Brandy said, "This should be fun, even if we do get raped, and that's not likely, since one of your relatives is dangling from the rear view mirror. I'm sure he'll protect us!"

During lunch, Brandy looked towards the beach, and saw Diego taking a shower with bottled water. "Oh look, we must have impressed El Gato. He's getting all cleaned up for us!"

"You must be really great at surveillance! You don't miss much, do you?"

"Well, my observational skills have improved considerably since I've been here. I can pick out sloths, monkeys, and birds other people can't see!"

"Do your skills tell you if our surfer has finished his douche? I can't wait to ride in that hot rod!"

"He just ran out of water, let's go join the party!"

When they got to the car, the surfers, and two adolescent boys were loading surfboards onto a car top rack."

Diego said, "These guys want to go with us; they're really good!"

Brandy nodded her head, I watched them the last time I was here, and I remember their names."

She pointed to the shorter of the two. "You are Pepe, and your buddy is Luis. Am I right?"

"Si, Senorita Brandy! I am Pepe."

"You're very polite, but we're going to surf together, so you can skip the Senorita! Just call me Brandy! Kawabunga!"

Before the last board was secured in the rack, Brandy pretended to take a picture of the ocean, but discreetly included the license plate, in case of an unpleasant turn of events, which she considered unlikely. Diego said, "You girls can ride in back. The boys will ride upon front with us. He held the door open, and Ducky climbed in. When Brandy joined her, she whispered, "I'd feel like Gidget, if I wasn't bigger than the guys!"

The little car bounded along the road for several minutes until it reached a beach which appeared to be relatively undeveloped. The waves were very large, and they rolled along the surface of the ocean for a long time, before they reached the shore. Pepe squealed with delight. "Hey Luis, look at those waves! We're going to ride like Vaqueros!"

Brandy was delighted by their reaction, and found it difficult to contain herself when they scrambled out of the window. Diego and Manuel got out on the driver's side. When Brandy exited, she said, "Those guys didn't even open the door, they're so excited!" Diego laughed. "The door's broken! It won't open!"

Once the boards were unloaded, Brandy asked Diego why he had "El Gato" tattooed on his arm, "My friends say I am quick like the cat, when I'm in the water."

"Brandy thought, *Ducky needs to have as many of the thrills of surfing as she can, so I think she should go out in the surf with a dude named "El Gato," who showers with bottled water!*

"Why don't you show Ducky how to surf! I'll go with Manny and the kids"

"No problem! We'll look for little waves to start!"

He handed a board to Ducky, and after he tucked another under his arm, they headed for the water. Brandy, Manuel, and the boys secured their boards, and followed. The first time Brandy got up on her board, her ankle began to throb, but as soon as she began skimming over the water, while watching Pepe, Luis, and Manny perform tricks she forgot about the pain. Manny showed her how to ride a wave left, and she began thinking, *This is awesome, I'm riding so long, I could take a nap before I reach the shore!*

When her ride ended, she looked towards Ducky, and was pleased to see that she was standing on her board, gliding towards the beach, closely followed by Diego. Then she turned around in time to see Manny doing a handstand on his board, while Pepe and Luis cavorted on theirs. She immediately paddled out, eager to join the competition. She caught a wave, began riding backwards, then moon-walked, and finally changed feet, by jumping. The others applauded and cheered, until she attempted to hang ten, which caused a massive wipeout. Pepe and Luis rushed to her, and Luis shoved her onto her board, and then pushed her to shore where Ducky was waiting. "That was spectacular, roomie! Why not try it again?"

"That's a great idea; I think I will!"

She again mounted her board, and started to paddle away from her friend, who called out, "I was kidding! Are you sure you want to do this?"

Brandy yelled, "Yes! I'm going to hang ten. You guys can watch me reach my goal!"

Determined, she paddled away from the shore, and prepared to catch a wave. When she did, she stood up, then scrambled forward, until she was inches from reaching her objective, when she started to lose her balance, and leaned backward to try to compensate. She didn't succeed, and failed to stabilize, with the result that her feet flew over her head, and she landed flat on her back, on the board, then bounced off to be clobbered by a wave. When Ducky was assured that her pal was not hurt, "She said, "Now, that was classic! You should get style points for that! Have you had enough?"

"Not really, I'm going to give it one more shot!"

Almost instantly, a storm erupted, and the group began running towards the car. When the boards were secured on top, they jumped into the Nova, and rode up the mountain to the hotel. Brady and Ducky said goodbye to the surfers, and went up to their room.

Chapter 46

The Last Night of the Odyssey and the Return Flight

Brandy went out on the balcony as soon as she entered the room. Ducky undressed, and got into the shower. An instant later, Brandy spotted a sloth in the top of a tree in the forest below.

"There's a sloth down there, and he looks like that guy you dated in college!"

Although the shower was partially open and overlooking the forest, Ducky could not see the creature. "I don't see him!"

She jumped out of the shower, and ran onto the balcony with a towel draped around her. When Brandy pointed out the sloth, Ducky exclaimed, "Oh, he's a lot cuter than Jimmy, and his body's not nearly as hairy!"

She ran back into the shower, and Brandy continued to scout the rainforest. After she had showered, she quickly put on fresh clothing. Then the girls went to Quepos to go shopping. After they had purchased souvenirs as gifts for friends and relatives, they decided to have Mexican food at Dos Locos. When they were seated, Ducky said, "It's our last night, so I'm going to have a yard of daiquiris, how about you?'

"That sounds good, but after this journey, I will probably have diabetes and no liver! Let's drink to that! "

After dinner they returned to the hotel, where they packed their bags, and went to bed before nine o'clock. They arose early in the morning, and checked out of the hotel. After they had fruit smoothies for breakfast, they went directly to the airport by taxi in pouring rain. They sat in the Tiki hut watching the wind blow in all directions. Brandy became concerned when an attendant told them the flight may be canceled, which meant that they might have to travel on a bus over the mountains for three and one half hours. "What will we do if you miss you flight? "I'll be stranded in the rainforest with the sloths and monkeys! What's so bad about that? It'll be like being back in college, and that was fun."

A short time later, the weather cleared, and they were soon aboard a Cessna Caravan flying across the far side of the mountains, and to Brandy's surprise, she could see the volcano. The flight was smooth, with no turbulence. A portly man seated next to Brandy became alarmed because he could not fasten his seat belt. Why worry? If we crash, we'll all die, anyway, so what good is a seatbelt?"

The man began to laugh, and the plane landed without incident. Brandy traveled with Ducky to International Airport, where she said goodbye. Saddened, and depressed, she dropped her luggage off at Rosita's, and went to her favorite Japanese Restaurant to seek solace her favorite food. She sat by the window and watched the rain. When the waiter took her order, she said, "I'll have the usual." As she spoke, she thought, *I've been here so many times that the waiters all know what I'm going to order, and I've always wanted to be able to do that!* The waiter smiled, and then said, "Yes Mam'! Seaweed soup, kappa maki, tekka maki, futo maki, and a California roll, coming right up!"

She walked home in the rain, and told Rosita about her visit with Ducky while they watched television with Guido and Tuffino, who were both fighting unsuccessfully to stay awake. Finally, Rosita ran Guido and his canine friend off to bed, and Brandy excused herself and went to her room to prepare foe her morning classes.

Chapter 47

Relentless Rain and Malicious Maybugs

On Wednesday morning, when she awoke, Brandy could hear the rain outside, and when she drew back the curtain on her window, she could barely see the cactus plant in the garden. She started thinking back to when she began planning her trip to Costa Rica. *I was so pleased that my plan was to leave after only one week here during the rainy season. Now they tell me that it came unusually early this year!*

She had breakfast with Rosita, then, umbrella in hand, she walked to school in the drizzle. Six hours later, she went running in the downpour, and then walked to the gym as the deluge continued. After her workout, she walked home in the torrential precipitation. After dinner, she excused herself and went to bed. She was reluctant to get up on Thursday morning, because the heavy rain was still pounding on the roof of the house. The darkness which had replaced the sunlight which had announced the arrival of miorning each day appeared to be eternal.

After trudging to school while droplets of water pounded on her umbrella, she felt very weary, and, once in class, she fought to stay awake until the bell rang. She walked to the daycare center, where she played for several hours with children who were hyperactive from being kept indoors. The rain continued as she walked to her aerobics classs. Virtually exhausted, she returned home for dinner. When the meal was finished, she helped Rosita clear the table, and went to bed, where she drifted off to sleep listening to the rain. It was still raining when she opened her eyes on Friday morning. Her first instinct was to pull the covers up over her head, and go back to sleep, hoping to dream about the sunshine which had greeted her for so many mornings in the past. Instead, she cast her blanket aside, and rose quickly from her bed. While she was taking a shower, she began to think about how the rainy season was only four days old. *This is only the beginning, and I'm starting to sympathize with Noah! Maybe I ought to start designing my own personal Ark. I could call it Brandy's Salvation, and float all the way back to the States. I'm sure that it would be cheaper than flying, and I wouldn't have to make it forty cubits long! That's good, because I don't have any idea what a cubit is, anyway!*

While Brandy was getting dressed, Rosita called from the kitchen, "Child, your breakfast is ready! You will be late for school!"

She gathered her school supplies and stuffed them into her backpack. *Gosh, that makes me homesick! My mom used to say that every morning when I was a kid!* She quickly devoured a plate of fruit, and headed for the door. Once in the classroom, she struggled again to stay alert, and found it difficult to stop thinking of the darkness and foul weather. She went to the gym immediately after class, and spent an hour riding an exercise bike which she thought might have been built by the Wright brothers before they got into the airplane business. It was not long before the battered metal seat began to generate friction on her buttocks, and soon after that, one of the trainers turned the volume up on the radio.

After several minutes of listening to Britney Spears, followed by Boys to Men, while blisters began to gather on her rump, she began to think about her situation. *I believe I'm having a premonition of my own personal hell! The humidity has me sweating like a pig, my ears are aching from listening to music I hate, and I'm getting blisters on my big fat ass!* An hour after she had started, she climbed off the bike. *I feel like I just rode a starving mule from here to Tierra del Fuego!* She walked home from the gym in the rain, and when she entered the house, Rosita was watching film of flooding in Limon on the news. Houses were floating away, and people were riding horses and boats in the streets. She turned to Rosita, and asked," Is that unusual?"

"No, it happens once or twice a year, and those people just rebuild their homes in exactly the same place."

"That's ludicrous! You'd think they would learn eventually."

Rosita said, "Some people never learn! Not everyone can be Italian!"

After dinner, Brandy and Rosita watched "Scream" together. While Neve Campbell was trying to lose her virginity to the insipid character played by Matthew Lillard, Brandy jumped out of her chair and screamed when a large insect flew onto her head.

"What is that thing?"

"Oh, it won't hurt you. We call them Maybugs, and they always come around this time of the year."

Brandy looked at the fleeing insect, and said, "Well, it looks like what we call a June bug back home, and it just scared me more than those two creepy killers we're watching!"

She sat back in her chair, and regained her composure. Finally, after Neve stabbed Skeet Ulrich with her umbrella and her arch rival, Courtney Cox finished him off with bullets. Rosita turned off the TV set, awakened Guido and Tuffy, who managed to sleep through all of the commotion, and sent them off to bed. Brandy excused herself, and went to her room. Five minutes later she was sound asleep until she was awakened three hours before sunrise by the sound of something, or someone rattling the glass in the shower door. She grabbed her umbrella with renewed confidence in its adaptability as a weapon, having just seen the heroine in the movie she had just watched use one to render a crazed killer harmless.

When she went to investigate the source of the noise, she came face to face with a larger beetle than the one which had attacked her earlier. The intruder had entered through the barred window in the shower stall, which remained open at all times. The brazen creature made the first move, flying directly at Brandy's face. Brandy countered with catlike grace, swinging her umbrella as she had seen Robert Redford do many times with a baseball bat in Chuck's favorite movie, "The Natural." She solidly connected with the insect, causing it to bounce off the window ledge, and scurry out into the garden. After she had returned to the safety of her bed, she could hear her antagonist buzzing angrily from the shelter of the foliage outdoors. She pulled the covers tightly around her, thinking, *That horrific mutant is probably calling for backup!* After a short time, the buzzing ceased, and Brandy was soon asleep again.

Chapter 48

A Stroll Through Town, and a Special Guest for Dinner

Brandy left the house early on Saturday, having decided to spend the morning touring the city for possibly the last time. When she reached the bus stop, she saw a bus preparing to leave, so she climbed aboard. When she reached familiar territory, she got off , and began walking until she came to a small park, where she stopped to photograph two elderly gents carrying on an animated conversation while sitting on a bench. She then turned her attention to two little girls feeding pigeons, and a mischievous little boy who was chasing them away to irritate the girls..

She wandered from street to street, and from store to store. The smell of grilled chicken, pinto beans, and fresh fruit wafted past her nostrils from a cluster of tiny restaurants. She waved playfully at a group of men drinking beer in a bar, when they lost interest in the soccer game they were watching long enough to leer at her from their barstools. When she reached a street lined with art galleries, she began searching for the perfect painting to take home with her. As she passed the third shop in the row, she spied a painting of little children playing in the streets of San Jose. She considered buying it, but changed her mind when she discovered that it would cost more than she had paid for her plane ticket. She thought, *I have enough beautiful pictures of Costa Rica to cover a thousand walls!*

She continued walking for about two hours, until she reached a small cafe across the street from a soccer field where two teams of boys were playing enthusiastically. She decided to to have lunch. Once inside, she chose a table with a view of the field, so she could watch the game, and the people scurrying by. While she ate, she conversed with a heavyset waiter, who looked to her like a Hispanic Jackie Gleason. He was very friendly, and like most Costa Ricans she had met, very curious about the United States. He called her "Mi Amore," and when she spoke about Chuck, he said, "Your boyfriend is, "Un hombre muy fortunato!"

"I guess so, but I'm lucky, too! He's a very nice hombre, and I miss him very much!"

Immediately after returning home, she spent the next hour running in her neighborhood, and, as always, kept her eyes focused downward, looking for potholes obscured by water, and dodging traffic. When she staggered into the house, she discovered that Rosita and two of her cousins were preparing the dining room for a dinner party. She washed her hands, and began helping. While they were setting the table, Rosita said, "Brandy, tonight everything must be perfect. Bartolemeo is coming to dinner. He is the son of our family's lifelong friends, Augustino and Lenora Solari. He is very handsome, and comes here from Italy every five years or so to visit. You must go freshen up now. He loves beautiful women, and you will love him, but he is bringing a lady friend with him." She snickered, then added, "He brings a different one every time!"

Brandy showered quickly, and after she had dried her hair, she put on a short strapless pink dress adorned with white roses. After brushing her hair, and arranging it to her satisfaction, she headed for the dining room, just as Bartolemeo sauntered through the door with a beautiful woman by his side. When she saw him, Brandy thought, *Oh, my gosh! He looks like Dean Martin! My mom loved Dean Martin. It's a good thing she's not here, or daddy would be loading his old twelve gauge!*

It was at that moment that the party started. Guido kept the wine glasses full, and Rosita made sure the table was well stocked with salads, pasta, steaks, and condiments.

Brandy sat next to Bartolomeo's platinum blonde lady friend, Monique, who told her everything about him between sips of wine and dainty nibbles of food from her plate.

"I work for Armani in Paris, and I met Bartolomeo four years ago on the Concorde flight from Paris to New York. He's a design engineer for Ferrari, but he formerly worked for Formula One, and as an aeronautical engineer for Boeing. He is very modest, and seldom talks much about all he has done!"

The table-talk continued in Italian, French and Spanish. At one point Bartolomeo made eye contact with Brandy, then asked her if she was enjoying her stay in Costa Rica. She intended to answer in Spanish, but, without thinking, surprised herself, and answered in Italian. When everyone laughed, Bartolmeo said. "I'm impressed by your beauty, but also by your intellect. Do you speak Italian?"

She smiled daintily, took a sip of wine from her glass, rolled her eyes, and answered, "I have no idea!"

While all present roared with laughter, she ruminated, *They think I'm kidding! I know a few words from hanging out with these people, but it must be that the synapse is firing so hard that my brain is short circuiting!*

After dinner, as the guests began leaving, Bartolomeo took Brandy aside. "Good night, pretty one, I will see you domani, manana, or in the morning, whatever you prefer! Rosita has invited me for breakfast, and then I'm going to drive her to the market. I hope you will join us!"

"Yes, I would consider it an honor, if you're sure Rosita won't be jealous!"

"It was her idea. I'll see you then!"

Brandy helped clear the table, then went to bed exhausted. When she woke up at daybreak, she was dreaming that Bartolomeo was making love to her in the back of Chuck's old van. When she heard the rain beating down on the roof, she rolled over and went back to sleep.

Chapter 49

A Trip to the Market, and a Neglected Child

Rosita knocked on the door, and said, "Brandy, your breakfast is ready."

"I'll get dressed, and will be there in a minute!"

She threw off the covers, and dashed to the shower. A few minutes later, she put on a pair of white shorts and a hot pink tank top, slipped into her shoes, and headed for the kitchen. When she arrived, Bartholomeo and Guido were seated at the dining table drinking coffee. Brandy's mind raced back to her dream. *Gosh, maybe I wasn't dreaming! It seemed real, and if Chuck's van is parked outside, I'm going to have to run to the bathroom!*

"Buon giormi! I hope you slept well, because, as promised, I am here to take you shopping. I tried to convince Rosa that we didn't need a chaperone, but she insists on coming along!"

Rosita pretended to throw a plate in the direction of the handsome curly haired man. "Shame on you, Barto! You know that I'm the only woman you've ever loved!"

"Ah yes, but Guido has your heart, and Brandy is so beautiful!"

Brandy laughed, then kissed Bartolomeo on the forehead, and sat down beside him.

"You're really cute, but you have so many women already! One of them might get jealous and kill me!"

When the meal was finished, Brandy followed Bartolomeo and Rosita outside, where a four-door Geo Tracker Wagon was parked in the driveway. Rosita climbed into rear seat, and motioned for Brandy to sit next to Bartolomeo. When he started the motor, it became apparent that he was having difficulty with the clutch, though he didn't utter a word. He laughed when Brandy teased him, saying, "These wheels are a bit different from your Ferrari, aren't they?"

"Yes, my love, and it is not quite a Maserati, either, but it is better than riding a donkey!"

At the market, Rosita led the way, and Brandy helped fill the cart with produce, while Batholomeo pushed it along. Brandy noticed that a shapely girl behind the pastry counter appeared too be very interested in Bartoleneo, but he seemed oblivious to her. During the trip back to Rosita's house, he spoke of his travels in the United States, including business trips to Washington, especially to Andrews Air Force Base, when he was with Boeing. When the groceries were unloaded, he reached under the driver' seat, and brought out a dozen long stemmed roses, which he handed to her.

"Arrividerci, my little flower. I will remember you always. My only regret is that you were not the first woman in my life. If that were true, I would not have to keep looking!"

"That's very sweet, and a wonderful compliment, but even though you've traveled the world and know many languages, I hope you won't mind if I tell you in plain English that you're full of shIt!"

Bartolomeo laughed heartily, and said, "You have a sense of humor! That is why I love you! Goodbye!"

He drove away, and Brandy went into the house and handed the flowers to Roaita. "Bartholomeo asked me to give these to you. He said goodbye, and I got the impression that he was leaving the country. Is that true?"

"He'll be here tonight for dinner! I've known that man all of his life, and he loves to make jokes! I was with him when he bought the flowers for you. He hid them when you weren't looking. I'll put them in a vase, and you can take them to your room."

"Just put them on the dining room tabled, so we can all enjoy them. I'm going to the hospital, but I'll be back for dinner. I have a few things to say to your playful friend!"

When she walked into the ward, Brandy was confronted by a two year old boy, who seemed very distressed. "What's wrong, Araldo?"

"My momma was supposed to come see me, but she isn't here!"

He began sobbing uncontrollably, so she picked him up and carried him to a chair by the window, then sat down. She spoke softly, trying to console him, then began to sing, but he continued to cry and scream almost constantly until his mother arrived almost three hours later.

Brandy stood up, and put the toddler in his mother's arms. The woman shrugged her shoulders, then she set the boy down and sat in the chair Brandy had vacated. She quickly parted company with the woman, thinking *She couldn't care less! My clothes are soaked with the poor kid's tears, and my eardrums are aching from his screams, and she obviously doesn't give a damn about anyone but herself!*

She spent the rest of the day in the playroom with several children. Because all of the toys, crayons and books had again been stolen again, they told stories and played games until she departed. When she reached Rosita's, the

Geo was parked in the driveway. She entered the house, and pretended that she was surprised to see Bartolomeo.

"Well, hello there handsome! I see that you missed me so much, that you decided to stay awhile longer. I bet you r other girlfriends don't know what you're up to!"

"You hurt me deeply, little flower, you're the only woman who has my heart!"

Brandy went to her room to shower and change clothes, and then returned to help Rosita carry plates of bread, salad, pasta, and sauce to the table. When they were seated at the table, she mentioned that she had not seen many helicopters since she had been in Costa Rica' and Bartolomeo said, "Do you like helicopters? I am a helicopter pilot. If you come to Rome, you can stay at my villa, and I'll fly you all around the city!"

"Is there anything you haven't done? Anyway, I love helicopters! I got to hover a Black Hawk once back home. Did you ever fly one of those?"

"Yes, and I've, flown the Italian Military's A129 Mangusa, or, in English, the Mongoose, but I do not wish to discuss helicopters! I would rather talk about you!"

After dinner, Bartolomeo excused himself, saying that he had to meet with some business associates. Brandy, Guido, and Rosita started to watch a news report about the devastation caused by flooding in Limon. Guido fell asleep soon after the broadcast began, and Rosita sent him off to bed, then went to the kitchen and returned with two glasses of beer. They sat and talked for about an hour, and then Brandy said good night.

Chapter 50

A Doctor Who Makes House Calls

Brandy walked to school in the gently falling rain, and once in the classroom, she had to fight to stay awake because it was dark and dreary. Her problem was exacerbated by the fact that there was a new professor in her conversation class named Annetta Delgado, who seemed enamored with the sound of her own voice. As she spoke, Brandy began to think of the rain, and her plan to emulate Noah. She started fantasizing as to which animals she would take when she built her personal ark. She was grateful when class was dismissed, and, once outside, she decided to walk to the market. As she approached, she caught sight of a small open field upon which stood an enormous pile of garbage. She looked back, and saw steam rising from the mountains hovering in the background against the sky, which was painted with shades of blue, pink, and purple by the setting sun. At that moment, she thought, *What a contrast! It's kind of a life lesson! If you can look past the garbage, you can find beauty almost anywhere!*

The next afternoon, after class, she went running in the rain, side stepping potholes, and trying to avoid being killed by a speeding vehicle, tasks made more difficult because her eyes were burning from the acid rain. When she entered the house, she passed a mirror, and her eyes were red and swollen, and was greeted by Rosita. "

"My goodness, child, what is wrong with your eyes?"

"I think it's acid rain, but I'm not sure."

"Well, the first several weeks of every winter, the acid is so strong that I have to move most of my less hardy plants indoors!"

After dinner, Brandy went to her room to read a book for school. As she read, she munched chocolates from a box of candy Chuck had sent to her. She soon became drowsy, so she went bed, and was sound asleep within minutes. She woke up two hours later because her skin seemed irritated, then arose from bed and turned on the light. When she looked in the mirror she was horrified to see that she had broken out with hives. She went to Rosita's room in panic, fearing that acid rain or some exotic Costa Rican insect was devouring her flesh. Rosita led her into the bathroom for a closer look. "Do I have Dengue Fever, Elboa, or Papaomoya?"

"I think that you're having an allergic reaction to something you've eaten. What have you eaten recently other than what we had for dinner?"

"I ate several pieces of chocolate just before I went to sleep."

"That's probably what caused your problem; I'll fix you some hot milk and honey. It helps sometimes with allergies, and we'll go to the pharmacy in the morning."

Brandy went back to bed, but couldn't sleep because her head was pounding, and she was having difficulty breathing. After breakfast, Rosita took her to the pharmacy where she purchased skin cream and headache medicine. She went back to bed as soon as she reached home, and slept for several hours. When she awakened, Rosita called her and said, "Bartolomeo and Monique are here, and I've asked them to take you to the Country Club at Heredia. I think the fresh mountain air might do you some good!"\

That afternoon, at Heredia, they walked around the grounds, and when they returned to the main building, Bartolomeo saw an old friend, and stopped to chat. Brandy and Monique went to the balcony overlooking the city of San Jose, and sat down. Monique told of her experiences as General Manager of the Armani Women's Department in Paris.

"Jodie Foster comes to our shop frequently. She speaks perfect French! She has no American accent whatsoever. Bruce Willis buys a lot of children's clothes from us; Denzel Washington brings his whole family to shop for clothes, and Beyonce is often dressed in our store before her concerts in Paris. Anytime you, and anyone you want to bring along, want to come to Paris, you can stay with me, and shop at our boutique!"

Brandy smiled, and said, "That's very sweet of you, and I'll keep it in mind!" Silently, she was thinking, *Oh, sure, I've never paid more than ninety bucks for a pair of shoes, and sadly, those were running shoes, and I'm going shopping at Armani's in Paris! If anybody volunteers to foot my bill, I'll invite them on that little junket in a heartbeat!*

When the trio returned to Rosita's, they discovered that the house was filled with relatives ad friends, and that the dinning table was overloaded with platters of barbequed meat and a variety of side dishes. As usual, dinner was followed by the telling of stories and boisterous behavior. When desert was served, Brandy consumed a small portion of Tiramazu without realizing that it contained chocolate.

By the time the guests had departed, she had developed a severe headache, and began having difficulty breathing.

She managed to sleep intermittingly, but was miserable all night. By early morning, her head seemed close to exploding, her throat was burning, her skin itched, and her breathing was labored. Rosita immediately called her doctor. One hour later a tall slender man walked into the house carrying a large black bag. When she saw him, Brandy had the feeling that a miracle was occurring in her presence. *My Lord! A doctor who makes house calls, and on a Saturday!*

After he had finishing his examination, the doctor said, "You have a sinus infection. Also, I think that Rosita is correct. Chocolate is the cause of your hives. You will need an injection for that. Here is my cell phone number. Call me if you do not feel better soon."

Brandy thought, *I think I'm going to faint, or wake up and find out that I've been dreaming! Back home, I could be at death's door, and this would never happen!*""

Chapter 51

Dejection over an Injection

Gina arrived as the doctor was leaving, and drove Brandy to the Farmacia Central. She was amazed that almost any drug, other than those for treatment of psychiatric disorders could be purchased without a prescription. Within minutes, a female pharmacist, needle in hand, led her behind a row of shelves to administer an injection, and to her chagrin, she was less than pleased to hear the Spanish word for posterior, instead of arm. She asked three times where the injection was to be given, even though she knew she had heard right the first time. She finally acquiesced, realizing that she was in a different culture, and might as well drop her jeans, thinking, *So what if I'm behind a shelf in a drug store with my bum in the air, waiting for a pharmacist to stick me with a needle, while half of Costa Rica is watching? If I were in the states, I'd run like hell, but I'm not! I'm here, and I'm sick, so who cares?*

When she got home, she went directly to bed and slept for several hours. When she woke up late in the afternoon, she went to the computer lab to write a letter to Chuck. When she finished, because of the rain, humidity. and pollution, she headed for a shopping mall to walk for awhile, but soon became exhausted. After exiting, she had walked less than a block; when a bolt of lightning struck the surface of the street a short distance ahead of her. She was terrified, and, took refuge in an interior decorating store. When the lightning stopped, she ran all the way home, where Rosita, was standing in the door shaking her head. "Where have you been, child? You look terrible! Go take a hot shower, and I will make some tea. The school would never forgive me if I let you die while you're staying with me!"

Brandy meekly complied with Rosita's commands, and then returned to the kitchen to help her roll dough, and make pizza sauce on a large wooden table in the pantry room. Rosita put the pizzas in the oven, and when they were cooked to her satisfaction, she called Guido, and they dined together on pizza, salad, and beer.

When she awakened on Sunday morning, Brandy still did not feel well, despite the fact that the sun was shining brightly for the first time in days. Gina had arrived right after breakfast to take Rosita to the market. Brandy declined an invitation to join them, and went out to the garden to enjoy the sun. Five minutes later, Guido and Tuffy came out and Guido sat beside her and began throwing a rubber bone for Tuffy to fetch. "You have the right idea,! The sunshine is good medicine."

"I love the sun, but I detest the rain."

"You forget that the rain makes the flowers grow."

"That's true, but I'm not a flower."

"No, but you have the beauty of the fairest flower in the world!"

Brandy began to think, *I wonder where this is going!* She got up, and began to walk around the yard. Guido went back to entertaining Tuffy, and eventually went into the house to search for a soccer game on television. Tuffy followed, and Brandy retuned to her bench. When Rosita and Gina retuned, Brandy helped them carry the usual large quantity of fruits and vegetables into the house. When the produce was safely stored, Gina announced that they were going to go to Heridia for lunch, and asked Brandy to join them. She explained, "Sunday is the day I usually spend at the hospital, but the children have very fragile immune systems! I'll be very happy to join you. Is Guido coming along/"

"No, since it is a nice day, one of his friends is going to pick him up, and they are going to the park to play Bocce ball."

"That sounds like fun! Maybe I'll go with him!'

Gina smirked, "If you do, your fondoschina will be purple! Those are dirty old men!" She giggled, pointed to her backside, and said, "They are all Veijo Verdes!"

"Oh I'm sure Guido would protect me, He's so sweet!"?

Rosita did not speak, but she and Gina laughed heartily, and rolled their eyes. Soon Gina's car was zig-zagging through traffic in the rain. She hesitated frequently to ask her passengers if she was going in the right direction. They laughed and teased her about her shortcomings as a navigator. Brandy began to have empathy with her, and the song by the Irish rock band,U2, "Where The Streets Have No Names", began running through her head. The little Toyota slid rapidly along on the wet pavement, as Rosita occasionally screamed directions, sometimes in Spanish, and often in Italian, in a loud, shrill voice, until they were entering the country club grounds.

After eating their lunch, they went back into town, and stopped at the home of some family friends, where they watched "The OC" on television, which amused Brandy, because she was the only American in the room, and the only person there who had never seen the show. She soon began entertaining a little boy by making monsters out of playdough.

When she got home, she went to bed, but her head soon began pounding in unison with the rain on the roof. She began to think about her arrival in Costa Rica, the strong bond she had formed with her surrogate family, and how she had come to love each of them in a special way. She had been greeted with warm hugs and kisses from the first night she had arrived at Rosita's door, and treated like a daughter by her and Guido from the outset. She recalled how Rosita had walked her to school on her first day, and introduced her to her instructors. The whole family had patiently talked with her to help her learn the Spanish language. They comforted her when she was tired, homesick, or frustrated. They gave her advice, worried about her when she traveled, taught her how to cook Italian food, and included her in family activities. Rosita had even ironed her clothes, including her socks and underwear. She had spent many wonderful nights and afternoons with friendly, loving people, and had relished every opportunity she had had to spend time with them, even when it involved such mundane activities like shopping at the local markets.

She began to think of her other classmates, especially Paul, who spent many afternoons and most of their nights in bars. They teased her, and couldn't understand why she would prefer the company of old people to the excitement of Costa Rica's night life. They couldn't understand why a beautiful, vibrant, young woman would enjoy eating dinner, watching Senor Frijole, or sitting around talking with foreigners who were old enough to be her grandparents. Further, they didn't seem to comprehend how she could consider people with whom she had little in common as family. She was very eager to get back home to the United States, to be with her own family, and to have Chuck hold her in his arms, but knew that there would always be a place in her heart for her surrogate family. She felt that of all of the memories, she would cherish about the beautiful country, the school, and her classmates, her second family of jovial Italians would always be at the top of the list.

Chapter 52

Saying Goodbye to the Kids and The City

On Monday morning, when Brandy arose from a restless night, the sun was shining brightly, and the welcome sight buoyed her sagging spirits. She showered, dressed, and headed for the kitchen, where Rosita had her breakfast on the table. She began to sample from a plate of fresh strawberries, pineapple, bananas and mangoes, when she notice that there was a dead gnat, or a Costa Rican relative of the species, on a piece of pineapple she had just bitten into. Knowing that Rosita was very picky about her food, and its presentation, she feared that the most discreet effort to remove it might cause her sensitive hostess grave concern, so she continued eating, and thought, *Oh, what the heck! I feel like I'm already sick, possibly near death's door. Down the hatch! What's the worst thing that could happen – Malaria?*

She finished her meal and started out for school, not minding in the least that the bright sun actually hurt her eyes. As she passed several rows of flowers, she tried to imagine what they would smell like if she were able to breathe normally. At the end of her schoolday, she returned home, physically exhausted, severely congested, and incapable of breathing through her nose. Rosita made her a large bowl of chicken broth and a pot of hot tea. Brandy wasn't willing to accept the fact that she had used three days worth of Afrin in one night might have worsened her problems. She went to bed, but was so miserable because of her inability to breathe normally, that she decided to go to the daycare center to say goodbye to the children. She got dressed and started to leave the house, when she became aware that rain was pounding on the roof. She had opened the door to peer out into the darkness, when Rosita screamed, "Are you loco? It is cold and wet out there! Get back in bed, this instant! Where do you think you're going?"

"I can't sleep, and I promised I would go to the daycare center to say goodbye to the kids! I won't stay long."

At Rosita's insistence, she donned three layers of clothing, a hat, a poncho, and a pair of rain boots. Rosita, remained distraught, but handed her an umbrella, then retreated to the kitchen, shaking her head in a manner with which Brandy had noticed frequently during the past few days.

She jumped over a number of huge puddles in the flooded streets on the way to the center, where she discovered that half of the children were sick, and had remained at their homes. She was greeted enthusiastically by the nine who were present, and she sat down at a child size table surrounded by excited little tots while they chattered, scribbled on coloring pages or drew pictures for her. When the conversation began to focus on Brandy's return to the United States, a little boy asked her how big her country was, and she replied, "Oh, it's very big!"

"Is it bigger than Costa Rica?"

"Oh, yes it is much bigger! I'll show you."

She removed maps of each country from her bag, and unfolded them on the table. Because, by coincidence, she had heard the answer to his question in a class discussion a week earlier at CASA, she pointed to West Virginia on the U.S. map. "This is West Virginia, the state right next to Virginia, where I grew up. Costa Rica is just a little bit smaller."

"Un poquito mas pequeno?"

"Si! Un poquito pequeno! A little bit smaller!"

The children began asking questions about West Virginia and Virginia. Brandy told them about the mountains near her home, and the gringo animals who lived in them, Senor Bear, Senorita Deer and Maestro Hoot Owl." When she started to leave, she was given a large bag of cards, drawings, chocolate hearts, playdough animals, and notes scribbled on scrap paper, some of which were done with crayons. She had to fight back tears as she walked away, knowing she would always remember their big brown eyes, sticky little hands and faces, and the cutest Spanish accents she could ever hope to hear. She started to go home, but felt that she would get no rest because of her illness, and began walking to the gym in the rain, wondering what the tykes' lives would be like when they grew up, whether or not they would remember her, and whether she would ever see them again. When she got to the gym, she attempted to work out, but soon was completely worn-out. She managed to reach home, and was greeted there by Rosita, who ordered her to take a hot shower, don her pajamas, and go directly to bed after dinner.

When the meal was finished, Rosita boiled some manzarilla tea, and Brandy spent fifteen minutes leaning over the pot with a towel over her head inhaling the vapors until she could breathe through one of her nostrils. Rosita laughed, and said, "You look like a lobster! Now go to bed, and try to get some rest."

She meekly retreated to her bedroom, and crawled under the covers, only to wake up again in the middle of the night. She got out of bed and hurried to her medicine cabinet in search of her Afrin, then remembered that she had already packed it in a suitcase to avoid overdosing again. She got back in bed, and although she was unable to sleep, when morning came, she managed to get out of bed, and walk to school, where she struggled all morning to stay awake. Having survived that experience, she tried to go running, but soon abandoned the effort and went home to take a nap.

Later in the afternoon, Amanda Ruiz called, and invited her to have tea at the country club. She had bonded with several of her teachers, but she and Amanda had become close friends. They spent two hours talking about Brandy's escapades at the school, particularly the manner in which Paul had pursued her. When Amanda drove her home, she asked her if she would like to make one last tour of San Jose before she left.

"We can meet tomorrow morning, if you wish."

"Yes, that sounds like fun! What time should I meet you?

"I'll pick you up after breakfast. Is there anything you would like to see?'

"I don't care, we can just ride around and play it by ear. I'll see you in the morning."

That evening, Gina, Brandy, Guido, and Rosita ate lasagna and drank beer, then they watched television together. When the program ended she went her room, brushed her teeth, and got into bed. Although her congestion had not completely subsided, her nasal passages had cleared enough to allow her to breathe almost normally, and she slept through the night.

Amanda arrived the next morning after breakfast as promised. "Good morning Brandy, where do you want to go first?"

'I don't really care, why don't we cruise around a bit, and see what happens."

For the next hour, the two women talked, while Amana drove around the city, stopping occasionally to admire flowers in a park or to watch people shopping or hurrying to work. When they drove past the Supreme Court Building, Brandy noticed a large sign in front, which read "Organisomo de Investiaciones Judiciales."

Brandy said, "So this is your country's equivalent of our Federal Bureau of Investigation! That's the agency I would like to work for someday! I wonder if they have tours!"

Amanda parked her car, and they walked to the building and entered. Brandy asked the security guard if it was possible to tour the facility. He picked up the phone, and a few minutes later, an attractive young woman appeared. "Hello, I understand that you are from the United States. I am Agent Desideria Ortega. What can I do for you? "

Brandy replied, "I work for our Homeland Security Department in Washington, but right now I am on a leave of absence, and a student at CASA. Mrs., Ruiz is my teacher, and one of a very few people here who know what I do for a living back home! Is there any chance we can look around?"

"Certainly, I'll be glad to give you a tour. I am sure that you understand that we will not be going to any restricted areas!"

"Of course, I understand. Our agency is as tight as a drum since Nine One One! You can't be too careful these day!"

When the tour ended, Amanda glanced at her watch, and said, "Goodness! I must get back to school! I lost track of time!"

"That's fine! Thanks for last night and this morning. I'll ride to school with you, and then I'll walk to the hospital for my last visit. I'm going to miss those kids, although I won't be able to get close to many of them, because I'm not exactly well, and several of the kids have very fragile immune systems."

Chapter 53

Brandy Meets the Victim of an Unspeakable Act

The head nurse, Lily Guzman, was standing in the hallway of the children's ward when Brandy arrived, "Hola, Brandy, I understand that you will be going home soon!"

"Yes, in fact, my visa expires in eight days, but I'm leaving San Jose on Saturday to travel on the Pacific Coast before I fly out. By the way, I have some kind of bug, so I'll have to keep my distance from most of the kids."

"I agree, but there is one child here that you can visit. She's a two-year old girl named Dora. She has no one who spends time with her. I should tell you, though, that she will not, or cannot speak. It is very sad!"

Lily led Brandy over to a bed where a chubby-cheeked little girl with shoulder length black pigtails, was eating cake and drinking milk. As soon as she saw Brandy, she stretched her arms in the air. Her beautiful brown eyes seemed to say, "Pick me up, please?"

"Come here, sweetie, let's take a walk!"

The child rested her head on Brandy's shoulder the instant she was lifted from her crib. Brandy started walking while singing softly. Dora began rubbing her shoulder with one tiny hand, and gently touching her hair with the other. Finally, Brandy sat down in rocking chair, and she snuggled to her neck. Brandy turned her so she could look at her face, her milk mustache, and cheeks covered with cake crumbs. She didn't divert her eyes from Brandy's until she fell asleep, never removing her hand from its gentle grasp of the arm which held her. She slept peacefully until Lily came into the room, and said, 'It is time for the baby to go back to her bed, but we must change her clothes, especially her diaper!'

She removed the diaper, and Brandy stared in disbelief at multiple lacerations in the child's pelvic area. Lily explained, "This poor little angel was repeatedly raped by a member of her own family, but the police have not found out who it was! They suspect that it was her father. Of course, he won't admit it, and her mother has not been cooperative, probably because she's afraid to speak out. The authorities brought her here, and no one ever comes to see her or even inquire about her. She has no one who seems to care!"

Brandy was infuriated. "That is monstrous! If I had time; I'd hunt that miserable creep down, and cut off his private parts! If somebody wanted to adopt her, how would they go about it?"

"One problem is that she is being treated for venereal disease, and we're waiting for the results of AIDS tests. Another thing is that parental rights would have to be terminated, or the courts would have to issue a decree of abandonment."

"Well, if I had time to work it out, little Dora would be flying back to the U.S.A. with me!"

"Oh, Brandy, I know that you're sincere, but a child is not a homeless animal, that you can take in and feed with table scraps! A child like Dora may need constant care for many years, perhaps for her whole life.! We have become very close in the past months, and to use what you Gringos call a cliché, 'Your plate is full!' "

'Well, I'll never forget about her, nor will I ever forgive the monster who assaulted her!"

When Brandy went back to Rosita's house, she was surprised to find several members of her surrogate family gathered to say goodbye. When she entered the house with tears in her eyes, she told them about Dora.

"I just spent the afternoon with a beautiful little girl who was brutally raped by a demented savage, and her father is the prime suspect! She's so sweet, and so helpless that it breaks my heart!"

Bartolomeo told her that he knew some people with considerable influence, and promised to look into the situation. "Don't worry about the child, I'll see that she gets the best of care, and all of us will pray for her."

Rosita led her into the dining room, and seated her at the place of honor. Guido started pouring wine, and the festivities were underway. The party lasted until almost midnight, and after the guests had presented Brandy with gifts and photographs, they embraced her and kissed her until she almost suffocated.

The next day she flew to the Pacific Coast, and spent a week traveling through rainforest resorts and fishing villages before returning to San Jose to pick up the rest of her baggage and say goodbye to her hopst and hostess.

Chapter 54

Exit from Paradise

After staying overnight at Rosita's, Brandy flew to Dulles Airport on the twenty-eighth day of May. Chuck, who had flown from Georgia to spend the weekend with her, was waiting when she disembarked. When he saw her, he ran to meet her, wrapped his arms around her and kissed her passionately, oblivious to the hordes of people around them. After Brandy picked up her baggage, the young lovers went to the townhouse she shared in Vienna. During the cab ride, she moved close to Chuck, placed her head on his shoulder, nibbled at his ear, and whispered, "Did you miss me? I bet the girls in your class are crazy about you!"

He kissed her gently, and said, "I won't lie, because there are a couple of real hot trainees from Alcohol, Tax, and Firearms, who are very friendly, but they keep our butts dragging during the week, and I've buddied up with a guy named Tim Hill, and he keeps me out of trouble on the weekends. He's a Catholic, about three years older than I, and has four kids already. We went fishing a couple of times, and managed to take in a few minor league ball games. We can't go far on weekends, because if we're not back to start humping early on Monday, that's the end of the road! It means dismissal. You know that you're my one and only girl! Besides who are these bozos you've been traveling with? I'm the one who should be asking questions. You know how I feel about you! You own my heart!"

"Well, your heart isn't the body part I was concerned about! But don't worry, I won't lie, either. I was hit on by a few guys, but the Tico men are all almost a foot shorter than I am, and the gringos didn't turn me on, including the one male I traveled with. Also there was another girl with us both times. I went down to Costa Rica to learn Spanish. I wasn't looking for action! You've been my guy since high school, and I haven't changed my mind. Not yet, anyway."

"Okay, then, let's get married. I have a surprise for you I bought a three-bedroom house in Chesapeake, about twenty minutes from Virginia Beach, so when you move to Norfolk, you can move in with me!"

"That's nice, but I made arrangements online to rent an efficiency apartment right on Virginia Beach, so my Dad won't shoot you because we're shacking up! That way we can get married when we're ready for that kind of commitment"

Chuck shook his head and smiled. He started to tell her that it was she, and not he, who feared commitment, but then he quickly changed the subject, asking, "What's a Tico man?"

"It's slang for Costa Rican male, and some of them are even bigger pigs than you Gringos!"

The taxi pulled in front of Brandy's dwelling, and Chuck paid him. They took their bags into Brandy's room, where they spent the next hour before going to dinner at the Amphora Restaurant.

On Saturday morning they set out for the mountains in Brandy's car, to spend the weekend with their parents. On the way, Brandy told Chuck about Dora, and how she thought of trying to adopt her.

"Hey, babe--that's cool! We could start our married life with a kid, before we make some of our own!"

"There are too many things I want to do. I'm not saying that I'll never marry you; I'm just not ready for a lifetime commitment yet."

At that point, they mutually agreed to change the subject. Brandy listened intently to Chuck's stories about his experiences at Glynco. She reciprocated as she filled him in on her adventures with Guido, Rosita, and their various relatives. She made him laugh when she spoke of her travels with Kitty, and of Ducky's visit, while discreetly avoiding references to her travels with Paul. When they reached the mountains, Brand y said, "Except for the absence of volcanoes, these mountains are very much like the ones in Costa Rica!"

"You know what? There are mountains in Georgia, and all mountains look the same, especially when you're running up and down them with a hard-ass instructor ragging your butt! When I graduate, we're going to Florida for a week, without a mountain in sight. We'll run on the beach, and sleep in the same bed every night."

"Well, we both know that won't happen tonight! We're almost to my house, so you can come in and say hello to my parents, then I'll take you to your house and drop you off! After I say hello to your Mom and Dad, I'll go back home and start pretending like I'm a virgin, so Daddy won't shoot you!"

"You don't really believe your Dad doesn't know that we stopped holding hands back in high school, do you?"

"Of course not, but he'll l be in denial until I decide to marry you. He'll never approve of us living at the same address before we marry. That's why I've arranged for my own apartment, and it happens to be right on the beach, which makes the fact that summer starts on June 21, a definite plus!"

Chapter 55

Chuck Graduates, and Brandy Starts Her New Job

On Sunday night, Brandy drove Chuck to the airport, then drove back to pick up her Grandmother in Newmarket. On Monday, she drove back to the airport with her Grandmother and they flew to Savannah to spend a week with relatives. On Saturday, June 5, they flew back to Virginia, were she stayed with her parents for one week, before flying to Georgia to attend Chuck's graduation. After the ceremony at the Federal Law Enforcement Training Center, they attended a reception for the newly trained Federal Agents and their families in a building, which had housed the officer's club when the center was a Naval Air Station. Soon after they entered, a statuesque, well endowed blonde in a very tight mini-skirt approached them. "Hey, Chuck, is that your wife? She's really cute!"

"No, Wendy, she's my girlfriend! Brandy, this is Wendy, and she's with the ATF. We were in the same dormitory."

"Nice to know you, Brandy, you've got the cutest guy I've met since I got my divorce. He can handcuff me any time he wants to! I tried to get him to practice in the dorm, but he blew me off! He's really hung up on you; now I see why!"

"Thank you, but I see some cute guys here who'd probably give you all the practice you could ever dream of!"

"Honey, I like you! Like I said, Chuckee is a very lucky guy! Nice meeting you, and I'll see you around!"

Brady kicked Chuck in the shins, as Wendy wiggled her way towards a group of men.

"Well, I'm glad that you made some friends while you were here! I was so worried that you'd be lonely!"

"Ouch! That really hurt!"

"I'm sorry, Chuckee!'"

She kissed him, and then purred, "Maybe you should handcuff me, if I've been a bad girl!"

That afternoon they drove to Miami, where they spent the next week surfing, swimming, sunbathing, running or walking along the shoreline, and getting reacquainted. When their idyllic hiatus came to an end, Brandy flew back to Virginia, and Chuck drove directly to Chesapeake to close on his house before reporting for duty at Fort Story on Monday.

Brandy drove to the mountains to spend the weekend with her parents before reporting to Washington, to assist in training her replacement for one week. On June 27, she started her new assignment in Norfolk, and that night, she drove to Chuck's house, having explained to Stony that her apartment on the beach was not yet vacant. Needless to say, he was less than pleased, and his parting words were,

"Christian couples do not live together under the same roof if they're not married!"

She had tried to placate him, and said, "Daddy, I'm just not ready to get married, but I'm a normal woman, and

Chuck and I love each other. Besides, I'll be moving to the beach as soon as my apartment is ready."

Chuck was waiting at the door when Brandy pulled into his driveway . "Welcome to your new home! I don't have a lot of furniture, but the bedroom is furnished, and the TV is hooked up to cable."

"You mean your new home! Daddy will be down here with his twelve gauge if I'm not living alone at the beach next time he calls."

Brandy stayed with Chuck during her first month in Norfolk, although her apartment was ready for occupancy, and they stayed there together when they wanted to be close to the water. When the month ended, she spent two weeks at a training facility, and then returned to living at Chuck's house.

Chapter 56

Stony Retires His Shotgun; Brandy Gets Welcome News

On Brandy's first night back from training, Chuck took her out to dinner at "Rudee's on the Inlet," a restaurant overlooking the marina in Virginia Beach. They drank beer while they gazed at the sun setting over the boats in the marina, and ate dinner by candle light. Suddenly, Chuck set his silverware down on his plate, and said, "Brandy, I have something I've thought about very carefully. We've been together since high school, and I've never stopped thinking that I'd marry you anytime you wanted me too. I still feel that way! You've kept putting me off because you want a career, and I respect that. I agree that a commitment like marriage would make that difficult, particularly in Law Enforcement. Hell, Glynco was loaded with people like Wendy! What I'm trying to say is that, though we've never used the word, we've had a commitment for years! Hell, that's why you changed jobs! We need to be together!"

"Oh, I know, but marriage is a lifetime commitment, and right now, I feel that you're the one I'd like to grow old with, if I have to grow up! But I'm not sure I ever want to grow up!"

"I'm not ready to grow up all the way, either but I'd like it if we were engaged. You can always give my ring back, but if you did, I'd throw it in the ocean!"

He reached in his pocket, and took out a diamond ring. He knelt in front of his chair, and said, "Brandy, I love you, and I hope that someday, you will be my wife. Will you marry me sometime before one of us dies?"

She smiled, and held out her left hand. "Yes, I will! But I'm keeping all of my agent job applications open!"

He slipped the ring on her finger, then stood up, took her in his arms, and kissed her. That weekend, her parents came to visit, and Stony's first question was, "Who sleeps on the couch, you or Chuck?"

"We both sleep in his room, on the bed, Daddy! After all, this is the twenty-first century, and we are engaged, she said, holding out her hand to display her ring.

Brandy's mother squalled with delight. "Oh, my! I have a wedding to plan! When're you getting married?"

"Oh, we hadn't thought about that! Maybe next spring; we're in no hurry!"

"Why wait? I can work things out. This is the first of August; I'll need a month or so. I've been talking to the minister ever since you told me you were going to move down here. I' m thinking December, a week or so before Christmas."

Stony grinned, and said, that's great, but I hope that couch is comfortable, because Chuck will be sleeping on it tonight!"

On December 15, 2004, in the Main Street Presbyterian Church in New Market, Stony Barton gave his oldest daughter in marriage to a man he had despised when he was a kid in a baseball cap, but had come to love as though he was his son. After the reception, the newlyweds flew to Florida for their honeymoon moon.

Two days before Christmas, Brandy received a letter from Bartolomeo, congratulating her on her marriage. At the end of the letter he wrote, "I have some good news. The week after you left, a young American doctor friend and his wife came to visit me, and I took them to the Children's Hospital to see little Dora. They fell in love with her almost immediately, and arranged for her to be treated by specialists. You will be pleased to know that the diseases she contracted when she was so brutally assaulted have responded to treatment, testing for AIDS was negative, and her physical wounds have miraculously healed! The doctor and his wife have consulted with an Abogado, who is also a friend of mine. They are going to adopt Dora, and raise her as their own child in Oklahoma. Your poor little Tica is going to be a wealthy Gringa, and with loving care, her mental scars should also heal. In fact, the doctors are almost certain that with time, she will soon be speaking normally!"

When Brandy finished reading, she sat down and as tears of joy began to trickle down her cheeks she whispered, "Gracias a Dios!"

* El Fin Casi

* That is not quite the end of this story, because in February, 2005, Brandy received an e-mail from Paul, which read:

"Dear Brandy:

Kerry and I were in Costa Rica last month on our honeymoon, when we stopped by CASA for old times sake. When we saw Amanda Ruiz, she told us that you and Chuck tied the knot! Congratulations!

Kerry? That's right! She dropped into our Jackson, Mississippi franchise last June when I was making a good will visit, and I soon realized that she was the girl I've been looking for all my life! She moved to Houston to live with me 2 weeks later! We're expecting our first child in June--a boy!

By the way, keep a lookout in your mail for a combination thank you and wedding gift which I picked especially for you.

Paul

Three days later, a package which contained a pair of Women's size six Savacony Progrid Hurricane 11 Running Shoes was delivered to Brandy's home. When she opened the box to remove the shoes, she found a note which said, "You were right! Thanks for running out on me!"

The End